THE MUSIC SHOP

Also by Rachel Joyce

The Unlikely Pilgrimage of Harold Fry
Perfect
The Love Song of Miss Queenie Hennessy
A Snow Garden & Other Stories

Listen to The Music Shop playlist at:
bit.ly/TheMusicShopPlaylist

The
Music
Shop
Rachel
Joyce

Doubleday

LONDON · TORONTO · SYDNEY · AUCKLAND · JOHANNESBURG

TRANSWORLD PUBLISHERS
61–63 Uxbridge Road, London W5 5SA
www.penguin.co.uk

Transworld is part of the Penguin Random House group of companies
whose addresses can be found at global.penguinrandomhouse.com

| Penguin
Random House
UK

First published in Great Britain in 2017 by Doubleday
an imprint of Transworld Publishers

A CIP catalogue record for this book
is available from the British Library.

ISBNs 9780857521927 (hb)
9780857521934 (tpb)

Typeset in 11.5/17pt Berkeley Old Style by Falcon Oast Graphic Art Ltd.
Printed and bound by Clays Ltd, Bungay, Suffolk.

Penguin Random House is committed to a sustainable
future for our business, our readers and our planet. This book
is made from Forest Stewardship Council® certified paper.

MIX
Paper from
responsible sources
FSC® C018179

1 3 5 7 9 10 8 6 4 2

For Hope

Time has told me
You're a rare, rare find
A troubled cure
For a troubled mind.

Nick Drake, 'Time Has Told Me'

It is a joy to be hidden and a disaster not to be found.

Donald Winnicott

THERE WAS ONCE a music shop.

From the outside it looked like any shop, in any backstreet. It had no name above the door. No record display in the window. There was just a homemade poster stuck to the glass. *For the music you need!!! Everyone welcome!! We only sell VINYL! If closed, please telephone* – though after that it was anyone's guess because, along with more happy exclamation marks, the only legible numbers were an 8 that could well be a 3, and two other things that might be triangles.

Inside, the shop was cram-packed. Boxes everywhere, stocked with every kind of record in every speed, size and colour, and not one of them classified. An old counter stood to the right of the door and, at the back, two listening booths towered either side of a turntable; more like bedroom furniture than regular booths. Behind the turntable sat the owner, Frank, a gentle bear of a man, smoking and playing records. His shop was often open into the night – just as it was often closed into the morning – music playing, coloured lamps waltzing, all sorts of people searching for records.

Classical, rock, jazz, blues, heavy metal, punk . . . As long as it was on vinyl, there were no taboos. And if you told Frank the kind of thing you wanted, or simply how you felt that day, he had the right track in minutes. It was a knack he had. A gift. He knew what people needed even when they didn't know it themselves.

'Now why not give this a try?' he'd say, shoving back his wild brown hair. 'I've got a *feeling*. I just think it will work—'

There was a music shop.

SIDE A: JANUARY 1988

1

The Man Who Only Liked Chopin

FRANK SAT SMOKING behind his turntable, same as always, watching the window. Mid-afternoon, and it was almost dark out there. The day had hardly been a day at all. A drop in temperature had brought the beginnings of a frost and Unity Street glittered beneath the street lights. The air had a kind of blue feel.

The other four shops on the parade were already closed but he had put on the lava lamps and the electric fire. The music shop was warm and colourfully lit. At the counter, Maud the tattooist stood flicking through fanzines while Father Anthony made an origami flower. Saturday Kit had collected all the Emmylou Harris and was trying to arrange them in alphabetical order without Frank noticing.

'I had no customers again,' said Maud, very loud. Even though Frank was at the back of the shop and she was at the front, there was technically no need to shout. The shops on Unity Street were only the size of a front room. 'Are you listening?'

'I'm listening.'

'You don't look like you're listening.'

Frank took off his headphones. Smiled. He felt laugh lines spring all over his face and his eyes crinkled at the corners. 'See? I'm always listening.'

Maud made a noise like '*Ham.*' Then she said, 'One man called in, but it wasn't for a tattoo. He just wanted directions to the new precinct.'

Father Anthony said he'd sold a paperweight in his gift shop. Also, a leather bookmark with the Lord's Prayer stamped on it. He seemed more than happy about that.

'If it stays like this, I'll be closed by summer.'

'You won't, Maud. You'll be fine.' They had this conversation all the time. She said how awful things were, and Frank said they weren't, Maud, they weren't. You two are like a stuck record, Kit told them, which might have been funny except that he said it every night, and besides, they weren't a couple. Frank was very much a single man.

'Do you know how many funerals the undertakers have had?'

'No, Maud.'

'*Two.* Two since Christmas. What's wrong with people?'

'Maybe they're not dying,' suggested Kit.

'Of course they're dying. People don't come here any more. All they want is that crap on the high street.'

Only last month the florist had gone. Her empty shop stood on one end of the parade like a bad tooth, and a few nights ago the baker's window – he was at the other end – had been defaced with slogans. Frank had fetched a bucket of soapy water but it took all morning to wash them off.

'There have always been shops on Unity Street,' said Father Anthony. 'We're a community. We belong here.'

Saturday Kit passed with a box of new twelve-inch singles, narrowly missing a lava lamp. He seemed to have abandoned Emmylou Harris. 'We had another shoplifter today,' he said, apropos of not very much at all. 'First he flipped because we had no CDs. Then he asked to look at a record and made a run for it.'

'What was it this time?'

'Genesis. *Invisible Touch.*'

'What did you do, Frank?'

'Oh, he did the usual,' said Kit.

Yes, Frank had done the sort of thing he always did. He'd grabbed his old suede jacket and loped after the young man until he caught him at the bus stop. (What kind of thief waited for the number 11?) He'd said, between deep breaths, that he would call the police unless the lad came back and tried something new in the listening booth. He could keep the Genesis record if he wanted the thing so much, though it broke Frank's heart that he was nicking the wrong one – their early stuff was tons better. He could have the album for nothing, and even the sleeve; 'so long as you try "Fingal's Cave". If you like Genesis, trust me. You'll love Mendelssohn.'

'I wish you'd think about selling the new CDs,' said Father Anthony.

'Are you joking?' laughed Kit. 'He'd rather die than sell CDs.'

Then the door opened and *ding-dong*; a new customer. Frank felt a ping of excitement.

A tidy, middle-aged man followed the Persian runner that led all the way to the turntable. Everything about this man seemed ordinary – his coat, his hair, even his ears – as if he had been deliberately assembled so that no one would look at him twice. Head bowed, he crept past the counter to his right, where Maud stood with Father Anthony and Kit, and behind them all the records stored in cardboard master bags.

He passed the old wooden shelving to his left, the door that led up to Frank's flat, the central table, and all the plastic crates piled with surplus stock. Not even a sideways glance at the patchwork of album sleeves and homemade posters thumbtacked by Kit all over the walls. At the turntable, he stopped and pulled out a handkerchief. His eyes were red dots.

'Are you all right?' Frank asked, in his boom of a voice. 'How can I help you today?'

'The thing is, you see, I only like Chopin.'

Frank remembered now. This man had come in a few months ago. He had been looking for something to calm his nerves before his wedding.

'You bought the *Nocturnes*,' he said.

The man wriggled his mouth. He didn't seem used to the idea that anyone would remember him. 'I've got myself in another spot of difficulty. I wondered if you might – find something else for me?' He had missed a patch on his chin when he was shaving. There was something lonesome about it, that scratchy patch of stubble, all on its own.

So Frank smiled because he always smiled when a customer asked for help. He asked the same questions he always asked. Did the man know what he was looking for? (Yes. Chopin.) Had he heard anything else that he liked? (Yes. Chopin.) Could he hum it? (No. He didn't think he could.)

The man shot a look over his shoulder to make sure no one was listening but they weren't. Over the years, they'd seen everything in the music shop. There were the regular customers, of course, who came to find new records, but often people wanted something more. Frank had helped them through illness, grief, loss of confidence and jobs, as well as the more everyday things like football results and the weather. Not that he knew about all those things but really it was a matter of listening, and he had endless patience. As a boy, he could stand for hours with a piece of bread in his hand, hoping for a bird.

But the man was gazing at Frank. He was waiting.

'You just want me to find you the right record? You don't know what, but so long as it's Chopin, you'll be OK?'

'Yes, yes,' said the man. That was it exactly.

So what did he need? Frank pushed away his fringe – it flopped straight back, but there it was, the thing had a life of its own – he cupped his chin in his hands and he listened as if he were trying to find a radio signal in the ether. Something beautiful? Something slow? He barely moved, he just listened.

But when it came, it was such a blast, it took Frank's breath away. Of course. What this man needed wasn't Chopin. It wasn't even a nocturne. What he needed was—

'Wait!' Frank was already on his feet.

He lumbered around the shop, tugging out album sleeves, skirting past Kit, and ducking his head to dodge a light fitting. He just needed to find the right match for the music he had heard from the man who only liked Chopin. Piano, yes. He could hear piano. But the man needed something else as well. Something that was both tender and huge. Where would Frank find that? Beethoven? No, that would be too much. Beethoven might just floor a man like this one. What he needed was a good friend.

'Can I help you, Frank?' asked Kit. Actually he said 'Ca' I hel'?' because his eighteen-year-old mouth was full of chocolate biscuit. Kit wasn't simple or even backward, as people sometimes suggested, he was just gauche and wildly overenthusiastic, raised in a small suburban house by a mother with dementia and a father who mainly watched television. Frank had grown fond of Kit in the last few years, in the way that he had once cared for his broken van and his mother's record player. He found that if you treated him like a young terrier, sending him out for regular walks and occupying him with easy tasks, he was less liable to cause serious damage.

But what was the music he was looking for? What was it?

Frank wanted a song that would arrive like a little raft and carry this man safely home.

Piano. Yes. Brass? That could work. A voice? Maybe. Something powerful and passionate that could sound both complicated and yet so simple it was obvious—

That was it. He got it. He knew what the man needed. He swung behind the counter and pulled out the right record. But when he rushed back to his turntable, mumbling, 'Side two, track five. This is it. Yes, this is the one!' the man gave a sigh that was almost a sob it was so desperate.

'No, no. Who's this? Aretha Franklin?'

'"Oh No Not My Baby". This is it. This is the song.'

'But I told you. I want Chopin. Pop isn't going to help.'

'Aretha is *soul*. You can't argue with Aretha.'

'*Spirit in the Dark*? No, no. I don't want this record. It's not what I came for.'

Frank looked down from his great height, while the man twisted and twisted his handkerchief. 'I know it's not what you want, but trust me, today it's what you need. What have you got to lose?'

The man sent one last look in the direction of the door. Father Anthony gave a sympathetic shrug, as if to say, *Why not? We've all been there.* 'Go on, then,' said the man who only liked Chopin.

Kit sprang forward and led him to a listening booth, not exactly holding his hand, but leading the way with outstretched arms as if parts of the man were in danger of dropping off at any moment. Light bloomed from the lava lamps in shifting patterns of pink and apple-green and gold. The booths were nothing like the ones in Woolworths – those were more like standing up in a hairdryer. Their headphones were so greasy, Maud said, you had to shower afterwards. No, these booths Frank had made himself from a pair of matching Victorian wardrobes of incredible magnitude he had spotted in a skip. He had sawn off the feet, removed the hanging rails and sets of drawers, and drilled small holes to connect each one with cable to his turntable. Frank had found two armchairs, small enough to fit inside, but comfortable. He had even polished the wood until it gleamed like black gloss paint, revealing a delicate inlay in the doors of mother-of-pearl birds and flowers. The booths were beautiful when you really looked.

The man stepped in and made a sideways shuffle – there was very little space; he was being asked to sit in a piece of bedroom furniture, after all – and took his place. Frank helped with the headphones and shut the door.

'Are you all right in there?'

'This won't work,' the man called back. 'I only like Chopin.'

At his turntable, Frank eased the record from its sleeve and lifted the stylus. *Tick, tick* went the needle, riding the grooves. He flicked the speaker switch so that it would play through the whole shop. *Tick, tick—*

Vinyl had a life of its own. All you could do was wait.

2

Oh No Not My Baby

TICK, TICK. IT WAS dark inside the booth, with a hushed feeling, like hiding in a cupboard. The silence fizzed.

Everyone had warned him. Be careful, they'd said. He just wouldn't listen. So he asked her to marry him and he couldn't believe his luck when she said yes – her so beautiful, him so ordinary. Then he took her a bottle of champagne after the wedding breakfast, and there she was, upside down in the honeymoon suite. At first he couldn't work it out. He had to take a really good look. He saw a dress like a sticky meringue with four legs poking out, two with black socks, one with a garter. And then he realized. It was his new wife and his best man. He left the bottle on the floor, along with two glasses, and shut the door.

He couldn't get that picture out of his head. He played Chopin, he took pills from the doctor, and none of it made a difference. He stopped going out; he cried at the drop of a hat. He felt so bad he called in sick at work.

Tick, tick—

The song started. A twang of guitar, a blast of horns, a chirruping 'sweet-sweet-ba-by' and then a bam-bam-bam-bam from percussion.

What was Frank thinking? This wasn't the music he needed. He went to pull off the headphones—

'*When ma friends tol' me you had someone noo,*' began the singer, this Aretha, her voice clear and steady, '*I didn' believe a single word was true.*'

It was like meeting a stranger in the dark, saying to them, 'You'll never guess what?' and the stranger saying, 'Hey, but that's exactly how it is for me.'

He stopped thinking about his wife and his sadness and he listened to Aretha as if she were a voice inside his head.

She told him her story – something like this. Everyone said her man was a cheat; even her own mother said it. But Aretha wouldn't believe them. He was not like those other BOYS who lead you ON. Who tell you LIES. She started the song calmly enough but by the time she got to the chorus she was practically screaming the words. Her voice was a little boat and the music was a Japanese wave, but Aretha kept riding it, up and down. It was downright pig-headed, the way she kept believing in him. There were strings, the bobble of the guitar, a horn riff, percussion, all telling her she was wrong – '*Wohhh!*' shrilled the backing vocals, like a Greek chorus of girlfriends – but no, she hung on tight. Her voice pulled the words this way and that, soaring up over the top and then scooping right down low. Aretha knew. She knew how desperate it felt, to love a cheat. How lonely.

He sat very, very still. And he listened.

3

It's a Kind of Magic

FRANK SHOOK A cigarette from the packet and as he smoked, he watched the door of the booth. He hoped he wasn't wrong about this song. Sometimes all that people needed was to know they were not alone. Other times it was more a question of keeping them in touch with their feelings until they wore them out – people clung to what was familiar, even when it was painful.

'The thing about vinyl,' his mother used to say, 'is that you have to look after it.' He could picture Peg now, in their white house by the sea, dressed in a turban and kimono as she played him Bach or Beethoven or whatever else she'd had delivered. Peg told stories about records, little things to help him listen, and she spoke about composers like lovers. She wore massive sunglasses even when it was raining, actually even when it was pitch black, and her arms were looped with so many bangles she jingled when she laughed. She had no interest in normal mothery things. Jam sandwiches, for instance, cut into triangles. A nice casserole for his supper or cherry linctus when he had a cough. If he showed her a shell, or a ribbon of seaweed, she tended to lob it straight back at the sea, and whenever she drove the old Rover into town it was Frank who had to remind her about the handbrake. (She had an unfortunate habit of rolling forward.) Yes, being a regular mother was anathema to Peg but when it came to vinyl, she displayed a care that verged on sacred. And she could talk music for hours.

The song began to fade. The door of the booth gave a click and opened. Off went those mother-of-pearl birds, shaking their wings and taking flight.

The man who only liked Chopin didn't come out. He stood at the door, looking candlewax-white and a bit sick.

'Well?' said Frank. 'How was it?'

'Well?' Over at the counter, Maud, Father Anthony and Saturday Kit were all waiting too. Kit jumped first on one leg and then on the other. Father Anthony had lifted his glasses on top of his head and wore them like a hairband. Maud frowned.

The man who only liked Chopin began to laugh. 'Wow, that was something. How did you know I needed Aretha? How did you *do* that, Frank?'

'Do what? I just played you a good song.'

'Did Aretha Franklin make any more records?'

Now it was Frank's turn to laugh. 'She did actually. You're in luck. She made a lot. She really liked singing.'

He played the whole record, side one and then side two. As he listened, Frank smoked and danced in the cramped space behind his turntable, rolling his shoulders and swinging his hips – watching him, even Maud began to sway – while Kit did something that was possibly the funky chicken, but could equally be to do with his new shoes hurting his feet. It was Aretha at her best. Everyone should own a copy of *Spirit in the Dark*.

Afterwards Kit made cups of tea and Frank listened at his turntable while the man told him more about his wife. How he couldn't so much as touch her after the wedding. How she'd moved out a month ago to live with his best man. It was a relief, he said, just to tell someone all this. Frank nodded as he listened and reassured the man, over and over, that he could come to the shop whenever he needed. 'Just bang on the door if I'm not open. It doesn't matter what time it is. I'm always here. You don't need to be on your own.'

They were small things really, and pretty obvious ones, but the man smiled as if Frank had given him a brand-new heart.

'Have *you* ever been in a mess like this?' he asked. 'Have you ever been in love?'

Frank laughed. 'I'm done with all that. My shop is all I need.'

'These days he hardly leaves,' piped up Father Anthony.

'Could I listen to my song again?'

'Of course you can listen again.'

The man shut himself back in the booth and Frank reset the needle on the vinyl. '*When ma friends tol' me you had someone noo . . .*' His gaze drifted to the window.

So empty and quiet out there. Nothing coming, nothing going, just the thin blue light, the cold. Frank could not play music, he could not read a score, he had no practical knowledge whatsoever, but when he sat in front of a customer and truly listened, he heard a kind of song. He wasn't talking a full-blown symphony. It would be a few notes; at the most, a strain. And it didn't happen all the time, only when he let go of being Frank and inhabited a space that was more in the middle. It had been this way ever since he could remember. 'Intuition,' Father Anthony called it. 'Weird shit': that was Maud.

16

So what did it matter if he had no one in particular in his life? He was happy alone. He lit up another smoke.

And then he saw her. She was looking straight at him.

4

The Shop on Unity Street

THE FIRST TIME Frank saw his shop, he burst out laughing. *Haw haw haw.* Great joyous lungfuls. It was fourteen years ago. 1974: Britain was in its first recession since the war. The miners were on strike and a three-day week was in force.

He had been wandering the city for hours. He had no idea where he was heading. He passed the cathedral, the network of old alleys, passages and cobbled lanes that surrounded it, with their trinket shops and cafés. He walked the length of Castlegate, the main shopping precinct in the city, staring at the big windows, and he visited the clock tower. Further on he noticed gates to a park, a queue at the dole office, he tried an amusement arcade and afterwards browsed a line of market stalls; then he followed several residential roads in the direction of the old docks. He only stopped at Unity Street because it was a cul-de-sac with a pub and six shops on one side, and a row of Victorian brown-brick houses on the other. Short of climbing rooftops, he couldn't physically go any further.

And so he paused and he really looked at it; this little run-down street. An Italian flag at the window of one house, the smell of spices bursting from its neighbour, a woman in a headdress shelling peas on her doorstep, a gang of kids pushing a trolley, a set of letters painted across another façade, advertising *Rooms to Let*. He stared at the parade of shops. An undertaker, a Polish bakery, a religious gift shop, the empty shell with a *For Sale* notice at the window, then a tattoo parlour, and finally a florist. He saw two old men in the undertaker's window offering tissues to a woman who was crying. He saw a boy pointing to a cake in the bakery; another man in his fifties helping a girl choose a plastic Jesus in Articles of Faith. He saw a young woman with painted skin mopping her floor, a pair of curtains at her window and the word TATTOUISTA on the glass, while an old lady in a sari emerged from the florist with an armful of flowers, calling her thank you as she closed the door. It was the everyday ordinariness of it that moved him. That, and the usefulness, as if this diverse mix of people had always been there, like mothers and fathers, helping others to find what they needed. In his mind's eye, the future appeared to him in the same way he had seen the distant horizon materializing out of a sea mist at the white house; blurred and remote, but beautiful and full of hope. That was when he began to laugh, and it was years since Frank had laughed like that. He went straight to the estate agent.

'Of course the shop needs a little love, sir,' said the agent, putting down his sandwich and searching for the keys. 'You will have to use your imagination once we're inside.'

A little love? The interior was a wreck. It was choked with rubbish and the stench was sickening – clearly people had been using it as a toilet. Someone had even ripped up the floorboards and lit a fire.

'I like it,' said Frank. And he touched the walls, just to reassure them. 'Yes, I'll pay the full asking price.'

'Really? You don't want to make an offer?'

'No. It's right for me. I don't want to haggle.'

Ask Frank to love a nice house with a garden, all mod cons, he would have turned on his heels. Ask him to fall in love with another human being, he'd have fled. But *this*. Broken as it was, and manky and misused – yes, this was on his level. He admitted to the estate agent he didn't have any experience with DIY but guessed it couldn't be so hard if you got a book from the library. He also admitted he didn't have much of a clue about shops. Peg had only ever had things sent by special delivery. He mentioned Harrods, Fortnum's and Deutsche Grammophon.

The estate agent – whose wife drove to the supermarket every Saturday – couldn't believe his luck. The property had been empty for a year and the parade was on its last legs; lumps of masonry had a habit of dropping to the ground whenever someone slammed a door. Beyond it lay an expanse of rubble where a bomb had hit the street in '41. Last time the agent looked, he'd seen scrappy children playing there, and also a tethered goat. The street was a complete mish-mash. One day a developer would have the sense to flatten the whole lot and build a car park.

But Frank didn't seem to notice. Instead he suggested a beer in England's Glory, the pub on the corner. There was something about this great big young man, with his wild hair and shabby clothes, his funny lollopy way of walking as if he still hadn't got the measure of his feet, that baffled the estate agent. A kind of innocence you didn't often see. His hands were soft as powder puffs; clearly he'd never done a day's hard work. And he couldn't stop talking about records.

When the agent asked what had brought him to this particular nook, Frank said his van had just stopped. (*Nook* was estate-agent speak. There was nothing *nookish* about this corner of England. It was an eyesore. Its main industry was processed food. Flavoured snacks, to be precise. When the wind blew in the wrong direction, the entire city smelt of cheese and onion.)

But the estate agent was not the only one who was being fanciful. Frank too could have been more specific. He could have said his van had not exactly been going for the last twenty miles. And he might also have mentioned that since the death of Peg, his life was a write-off; he didn't even have the white house by the sea. Recently he'd been on the move, and sleeping rough, and waiting for a solution to jump out at him. And now here it was. If he could run a small shop in a dead-end street, without the complications of love or ties – if he could put everything into serving ordinary people and avoid receiving anything in return – he thought he might just about get by. He sold his van for scrap and signed the paperwork that afternoon. He didn't even wait for a survey.

'So you're gonna open a music shop?' Maud asked, the first time they met. She was a short, blocky young woman with a Mohican that she dyed different colours to suit her mood – generally very dark colours that were not to be found in nature. Her skin was an inky web of hearts and flowers.

Frank looked up from the kerb where he was sitting in the sun. He held a notepad and pencil. He was drawing smiley faces.

'Yes,' he said. 'I'm going to help people find music.'

'What about Woolworths?'

'What about Woolworths?'

'There's one on Castlegate. It's a ten-minute walk from here.'

'Oh,' said Frank. 'I wondered where I was going to get chart singles.' He went back to the notebook.

21

'You mean you have no stock?'

'Stock?'

She rolled her eyes. 'Cassette tapes and stuff?'

'I have all my old records in my van. But I won't sell tapes. There's no beauty in tapes. I'll just sell vinyl.'

'What about the people who want to buy tapes?'

He smiled. To his confusion, she turned a scalded shade of red as if she'd just been attacked with a blowtorch. 'They can go to Woolworths.'

'The old woman who used to own your shop sold sewing stuff. No one came, you know. She lost her marbles. Ended up in a home.'

Frank made a mental note not to depend on Maud if he was ever in need of good cheer.

He began the refit straight away. In one morning alone, he dragged out a washing machine, a car battery, a mower and an iron cot. Ivy was uprooted, floors swept, window frames prised open. Now empty, the shop was suddenly full of potential. It seemed so much bigger from the inside than if you were just passing. A counter could go here to the side of the door, a turntable at the back. There was even room for two listening booths. He bought a bag of tools and set to work.

Frank might have cut a lonely figure but this did not make him unusual on Unity Street, where many people had once been alone. And barely a day went by without someone popping his head round the door – actually *through* the door, there was as yet no glass – to take over the work. Frank found them records by way of payment. The shopkeepers he had observed so carefully now took him under their wing. He learnt more about the ex-priest who had retired early for personal reasons and poured a drink around the same time he poured a bowl of

22

cornflakes. He learnt more about the old twin brothers whose family had run the funeral business for four generations, and sometimes held hands like children. He heard the story of the Polish baker, and he began to realize that when the tattooist scowled, it might actually be a smile.

Inside the shop, broken floorboards were replaced. Walls were replastered. Pipes were repaired, roof tiles fitted, and so were windows. The staircase to the flat was made safe and the building was replumbed. When his cash ran out, Frank applied to the bank for a loan.

'You won't get it,' said Maud.

It turned out the bank manager's wife had just had a baby. The poor woman had not slept in weeks. The bank manager confessed to Frank he had no idea how to help his wife; he'd tried everything. Frank sat forward – the chair was on the small side, in point of fact it was verging on miniature – and listened with his chin in his hands. He forgot all about the loan. He just listened. It was only at the very end of the interview that the bank manager read through Frank's paperwork and said that since he had no experience in retail, the bank would never agree. 'You seem a good man,' he said. 'But with inflation as high as it is, we can't take any risks.' As well as the recession, everyone was worrying about the Cold War. They fully expected to wake up one morning and find Soviet tanks parked outside the Co-op.

Frank returned to the bank the following day with two records – *Waltz For Debby* by Bill Evans, and the canticles of Hildegard von Bingen – along with a note, listing the tracks the manager's wife should play. He also included a lullaby. (*'Your wife doesn't have to listen to this,'* he had scribbled. *'This is just for the baby.'*) The lullaby was not an obvious choice and neither was it classical. It was 'Wild Thing' by The Troggs.

23

But it worked. The bank manager wrote to Frank. (Beautifully typed.) His wife had slept. And the moment the baby heard his lullaby, he too fell into a kind of trance, as if for the first time someone had recognized the animal inside him and made a safe place for it. The bank manager added that it would be a pleasure to provide the full loan. He enclosed the necessary paperwork – he had taken the liberty of filling in the form on Frank's behalf. He finished the letter with best wishes for the future and his name: 'Henry'. From that day on, they became good friends.

Simple wooden shelves were built. Frank bought a proper turntable and a pair of JBL speakers. In the early days the shop was stocked entirely with his own albums and singles. Because he loved them and knew everything about them, he arranged them carefully in boxes; not by genre, or letters of the alphabet, but more instinctively. He put Bach's *Brandenburg Concertos*, for instance, beside *Pet Sounds* by The Beach Boys and Miles Davis' *Bitches Brew*. ('Same thing, different time,' he said.) For Frank, music was like a garden – it sowed seeds in far-flung places. People would miss out on so many wonderful things if they only stuck with what they knew.

For a couple of years no reps would visit. It looked more like a shed than a shop, one of them said. There was the big Woolworths on Castlegate and a new Our Price Records had opened less than ten miles away. Then when *Never Mind the Bollocks* was released in '77, Frank was the only record shop owner within a twenty-mile radius who would take it. He sold out in two days. He had to borrow Maud's Cortina and drive to London to buy an entire new stock. He filled his shop with small independent labels he'd never even heard of until now. *Cherry Red Records, Good Vibrations, Object Music, Factory, Postcard, Rough Trade, Beggars Banquet, 4AD*. In the early eighties, a rep dropped by every day.

They unpacked promotional T-shirts, posters, tickets. Even freebies; ten records for the price of one. No matter that he refused to stock cassette tapes; the music shop was on the map, and so was Unity Street. Frank was so busy on Saturdays he advertised for an assistant, though Kit was the only applicant who produced a homemade CV, listing every club he had joined – Cubs, Scouts (both the landed and the sea variety), as well as St John Ambulance cadets, the National Philatelic Society and the Diana Ross fan club. He was clearly desperate to escape.

Now that CDs were on the rise, a few customers and reps had stopped calling at the music shop. Out of date, they called Frank. Pig-headed. But it was kind of cool, everyone else agreed. When a man has the passion to stand up for something crazy, it makes other problems in people's lives seem more straightforward. And anyway – as Frank was often pointing out – customers could go to Woolworths or Our Price if they wanted a cassette, or even a new CD. They had stacks of the things.

How could anyone get excited about a piece of shiny plastic? CDs wouldn't last, they were a gimmick, and so were cassettes. 'I don't care what anyone tells me. The future's vinyl,' he said.

5

The Woman Who Fell to Earth

SHE WAS STANDING outside. A woman in a green coat. Afterwards he could have sworn she was trying to tell him something, that there was a special glimmer in her eyes even then, but that was probably one of those details that come with hindsight. The simple fact was that one minute there she was, pale face pressed to the window, her hands cupped to her head like two small flaps, then – bang. The pavement seemed to swallow her. She was gone.

'Did you see that?' called Father Anthony. His mouth gave up and he stopped talking.

Frank loped to the door and threw it open, followed by Kit, Maud and the old priest. The woman was lying on her back on the pavement, caught in the river of light from the music shop. She was still and absolutely straight. Her hands were flat at her sides – she was wearing gloves – and her shoes poked upwards. He had never seen her before.

'What could have happened?' said Father Anthony.

'Oh my God. Is she dead?' asked Kit.

Frank was at her side and on his knees without noticing, though once he was down, he sort of wished he was back up. The woman's eyes were closed and there was no trace of blood. Her face was small and definite – her mouth and nose almost too big – slim eyebrows, a delicate chin that appeared even smaller given the exaggerated width of her jawbone, a neck as long as a stem, and the skin around her nose so freckled it was as if someone had dipped a brush in paint and spattered her, just for the fun of it. There was something about her that was both fragile and incredibly strong.

Father Anthony unbuttoned his cardigan and draped it over her. Kit's training as a St John Ambulance cadet now crashed to the fore and he too ran to help. The most important thing in an emergency, he said, was to assess the situation as quickly as possible, without panic, and then to offer the patient reassurance. If she required medical attention he would do his best, though the honest truth was that he hadn't progressed beyond bandaging a table leg.

'Her pulse, Frank,' whispered Father Anthony. 'Feel her pulse.'

Frank slipped his fingertips beneath her collar. The skin was so soft, it was like touching something you shouldn't.

'Is she breathing?' asked Kit. Sounding panicky.

'I don't know.'

At the age of forty, Frank had only seen one dead body and that was his mother's. This stillness didn't feel final; it was more as though the woman had put herself on hold. She might be in her late twenties. Thirty, at a push.

By now a few people had appeared from the houses opposite. Somebody said to fetch blankets, someone else said to get her into the warmth, another person said you shouldn't move her in case her neck was broken. Then a man began to shout about ringing for an ambulance. The chaos was completely at odds with the stillness that seemed to wind like the finest thread around Frank and this woman, pulling them together and away from everything else. The rest of the world had receded, irrelevant, watery, distant.

'Hello?' said Frank. 'Can you hear me? Hello?'

A flicker of life crept into her face. Slowly her eyelids lifted. It came as a shock to meet her eyes. They were astonishingly large, and black as vinyl.

'She's alive!' someone shouted. And someone else said, 'She opened her eyes!' They still sounded miles away.

She fixed Frank with those great big eyes. She didn't smile. She just stared as if she were seeing right through to the heart of him. Then they closed again.

Father Anthony bowed closer. 'Keep talking.'

Keep talking? What could Frank say? He was used to people standing at his turntable, a little nervous, a little ordinary, but not stretched out on the pavement and swinging in and out of wakefulness. 'You have to stay with me. You have to keep listening to me, OK?'

He realized how cold it was. Even with his jacket on, he was trembling.

'Stay with me,' he said; 'I'm here.' He thought that sounded pretty much like someone who knew what he was talking about, so he said it again, in a slightly extended Long Player version. 'You must stay with me because here I am.' She didn't respond.

'We'd better carry her inside,' said Father Anthony.

Frank bent closer. He attempted to lift the woman without appearing to do anything so intimate as touch her. As he brought her to sitting, her head flopped against his mouth and he smelt the musk of her hair. So now here he was, on his knees, with a sleeping or possibly unconscious woman in his arms – but not, he was pretty sure now, a dying one – and a crowd of people, urging him to stand up, stay put, wait for an ambulance, get her inside.

'Shall I help?' asked Kit, now blowing on her in an effort to keep her warm. *Woof, woof, woof.*

'Please don't,' said Frank.

To his relief, Father Anthony knelt opposite. He had clearly done this kind of thing before. He whispered, 'Ready?' and then he seemed to bear the weight of the woman as the two men rose to their feet.

'You take her now,' said Father Anthony.

'Me?'

'Don't look so terrified. I'm right beside you.'

Frank carried her towards the shop, feeling the way with his plimsolls. It seemed to take an unconscionably long time. Now that she was in his arms, there was more of her than he had imagined, and his legs were turned to mush. Years ago he had to help his mother up the stairs if she'd had one too many gin cocktails, but no one in their right mind would have attempted lifting Peg. She'd have flattened you.

Kit rushed ahead to swing open the door and inside the shop Father Anthony pulled crates out of the way to clear a space on the Persian runner, while Maud appeared with towels and an industrial-size bottle of Dettol. (What she intended to do with them, no one dared ask.) Frank lowered the woman to the ground.

'Go and fetch her a blanket.' Who said that? Probably Father Anthony.

Upstairs in his flat, Frank pushed past boxes of records. He couldn't

29

think straight. A feeling had welled up from somewhere deep inside him, he didn't even know where, some place out in the shadows where things happened from a different time, or a part of his life that he had left behind. It was the way she had gazed up at him. Eyes closed and then *bing*. A look of such radiance and intensity he could not see how he would ever get away from it.

Frank lumbered from room to room, grabbing things as he saw them, a blanket, a glass of water, some plasters, and then just as he reached the stairs it occurred to him she might be hungry so he ran back for a box of Ritz crackers.

By the time he made it down, the shop was full. People were offering coats – a few had fetched blankets – but the woman was already on her feet. She looked even lovelier now that she was vertical. Despite the excitement around her, she remained with her spine very straight, her neck tall, and her long arms folded back like a pair of wings. She just seemed to be in a different space from everyone else. Her dark hair was half pinned up, half falling down.

She checked her coat and tie belt – not that either of them was remotely wonky – and then her gaze roamed the crowd until it settled on Frank. Once again, their eyes locked and everything else in his shop gave way and disappeared.

'*Was mache ich hier?*' she murmured. Her voice was hushed and broken, as if she had a cold. Then in English: 'Excuse me.'

She made a rush for the door. People were saying, 'Who are you?' 'What happened?' 'Are you OK now?' Kit was calling, 'Wait! Wait!' and someone else was saying stop, stop, they had rung for an ambulance. But she took no notice. She pushed past, almost rudely, threw herself out of the shop and turned right in the direction of the city centre.

Frank stepped outside and watched as she rushed past the religious gift shop, the funeral parlour, the Polish bakery and the pub on the corner. Her shoes went *crack crack* on the sparkling pavement as if she were snapping things in half. Streetlamps bored funnels into the dark and the windows of the houses opposite were yellow squares. At the end of Unity Street she turned left towards Castlegate – she didn't look back.

It was years since Frank had felt so naked and light. He had to lean against the door, and breathe deeply.

He wondered if he was coming down with something.

When Frank was twenty-five, his mother hit the earth like a falling planet. Afterwards he sat every day at her bedside, unable to move, more clothes than man, staring at the tube taped to her mouth, the clipboard at the foot of her bed, not to mention the plastic cups of coffee or beef soup – it all looked the same – that he bought from the vending machine and failed to drink. She left him her entire music collection; the old Dansette Major, the endless boxes of vinyl. Then came the other news, and it was like being ripped open. He couldn't even sing 'Hallelujah' at her funeral.

'Who *was* that woman?' Father Anthony asked later in England's Glory. He held a glass of pineapple juice because he was teetotal these days. The man who only liked Chopin had bought a full round and was sharing a bar stool with Kit. Mr Novak, the baker, had joined them, his grey hair freshly slicked and his trousers pressed with a crease; it always came as a surprise to see him without a coating of flour. Plastic bunting hung above the bar from the Royal Wedding two years ago.

31

Everyone wanted to speculate about the foreign woman who had fainted. Even the regulars began to chip in. A line of old men at the bar agreed she must have been on holiday. A woman in curlers wondered if she was on the run, while a man with three teeth suggested she could have been a doctor. They wore green coats.

'So do leprechauns,' said Maud.

'She looked like a film star to me,' said Kit.

'Don't be a pillock. Why would a film star come all the way out here?'

'Well, I don't know. Maybe she was a lost film star.'

The man who only liked Chopin regretted he hadn't seen her properly. He'd been so caught up in Aretha, the first he knew of the woman fainting was when he opened the door of the booth and saw her running away. He asked if anyone fancied pork scratchings. ('I do,' said Kit.)

Father Anthony agreed that regardless of whether or not she was a tourist, a doctor or indeed a film star, she didn't look like the sort of person who usually came down Unity Street. She was elegantly dressed, for a start – her clothes were actually colour-coordinated and appeared to have no holes – though why a woman would fall to the ground outside a music shop remained a mystery. A wonderful accident.

'So why did she faint?' repeated Kit.

Why indeed? Again, everyone had a host of opinions. Even the people who had not been there; especially them, in fact. Was it the cold? Was she ill? Low blood pressure? Was she on drugs? Or had she just not eaten all day? The more they guessed, the more mysterious and enchanting she became.

Maud grabbed her drink and sucked with unnecessary violence on the straw. 'Anyone would think none of you had been with a woman before.' (She had a point.) 'Anyone would think you never left Unity Street.' (Yet again, Maud had a point.) 'The woman probably got hit by a piece of falling masonry. She'll probably sue you for damages, Frank.'

He sat hunched over his beer, not really drinking and not speaking either.

There was something completely different about her, something he had never met before. It wasn't the way she dressed. It wasn't even the way she looked or spoke. But what was it? He couldn't get it. His thoughts seemed made of wood.

The Williams brothers arrived from the funeral parlour, muffled up against the cold. Williams #1 ordered port and lemon at the bar while Williams #2 fetched chairs. They too had heard all about the woman.

'Apparently you almost dropped her,' said Williams. (Was this #1 or #2? Impossible to know. For a time they had worn different ties to help people tell them apart but there was a rumour they had swapped them, just for the fun of it.)

'Shame you two didn't get there first,' said Maud. 'She'd be in a hole by now.'

No one quite knew what to do with that remark. They decided to sit very still and wait for it to go away.

Pete the barman put down his tea towel and began to grin. 'Shame she didn't need the kiss of life. Eh, Frank? Know what I mean?' Well, everyone thought that was hilarious; Kit laughed so hard he almost catapulted Chopin Man off their bar stool.

33

'Are you all right there?' said Father Anthony. 'You've not made a sound.'

That was it. Frank got it. He realized the thing that was so different about her.

6

The Magic of Silence

'MUSIC IS ABOUT silence,' she said in the white house by the sea.

'Yes, Peg.' He never called her 'mother'.

A box of new Long Players stood on the table, this month's delivery from the subscription club. She pulled out the first one, and unwrapped the paper. Beethoven. Symphony No. 5.

'Music comes out of silence and at the end it goes back to it. It's a journey. You see?'

'Yes, Peg.' Though he didn't see. Not yet. He was only six.

Easing the new record from its sleeve, she raised it towards the window. She tipped it this way, that way. Black as liquorice and twice as shiny. He breathed in the beautiful smell.

'And of course the silence at the beginning of a piece of music is always different from the silence at the end.'

'Why, Peg?'

'Because if you listen, the world changes. It's like falling in love. Only no one gets hurt.' She gave a throaty laugh and reached for a cigarette. 'Now, then. Would you open the Dansette?'

Frank walked slowly towards the gramophone. This was the superior model

– the Dansette Major – with a grey leatherette finish and a deep red trim. When he twisted the top dial, the gramophone woke with a low buzzy growl. He lifted the lid open and eased it back on its hinges.

'Ready?'

'Yes, Peg.'

She lowered the disc on to the spindle and he held his breath as the tone arm jerked to life.

'Brace yourself,' she said. 'Here come the most famous four notes in history.'

Da da da dum. The sound crept out of the silence like a great beast emerging from the sea. Da da da dum.

'Hear that?' She lifted the needle.

'What, Peg?'

'You heard the little pause in the middle?'

'Yes.'

'You see? You see what Beethoven's doing? There is silence inside music too. It's like reaching a hole. You don't know what will happen next.'

After that, they lay side by side on the floor. Her, sucking a chain of Sobranie cigarettes. Frank in his pyjamas. If they wanted to speak, they whispered, as though they were watching the music from behind a tree. 'You hear that?' 'You hear this?' 'Yes, Peg, yes.' He had suggested once she might get a job as a teacher and to his confusion Peg howled with laughter. She knew about music because she loved it. Her father could have been a pianist if he hadn't married money. Instead he drank a lot and had affairs. 'But sometimes he told me about music,' she said another time. She went very still.

Over time, Peg played all the silences she loved. The more Frank listened, the more he understood. Silence could be exciting, it could be scary, it could be like flying, or even a really good joke. Years later, he would hear that final

36

pause in 'A Day In The Life' by The Beatles – the one that gave just enough time to breathe before the last chord fell like a piece of furniture from the sky – and he would dance with joy at the sheer audacity of it.

But Peg's favourite was the 'Hallelujah Chorus'. The brief moment of anticipation before the timpani-pounding climax. It had her in floods. Every time.

Silence was where the magic happened.

7

The Four Seasons

'FRANK, YOU NEED to help me. It went just like this.'

Three days later, old Mrs Roussos was singing in one of the booths with her white chihuahua on her lap. Frank sat behind his turntable, trying to help. The turntable was a large wooden unit and it doubled as an office; it held a drift of invoices as well as cigarettes, mugs, tissues, catalogues, replacement styluses, bananas – he seemed to live on them – and a large number of small broken things. The latest broken thing was Frank's yellow canister pencil sharpener, which had functioned as both a sharpener and a rubber until Kit borrowed it. Kit had an ability to fall over things that were not even there – Frank had given him a permanent job to save him from a lifetime in the food factory – so really the breaking of the pencil sharpener should not have come as any kind of surprise, but it had bothered Frank.

It was a small thing but he couldn't snap it back together.

And he liked that pencil sharpener.

'Are you listening to me?'

'Yes, Mrs Roussos.'

The old lady had a tune in her head and she would get no sleep until

Frank found the record. Mrs Roussos got a tune in her head at least once a week and it could take several hours to locate it. This one was something about a hill. At least she thought it was.

'Tell me where you heard it, Mrs Roussos,' said Frank, putting down the two halves of his pencil sharpener and lighting a cigarette instead. 'Was it on the radio?'

'Not the radio, Frank. I don't have a radio.'

'You do have a radio.'

'I did have a radio but I don't any more. It stopped.'

Mrs Roussos' radio was a huge old Bakelite thing about the size of a microwave, and Frank had visited her several times to fix it. He didn't know how to fix sharpeners and he didn't know how to fix old radios, but normally the problem was more a matter of plugging it in, or turning up the volume, and he knew how to do both those things. Besides, Mrs Roussos lived alone with her chihuahua across the street and she was one of Frank's oldest customers. 'How could it just *stop*?' he asked.

Mrs Roussos said she had no idea. It was now on its side with its legs in the air. If she didn't believe him, he should come and take a look. Then she began to sing again. Her voice was high and fine, surprisingly girlish for an old Greek woman in her eighties. Recently her hands had begun to shake, and her neck too, as if it couldn't quite get the right balance for her head.

'Is it Mozart?' asked Frank.

'Don't be ridiculous.'

'Sounds more like Petula Clark,' said Kit.

'Are you both fools?' Undeterred, Mrs Roussos lifted her chin and sang some more.

Frank closed his eyes. He dug his fingertips into the soft sockets, trying to concentrate. He felt churned up. It wasn't just the sharpener. He couldn't stop thinking about the woman who had fainted. It had been like this the first time Peg played him *La Bohème*. Again when he saw David Bowie on *Top of the Pops* performing 'Starman', and the night he heard John Peel playing 'New Rose' by The Damned. What he had felt in those moments was like being wired up to something explosive. It was so new to him, it had felt all wrong – and at the same time he had known it was entirely right. But that was *music*. Not a stranger in a pea-green coat.

And yet when Frank had knelt at her side on the pavement, when he had touched her neck for the pulse – when he carried her towards his shop – everything had changed. She had gazed at him as if she knew him, but she was a complete mystery. He had never heard such silence in a person. Nothing had come from her. Not one note.

'Pst, pst.'

Kit's warm mouth whispered violently in Frank's ear.

'Pst, pst. She's back. The woman who ran away.'

She was standing on the doormat, so that even though she was inside the shop, she appeared more outside it. Frank felt his heart surge as if on a wave. She was wearing the same coat and held a bag in one hand, a potted plant in the other. Something had happened with her hair – bits of it were piled up on top of her head like a flower, while other bits hung loose. Her too-short fringe only accentuated the roundness of her eyes and mouth. How could so much irregular loveliness have been put together in one small frame? He was terrified.

Saturday Kit was already skipping forward to help. 'It's you! It's you! Hello! Are you OK now? Are you better?'

'I am looking for the man,' she said in her wispy voice and choppy accent, 'who runs this shop.'

Kit swung his leg like a pendulum while explaining that he was the assistant manager. When he was excited or nervous, he had a way of talking in exclamation marks, suggesting everything was a marvellous surprise. He added that he wished he had a proper blue uniform!! Like the sales assistants at Woolworths!! With a badge that said 'KIT WELCOMES YOU'!! He made all his own pin badges, he said. He pointed to a selection on his camouflage jacket. *Wham!*, *Culture Club*, *Haircut 100*, as well as *I Shot JR*, *Frankie says Relax*, *Coal not Dole* and *Choose Life!!!!*

This was possibly more information than the woman required. She'd only walked into a record shop. She said, 'Is there another man who works here, please?' She spoke slowly, casting her gaze, as if she wasn't sure she would find the right words and was wondering if they might have the goodness to appear like cue cards somewhere to her left and right.

Frank eyeballed the door to his flat. It was only a matter of feet away. If he crawled on his hands and knees he might escape without her noticing—

'Yes, Frank is sitting right there,' said Kit, pointing expansively. 'Behind his turntable.'

So there was nothing for it. Frank shambled past the central table, only halfway he lost his nerve and stopped to rearrange a few record sleeves.

The woman crossed the floor as if she didn't quite trust it. She stood on one side of the unit. Frank stood on the other. She smelt of lemon and expensive soap.

'I was just passing,' she said. 'I'm new here.'

Frank's eyes were fixed on an album sleeve, and yet he had no idea what he was looking at. He listened and listened – and it was exactly the same as before. Nothing came from her. If anything, it was like listening to an absence of sound.

'I was just passing,' she repeated. 'That's all.'

Kit went the colour of a cooked prawn and rushed to the door, gabbling something about Blu-Tack from Woolworths. Before Frank could ask what the hell he was up to, he flew out.

What do you say to a woman with a potted plant, whose tender long neck you have touched even before you said 'Hello', and whom you have thought about ever since she ran out of your shop? In the circumstances, Frank thought the best thing would be to look like a shopkeeper who was extremely busy doing shop-like things. So he flipped through record sleeves. Kit had clearly been here before him – a stack of B's had been gathered up and placed together in something almost amounting to alphabetical order. Bach was beside Beethoven and Brahms, along with Count Basie, The Beat, The B-52s, Art Blakey, Big Star, Chuck Berry, The Beatles and Burt Bacharach. (But also Thin Lizzy.)

She said, 'What a lot of records.'

He said, 'Yes.'

She said, 'How many?'

'I don't know.' Then he said, 'I have even more upstairs.' Granted this was not the most exciting dialogue, but at least there was a lot of basic truth in it.

'I see you don't have any sections?'

'I put records where I think they should go. I am more interested in what it's like when you – when you, uh, you know . . .'

He dared a glance at her. Her eyes were so wide they were practically popping from their sockets. 'What?' she asked.

'When you – *listen*. So if a customer asks for *Rubber Soul*, they usually find something else they would like as well. Not just The Beatles but maybe something, uh, classical as well; a record they wouldn't have tried if the two weren't together.' This part of Frank's answer was addressed to his plimsolls. In fact now he examined his feet it occurred to him his shoes were the size of loaves and held together with electrical tape. He wondered why it hadn't occurred to him to buy new ones.

Her shoes were narrow – pointed toe, slim heel. He thought her bare foot would fit in his hand.

She said, 'You don't sell CDs?'

'I beg your pardon?'

'CDs? They are round things—'

'CDs aren't music. They're toys. And before you ask, I don't sell cassette tapes either.'

He hoped she hadn't read his mind – about her feet in his hands, and so on.

'Oh, by the way,' she said, 'this is for you.'

She held out the plant. It was about the size of a child's fist and covered in vicious prickles. He wasn't sure how you accepted a gift like that without getting hurt.

He said, 'Did you faint? The other day?'

'I decided to have a little nap.'

She stared straight at him with her huge, dark eyes. Then her great bud of a mouth did something funny.

It smiled.

Two dimples punctured her cheeks. His heart seemed to fall over.

She said, 'I didn't really. That was a joke.'

'A what?'

'A joke? To make you laugh?'

'Oh. I see. Yes.' HAW HAW HAW he went. HAW HAW HAW.

'Frank,' interrupted an imperious voice from behind. 'Are you intending to spend all day with that person?'

Mrs Roussos. Frank had completely forgotten her.

'Wait!' Frank said to the woman-in-green-with-a-cactus-plant. 'Don't go!'

He shot back to his turntable, in so far as he ever shot anywhere, and opening his *Music Master* catalogue he made a show of flipping through the pages. Words spilled. All he could think of was *her*, waiting still and silent. Never mind Mrs Roussos, what music did this woman need? Blues? Motown? Mozart? Patti Smith? He hadn't a clue. And he was still none the wiser as to why she had fainted. Where was Kit when you actually needed him?

'Frank, are you listening to me?'

'Of course I'm listening, Mrs Roussos.'

The old lady sat with her chihuahua in the booth, the door wide open – there was something mildly unsettling about that – while Frank moved around the shop, fetching one track after another. 'Solsbury Hill'? 'The Fool On The Hill'? 'Blueberry Hill'? And all the while the woman in her green coat was watching him—

'Wait.' He stopped in his tracks. '*There is a green hill far away*?'

That was it. Bingo. Mrs Roussos hobbled from the booth with her chihuahua clutched to her chest like a pop-eyed brooch. She told Frank he was a good man, there weren't many in the world; now she could sleep. He fetched the record from its sleeve behind the counter, and tapped the details into his sales return machine, same as always, only nothing about this was the same as always because here she was, this woman with her

44

rod-like back, her head lifted proudly, one heel dug deep and the toe pointing upwards, watching him steadily, but so unknown.

'You seem to have an audience.' She drifted towards his turntable but she pointed her finger over her shoulder at the window.

Five faces were smudged against the glass: Kit, the baker, Father Anthony and the two Williams brothers. Maud was also with them, but she was not looking inside the shop. She had her back to it and was apparently surveying the street, though it would be a small miracle if anything went and happened out there.

Clearly Kit had not gone to Woolworths at all – he'd run straight to the other shops along the parade to share the news about the return of the mysterious woman. You'd think a new star had been spotted in the sky and now here they all were, waiting for Frank to identify it.

Kit pushed open the door – *ding-dong* – and the shopkeepers shuffled inside in single file. They got extremely busy pretending they weren't there. The baker stood in a puddle of flour, Father Anthony began folding an origami bird, the Williams brothers passed their hats through their hands like wheels, while Kit unwrapped the foil from a chocolate biscuit in a meditative manner. Maud just scowled. She was dressed in Doc Martens, her leather jacket, stripy tights and a sort of sticking-out netting skirt. She looked every bit the bad fairy.

Frank felt both colossally large and vacuous. Everyone seemed to be waiting for him to say something enlightening.

'Is there anything I can help you with today? A record?' It was the best he could think of, in the circumstances.

At first the woman didn't reply. She just remained standing in her still and solemn way, as if she honestly believed he was addressing someone else. Then the penny must have dropped.

'Oh no,' she answered. 'I don't listen to music.'

A jolt passed through the shop. Everyone stopped what they (weren't) doing and all-out stared. Kit was open-mouthed. You could fit a whole plum in there.

'You don't listen to music?' Frank repeated her sentence very slowly and even so, it made no sense. 'Why not?'

She gave an awkward smile. 'I don't know.'

'Do you like jazz? Do you like classical?' This was Kit. He had obviously decided Frank required assistance and was rushing around the shop, pulling out record sleeves and holding them up. 'Do you like choral? We don't have the *Messiah* because Frank can't listen to that one, but we have loads of other stuff.'

'I don't know,' murmured the woman. 'I am not sure.'

'We have all sorts of music. Don't we, Frank?'

But now Frank seemed to have mislaid his vocabulary. Silences were springing out like potholes.

Father Anthony came to the rescue. He told the woman it was lovely to see her again, they had all been worried; she was always welcome on Unity Street. An ease came over her as she listened, as if she were breathing suddenly all the way to her feet. He repeated that he hoped she was feeling better and assured her that if they could help her in any way, they would.

Fortunately the woman remembered something. 'Do you know a record called the "Four Seasons"?'

'We have the "Four Seasons"!' sang Kit. 'We have that one!'

He fetched the album cover and gave it to her. She looked and looked, which was strange because it was only a picture of trees and some autumny leaves.

'Would you like to listen?' said Kit, already bounding towards the booth.

'No.' She sounded terrified. She turned again to Frank. Hitched up her chin. 'Couldn't you just tell me about it?'

'What do you want to know?' He stared at her, equally terrified.

'I have no idea. I was just hoping you could introduce me to this record. But that was a stupid idea. Sorry.' Her accent made the English words sound broken up; she hit her d's like t's. *Stupit*.

'You can introduce her to this record, Frank,' said Father Anthony softly. 'You can do that.'

So he told her the 'Four Seasons' were a set of concertos by a composer called Vivaldi. Vivaldi was Italian and lived in the Baroque period. In reply she nodded her exquisite head.

'Would I like it?' she asked. 'Do you like it?'

Would she *like* it? Frank hadn't a clue. 'Well, everyone likes the "Four Seasons".'

'I don't,' said Maud.

'I do,' said Father Anthony.

'Us too,' said the Williams brothers.

'Oh, I like it very much,' agreed Mr Novak.

'I love it,' sang Kit.

'Is there anything else could you tell me?' asked the woman.

So Frank attempted to explain that Vivaldi was telling a story in the 'Four Seasons'. It was why he kept it with his concept albums, like *Ziggy Stardust*, *At Folsom Prison* by Johnny Cash, ABC's *The Lexicon of Love* and John Coltrane's *A Love Supreme*. Concept albums told a story over a number of tracks; Vivaldi's happened to be one about the seasons. Sentences were falling out of Frank's mouth and he hoped they had verbs in them. He added that people knew the 'Four Seasons' so well that even when they listened they didn't actually hear it. They didn't get the little trills that were birds, or the staccato notes like slipping on ice. He reached for a smoke and realized he had one.

'Well,' said Maud, marching to Frank's side and folding her arms. 'Look at that. It must be closing time.' It was like being sweet-talked by a traffic warden. Not entirely without complications. 'Are you going to buy that record, or what?'

Humbled, the woman moved to the counter where she began to fill out a cheque in such a hurry she failed to remove her gloves. *Ilse Brauchmann.* Despite the funny way she gripped her pen, her signature was careful and neat. It gave away nothing.

Kit said, 'That's a very nice name.'

'Oh.' She unclipped her bag and replaced her chequebook. 'Do you know it?' She shot another glance at Frank.

'German?' asked Father Anthony.

She nodded.

'Are you visiting?'

'I just arrived.'

'To stay?'

'I don't know yet.'

'How do you say your name?' interrupted Kit.

'IlsA. Ilse BrOWKmann.'

Frank tried to repeat it but couldn't. His mouth just wasn't ready. But everyone else was ready. They couldn't wait to give it a try. Everyone; except Maud. 'IlsA, Ilse BrOWKmann,' they repeated, so that now it sounded less of a name and more like a blessing before dinner.

Taking hold of her record, she thanked Frank again and then, since she didn't seem to know what else to do, she moved to the door.

'I hope you like it,' called Frank. He was beginning to feel more confident. He even put his arm in a fatherly way around Kit. 'I hope you come back. I'm always here. I could find you another record—'

She hesitated at the door, lingering with a troubled expression, as if she were trying to make up her mind how to respond. Then she opened her mouth and said something so devastating it was like being whacked with a stick. 'I can't. I'm getting married. I'm an extremely busy person.' With that, she swung the door back on its hinges and all but threw herself into the street.

So it was over. The thing was lost before it had begun. Frank paced the Persian runner, up and down, trying to shake her off. Because if he thought too hard about her, he might want other things, and after that it would be a house of cards. No one would be able to put him back together. He lumbered over to his turntable. Well, he would never see her again. GOOD. She was getting married. She was an extremely busy person. That was all GOOD too. It had been a close shave but he was unscathed. He had his shop, his customers; yes, life was exactly as he had always wanted. No risk of loss or pain. Really he should be grateful she had someone else—

And there it was. Her prickly cactus. Beside it, his yellow pencil sharpener. The two broken halves neatly replaced to form a whole. So perfect, and so ordinary, it hurt to keep looking.

'Oh dear me,' called Father Anthony from the counter. 'She's left her handbag. What will you do now, Frank?'

8

The Red Priest

'PEOPLE CALLED VIVALDI *the Red Priest,' said Peg. 'Because he had this fabulous red hair.'*

Balancing the new LP in her hand, she began to clean it. Jingle, jingle, went her bracelets.

'But poor Vivaldi, he wasn't cut out to be a priest. He liked the ladies too much and he couldn't get through Mass because he had asthma.'

She lifted the vinyl towards the French windows and they checked for scratches. She tipped it this way. That way. Light spilled over it like water.

'So Vivaldi got a job as a violin teacher at an orphanage for girls. These girls, they were not your average girls, they were shit-hot musicians. So whenever Vivaldi wanted to show off how clever one of them was, he knocked out a new concerto. Now then. Can you open the Dansette?'

'Yes, Peg.'

She lowered the disc on to the spindle and he held his breath, afraid the slightest movement might distract it.

'People play Vivaldi as background music, but he was doing big new things in his time. He took one instrument and he made it the star of the show. No

one had tried that before. And he was painting pictures with music. That was new too. So you've got to listen. There will be wind and rain and a storm. There will be birds and flies, and a day so hot you can hardly move. There will even be a cuckoo and a sheepdog. You've got to lie on the floor and close your eyes and really listen.'

'Yes, Peg.'

'Vivaldi was so famous he was like a film star. There was a time everyone wanted to hear Vivaldi, but when he died, they'd all moved on. He had nothing at the end. Do you know the saddest thing?'

'No, Peg.'

'No one went to his funeral. There was no music for Vivaldi at the end.'

Other mothers told their boys bedtime stories; not this one. She took him to see Bambi for his eighth birthday and she had to lie in a darkened room afterwards. 'Never ask me to watch another film with a fucking talking fawn,' she said. Peg had been raised by nannies and the odd tutor – she said she just didn't know the mother recipe. When she saw her parents as a child, it was to bid them good night. Daddy, drunk at the piano – Lissen to thisss, Peggeee – mummy, sour and grieving. Mummy's true love had been felled at Ypres. Daddy was the back-up plan. She never forgave him for that.

Over time, Peg showed Frank other pictures in music. The trout in Schubert's quintet, the lark ascending in Vaughan Williams, the cuckoo in Beethoven's 'Pastoral'. Then, as Frank discovered music of his own, he showed her pictures too. 'Listen to this, Peg!' And she would. If it was music, she would come running. He showed her the way João Gilberto could whisper, so that you could hear a little buzzy bee in your ear, or the way Joni Mitchell sang 'Blu-oo-oo' and you saw her all alone in the dark. And what about the low baritone sax in Van Morrison's 'Into The Mystic', just like a real foghorn? There were pictures in all kinds of music, once you stopped to listen.

'It breaks my heart,' said Peg, the day she played Vivaldi. 'When I think of the Red Priest and no music for him at the end.'

9

The Problem of the Green Handbag

SOMETIMES, IF A sales rep was being particularly obtuse, Frank went through all the reasons vinyl was better than CD or cassette tape.

It wasn't just 1) the ARTWORK and SLEEVE NOTES on the album sleeve. It wasn't 2) the possibility of a HIDDEN TRACK, or a little MESSAGE carved in the final groove. It wasn't 3) the mahogany richness of the QUALITY of SOUND. (But CD sound was *clean*, the reps argued. It had no surface noise. To which Frank replied, 'Clean? What's music got to do with clean? Where is the humanity in *clean*? Life has surface noise! Do you want to listen to furniture polish?')

It wasn't even 4) the RITUAL of checking the record before carefully lowering the stylus. No, most of all it was about the JOURNEY. 5) The journey that an album made from one track to another, with a hiatus in the middle, when you had to get up and flip the record over in order to finish. With vinyl, you couldn't just sit there like a lemon. You had to GET UP OFF YOUR ARSE and TAKE PART.

'You see?' he would say. By this point he might be shouting. He could also be lumbering up and down the shop, in a glistening sweat. 'You see now why you will never get me to sell CDs? We are human beings. We need lovely things we can see and hold. Yes, vinyl can be a pain. It's not convenient. It gets scratched. But that's the *point*. We are acknowledging the importance of music and beauty in our lives. You don't get that if you're not prepared to make AN EFFORT.'

And the reps would laugh and say yeah, yeah, they got it, Frank. But they had their jobs to do. They had their sales targets to meet. Phil the EMI rep, who had been coming since the early days of punk, warned that record companies would soon be fading out vinyl altogether. Production costs were too high. 'End of story, mate.' If you wanted to run a music shop in 1988, you had to stock CDs.

To which Frank would reply, 'Get out of here.' And possibly throw something. 'I'm never going to change.'

So what was Frank going to do about Ilse Brauchmann's green bag? Frank was going to do what he always did when life got confusing, and that was absolutely nothing. If that didn't work, he would do the next thing he always did when life was confusing, and hide. ('You have a talent for it,' a girlfriend told him once.)

'But IlsA BrOWKmann will need it,' said Kit in England's Glory, where the shopkeepers of Unity Street had met to discuss the latest development. 'It matches IlsA BrOWKmann's coat.' Kit had been practising her name ever since she left. Now that he had mastered it, he was keen to demonstrate his new skill wherever he spied an opportunity.

'If she wants her handbag,' said Frank, 'she knows where to find it.'

'Exactly,' agreed Maud, 'the woman's got legs.' Only, the way she said 'legs' made them sound mildly unsavoury. Like an infection, for instance. Or horns. 'I don't know why you're all so keen to see her again.'

'She was just very lovely,' said Kit, who tended to say things as he saw and felt them. 'I wonder who she's getting married to?'

There followed yet more speculation that got wilder the more they speculated. Father Anthony suggested someone involved in finance, the Williams brothers thought the man would be a lawyer, Kit was sticking with the film theme for Ilse Brauchmann and was certain her fiancé must be a famous American actor, while the man with three teeth suggested foreign royalty.

Kit had already checked the contents of the bag; nothing other than her chequebook and a tube of hand cream. She'd left no clue as to who she was or where she and her fiancé were staying. He had wrapped the bag in bubble wrap and tucked it in the drawer beneath the counter for safe-keeping.

'I still don't understand,' he said. 'Why does she not listen to music? And what was she doing outside our shop?' Confusion got the better of him and he sat with both hands on top of his head.

He had made a good point, though, and no one knew the answer. Why would a woman come to a record shop if she didn't listen to music? Why would she want Frank to tell her about the 'Four Seasons'? And never mind those questions, WHY had she fainted? What was she doing in Unity Street in the first place?

'In my opinion,' said Father Anthony, 'she came for a reason. Just as she left her bag for a reason.' He gazed over his spectacles with a lop-sided smile; it had become that way after he'd once tried balancing on a spiked railing. Apparently he was remonstrating with God at the time. Frank had carried him all the way to the ambulance. He was lucky he hadn't lost his eye, the doctors said.

'Do you mean that she left her bag *deliberately*?' asked one of the Williams brothers.

Father Anthony said yes. She had made an unconscious decision to leave her bag. It was her soul speaking. She said she was too busy to return but actually she needed to come back.

'The woman sounds a right psycho,' said Maud. She laughed and tried to catch Frank's eye, but he hadn't the stomach for connection of any kind. He sat with his arms hugged around his shoulders, adrift and confused. He couldn't seem to get warm.

'I still don't know what Frank should do about her handbag,' admitted Mr Novak.

Kit scratched his hair as if he had something alive in there. 'I could make posters. Saying, *Have you lost your bag?* I could put one in the shop window, and another in the bus stop. Then she'll come back and we can find out who she really is.'

'We could all put up posters,' said one of the Williams brothers.

And so it was agreed. Kit would make posters. They would tape one in every window and they would put them up on Castlegate. So long as she was still in the city, she was bound to return.

As they left the pub Father Anthony touched Frank's arm and asked if he needed to talk.

'Not really,' said Frank.

But Father Anthony followed him anyway.

The music shop glowed a beautiful deep blue in the dark. At the far end, light flickered on the booths as if they were breathing. Frank led the way past the central table and opened the door to his flat. If it was cramped in the shop, the double-storeyed flat was even more so. A kitchen and double bedroom on the first floor, two single rooms and a bathroom on the second; all of them crowded with boxes of vinyl. There were no curtains as such, just an old Indian coverlet that Maud had given him one Christmas and he'd nailed above the bedroom window.

Father Anthony made his way to the kitchen sink and stepped in a bucket.

'Oh yes,' said Frank, too late. 'Mind that.' There was also a new leak in the ceiling.

He found eggs at the back of the fridge, along with butter, and a loaf of Polish bread.

'Something's wrong,' said Father Anthony. 'I can tell.'

Frank stood with his back towards the priest, stirring the eggs over the heat. 'Do you want beans?'

Father Anthony said yes, please. He would like beans. Then he said, 'Are you in trouble?'

For a moment, Frank stood eyeing the eggs in the pan. They were on the point of solidifying into a texture that was more like omelette. Frank tipped them on to plates, pushed old magazines out of the way and the two men – one music, the other church – sat opposite each other in the yellow cone of light from the overhead bulb.

'If you need a napkin, it will have to be the tea towel,' said Frank.

Father Anthony watched him solemnly from across the table. 'This is a feast. Thank you.'

They ate in silence. Afterwards Frank poured tea from the pot and they stood at the kitchen window looking out. It was one of the highest points of the city. You could see the old gas works, the tower blocks, the endless streets of houses. In windows all around them, people did the small, routine things they always did. Watching television, washing dishes, getting ready for bed. Moonlight cast a shine over the rooftops; they stretched, like thousands of fish scales, all the way down to the factories and docks, where smoke melted upwards in pale columns. Stars were tiny, cold points speckling the sky.

'Remember when you and I used to go night-walking?'

Frank nodded and lit up.

'You saved my life, Frank.'

'You saved your life. I just found you jazz.'

They kept looking to the window. Their reflections were ghosts on the glass; great big Frank and the ageing ex-priest. Far away a blue light flashed its passage towards the docks.

'She likes you.'

'Who likes me?'

'Ilse Brauchmann.'

'In case you didn't hear, she has a fiancé. She's getting married. I don't know why you all keep going on about her.'

'I'm just making a simple observation.'

'Well, would you stop? With your simple observations? Can we drink our tea and look out the window?' There was an impatience in his voice that made him ashamed.

'I'm only saying that beneath that fringe, you're an attractive man. It's too late for me but you've got years. And it pains me, the way you insist on being alone.'

'It's easier.'

'CDs are easier. You don't want those.'

They carried their mugs through to the bedroom and played jazz for the rest of the night. All their old favourites – Miles Davis, John Coltrane, Sonny Rollins, Grant Green – not saying much, just sitting on the mattress and listening to records like in the old days when Frank had kept Father Anthony company through the worst, fetching him buckets when he needed to be sick, or blankets when he was shaking so hard he wanted to scream and his joints hurt as if they were being twisted. Round about seven in the morning, a faint silvery light eased into the sky, and then came other colours, tangerine and gold and green. Clouds hung like black bones and smoke lifted from the food factories. The morning shift had started.

'God help them,' said Father Anthony. 'Poor souls.' His eyelids dropped and snapped open and dropped again.

Frank said, 'I am in trouble. You're right. I like her. I don't know why.' He spoke very quietly and slowly, more a shaping of his mouth than a full-blown sentence. He just wanted to know how it felt, to say those things, whether or not it hurt. He reached for a new cigarette and his hand shook a little as he struck a match but he was still breathing, wasn't he, the world was still turning. The lit-up tip of his cigarette was an orange flower in the dark. 'But she's got someone else. She'll probably be gone tomorrow. So, hey. That's that. Finito. End of story.'

The old priest lay asleep with his arms crossed over his chest, his hands thin and papery. In the distance, traffic was already moving and it was a soft sound, more a lullaby than anything else.

Finally Frank slept too. He dreamt he was back in the white house by the sea, with its jumble of turrets and gabled windows, ornate chimneys and overlapping roofs, perched on the edge of a clifftop. Peg's family had made their fortune in cigarettes but the house was all that was left. It had turned out her daddy was a gambler and a coke head. Dead by fifty. Her mother died months later.

In Frank's dream, the tall windows were wide open, sucking the curtains in and out with a life of their own. 'Peg!' he began to shout. 'Peg!' He chased from one room to another. The drawing room, the ballroom, the old billiard room. He threw open the French doors and tore out to the garden where tamarind trees grew with their feathery plumes of pink blossom. He even jogged down the limestone stairway to the beach that was bordered with thousands of orange flowers. But wherever he went, there was no sign of her. Nothing but the waves breaking in twos and threes on the sand. The fizz of the end.

Shaken, Frank rose and washed his face and made a mug of tea for Father Anthony. He couldn't stop seeing the white house by the sea. He couldn't put away the loneliness that swallowed him.

10

Adagio for Strings

MAUD UNLOCKED THE door of her salon and flipped the *Closed!* sign to *Open!* She arranged a few magazines in a fan shape and then she put them in a line shape and then she stuffed them back in a regular pile.

Outside, people were stepping from their houses, bundled up against the cold, parents and kids off to school, others to work. One man scraped the frost from his car window; another was trying to fix a gutter by tying it up with string. Two little olive-skinned girls stood shivering in pink coats. Then Kit appeared from the corner, arms flailing, skidding on ice and swerving at the last minute to avoid flooring Mrs Roussos as she emerged from her gate with a bag of rubbish. Its contents spilled everywhere. He dropped to the ground, scooped everything back into the bag, and carried it for her to the bin.

Spotting Maud, Kit did an elaborate mime that made no sense whatsoever. Before she had time to hide, he had exploded into her salon, bringing with him a gust of cold air and a smell of toothpaste.

'I'm putting up my posters today.'

'What posters?'

'My posters to find Ilse Brauchmann. To say we have her green bag.

I am going to launch a campaign. They will be on all the lamp posts. Can I count on your support?'

'As a what?'

Kit looked baffled. 'As a friend.'

Now it was Maud's turn to look baffled. 'As a what?' she repeated.

Frank's name was written in Maud's heart; or – more truthfully – it was tattooed above her right breast, just inside her bra strap. Sometimes when she spoke to him, or while she listened, she placed her hand where the tattoo lay and it was like sending a message in code.

Don't get her wrong. Maud knew Frank didn't love her. The problem was that he had a kind of empathy for everyone. There seemed to be no end to the amount of bad news the man could absorb. His shop was permanently occupied by people who would otherwise be roaming the streets or weeping in bedsits. And women were the worst. Anorexic girls, unmarried mothers, battered wives. Frank was so busy loving other people he had no room to accommodate the fact that someone might turn round one day and love him back.

Or maybe he just didn't want to. She thought that sometimes.

It had happened – Maud's love – the first time Frank found her a record.

'Try this,' he'd said.

'Try what?' she'd replied.

'Go on. Sit in there. Put on the headphones. There's something I want you to hear.'

'But that's an old wardrobe, Frank. I'm not sitting in that.'

Here she was wrong, apparently. It was a new listening booth. Yes, this crappy cupboard with small jewelly birds in the door now housed a velvet chair, trimmed with little tassels, and a headset so large it was like wearing a hatful of music.

So she'd sat on the chair, just as Frank asked. She'd shut the door, and it was strange, it was the same as hiding when you were a kid, only this time you weren't surrounded by your mum's dresses and your dad's suits and trying not to breathe in case they found you, it was like hiding inside a record. Time stopped.

Tick, tick.

'I think you'll like this,' Frank's voice had boomed from the other side of the door.

Tick, tick.

Barber. Adagio for Strings. She'd never even heard of the guy. Maud played Def Leppard, the louder the better. Anything to silence the voice inside her. *Where is that child? Fetch the belt. Why can't she be a good little girl?* But Frank played her the record and it was like walking through a magic door. It was so sad and so simple it could break your heart, but it didn't. From the softest of beginnings, it built and built as if it were climbing a set of stairs, until the violins were practically screaming AHHHHHHHH – and then it stopped. Nothing. Her heart had swooped to her mouth. When the music started again, she was in tears. Like a switch had been flicked, and her eyes were spouts. Because life goes on, the music told her, even when you think it can't. Yes, there is fear. There is real cruelty. Not knowing what the fuck. Those things are there. But listen because there is this too – this beauty. The human adventure is worth it, after all.

As she left that booth, the music was in her heart. The shop was just the same, the past was just the same, but now there was also this. This whatever it was. This truth. It was no less than a small miracle. And Frank had given her that.

'Was it OK?' he'd asked afterwards. How could she say? How can you tell a man with eyes like chocolate drops that by sticking you for eight minutes in a cupboard, he has changed your life? He knelt at her feet, gazing at her from beneath that floppy fringe – well, she assumed he was gazing – and smiling with his soft mouth, the lower lip cleft with a dimple like a segment of fruit. It was so intimate it was almost post-coital.

So here she was. All these years later. How many nights had she sat with him in England's Glory as he told another story about a customer who needed his help? How many times had she fetched a takeaway and pushed open the door of his shop, pretending a date had not turned up? How many Christmases? New Years? Birthdays? One day they'd jack it all in. Move out of the city altogether. Real love was not a bolt out of the blue, it was not the playing of violins, it was like anything else, it was a habit of the heart. You got up every day and you put it on, same as your pants, your boots, and you kept treading the constant path.

Maud thought of the woman lying on the pavement. She'd seen the expression on Frank's face as he gazed down at her, a kind of wonder mixed with barefaced terror. She had seen too the way the woman had stared up at him, as if she had found the thing she was looking for. Maud had waited years for Frank. There was no way a Kraut in a green coat was going to cock it up.

'So?' asked Kit, nervous now. 'Can I count on your support?'

'What?'

'With my posters?'

Maud felt a little flame lick and curl beneath her breastbone.

'Tell you what,' she said, smiling sweetly. 'Why don't you give them to me?'

11

A Hard Rain's A-Gonna Fall

KIT'S POSTERS HUNG in the shop windows along Unity Street. 'HAVE YOU LOST YOUR GREEN HANDBAG?' He had decorated them with other green things. Leaves and some little shapes that looked like nuts but were actually hearts, along with a green hat, a green pair of boots and a green umbrella. There was also a lettuce, a sprout and a cucumber. You'd think the owner of the bag was some kind of hapless small green vegan.

Strangely the posters all disappeared from Castlegate, and the lamp posts too. When questioned, Maud folded her arms and looked aggressive.

For the rest of the week, there was wind, there was rain, but not so much as a word from Ilse Brauchmann. Was Father Anthony right? *Had* she left her bag for a reason? The more time passed, the more Frank found he thought of her and yet this was madness because he knew nothing, except for the fact she very definitely had someone else.

Teenagers came to the shop, along with musicians, would-be musicians, punks, heavy metal fans, classical lovers and New Romantics. Several people enquired if Frank would be interested in buying their vinyl because they were replacing it with the new CDs. The man who only liked Chopin returned for more Aretha and asked Frank's advice about joining a dating agency. But Ilse Brauchmann? No sign of her.

'Well good,' said Frank. 'I'm glad.'

Fresh graffiti appeared on the baker's window. *Sharon loves Ian*, and *NF*, the two letters stuck to each other like an ugly claw. Frank fetched another bucket of soapy water.

'What does this mean, Frank? *NF*?'

'It's nothing, Mr Novak. It's kids being stupid.'

Rain fell hard and the baker cowered at the open door. The shop smelt sweet and warm.

'We came here before the war. I was a soldier for Mr Churchill.'

'I know that, Mr Novak.'

'I still talk to my wife. As I bake. And she watches me and she says, "You stupid old man, why you cry? Why you miss me?" But I am glad she never saw what those kids do to my window. It would have broken her heart.' The baker fetched cinnamon rolls, fresh out of the oven; two each for Frank and Kit.

'Ring me if you're worried,' said Frank. 'It will be OK.'

Nevertheless, as he walked through the rain he couldn't help thinking about the graffiti, and the baker talking to his wife at night and crying. He stared at the items beyond the yellow cellophane in the other shop windows – an urn in the funeral parlour; several bookmarks in Father Anthony's gift shop alongside a plastic Jesus – and as if for the first time, he saw how temporary it all looked. Here they were, living together on Unity Street, trying to make a difference in the world, knowing they couldn't, but still doing it anyway. Clearly some of the houses opposite, with their peeling paintwork and curtains that stayed closed, had seen better days. So had it been this way a while, and he just hadn't noticed? Or was something in Frank changing? Even his jacket felt too small.

HAVE YOU LOST YOUR GREEN HANDBAG? read Kit's posters in jumpy big letters. The last thing Frank needed was Ilse Brauchmann. He'd get Kit to take her bag to the police station. He pushed open the door of his shop.

But where was Kit? And where was the *ding-dong*?

'Here I am!'

Kit was perched against the window ledge, as if he had put himself on display.

'What are you doing? And why is the bell not working?'

'There is nothing at all to worry about!'

'What's happened?' asked Frank, feeling immediately worried.

Kit had been hoping for a random sighting of Ilse Brauchmann. He had climbed on to the window ledge for a better view but his foot must have slipped and as he fell he had pulled something out of the bell and kicked the window frame. So now there was no bell, but there *was* a leak. Yes: rain was coming in the bottom half of the window. The only way Kit could think of stopping the leak was to use his body as a wedge but unfortunately he had wedged himself a little too hard and now he was stuck. Also, he had made the leak worse because he had inadvertently knocked out some of the putty that held the window in place.

'You mean, the window is loose?'

In a manner of speaking, yes. Kit did mean that. He was happy to keep it in place for the rest of the day but he would need to go home at teatime to sort his mum's pills. His dad tended to fall asleep in front of the six o'clock news.

Frank helped Kit out of the window and fetched towels. He leant a length of hardboard against the lower part but the job needed a glazier – and that would be another twenty quid. He'd barely made a decent sale all week. He was so absorbed in doing the sums, he failed to notice a car parking up outside.

'Oh oh!' sang Kit. 'I think it's her! I think it's Ilse Brauchmann! Oh my God! This is so exciting—'

But it wasn't. It was Phil from EMI. He had a business proposition.

'Hey, Frank. How's things?' Phil was a heavy man in his forties with a quiff like a pointy hat and vast sideburns to match. 'Remember the old days? Remember that time you took me to see The Ruts and The Damned? Along with that other guy? What was his name?'

'Aunty Pus.'

Phil laughed. His eyes were bloodshot and small, and he was beginning to sweat. He'd always been a drinker but recently it had got more serious. Some days he could barely walk a straight line, and this was one of them. 'Then Malcolm Owen smashed his head with the cymbal and St John Ambulance had to take him off on a stretcher.'

Frank laughed too. There had been an issue back then with Phil's quiff: Maud had done her best to spray it into a Mohican but Frank had spent most of the night trying to hide him. 'Those were the days,' said Phil, 'when music had bollocks. Now it's all George Michael and gay boys.'

'I like George Michael.'

Phil threw his hands up as if he were hailing the arrival of a minor deity. 'This is why we all come back to you, Frank. You don't just love one thing. You love *music*. So listen, I'm not going to beat around the bush. It's time to drop this crap about CDs.'

'That's your business proposition?' Frank laughed.

'You don't want to sell cassettes? I get that. But CDs are new. They're *shiny*. It's a *lifestyle* thing. And they're virtually indestructible. You can drive over them and they still won't break—'

'Why would I want to drive over my music, Phil?'

'You know he'll never sell CDs,' piped up Kit from the counter. He was making a new poster.

'The word from the top is this. We have to get you guys giving more floor space to CDs, otherwise we can't supply you any more. By the end of the year, CD sales will have overtaken vinyl. So come on. You're a big boy. You can manage one rack.' Phil's face was so shiny he looked varnished. 'I'll throw in T-shirts. Badges. I'll even throw in ashtrays.'

'I don't need ashtrays.'

('I would like some ashtrays,' said Kit.)

A new customer slipped in the door but no one paid any attention.

Phil said, 'Make an order for a CD, I can sell you one and give you three. Are you hearing me, Frank? I can *give* you three CDs for nothing. But vinyl, it's completely different. We're deleting titles. In ten years, kids won't even know what vinyl *was*. It's dying, Frank. Move on.'

Frank stared at his turntable. A small yellow thing came into focus. He picked up his pencil sharpener, neatly returned to a whole. He twisted it in his hands, over and over. Why did it unsettle him so much? 'I can't do it,' he said.

Phil drew a huge breath, as if he were sucking it up through a straw. 'It's OK, Frank. I get it. But there's still a way we can make this work.' Nipping a scrap of paper out of his back pocket, he glanced round the shop. The new customer was busy searching through album sleeves, and wearing a plastic rain mac with a hood. Phil passed Frank the paper. It was a series of pencilled numbers.

'All you've got to do is enter this catalogue number a couple of times an hour in your sales return machine.'

'Without selling it?'

'It needs some help in the charts. Do this and we can forget about CDs. It's just a little arrangement between you and me.'

'But that's fraud.'

'Come on, Frank. My job's on the line.'

Phil looked very pale now, properly queasy. Two wet moons hung at his armpits. He stared a moment more at Frank and then a little switch seemed to flick inside him. He turned to the boxes packed with record sleeves and began to pull them out, first one, then another, chucking them to the floor. 'After everything I've done for you—' He was tugging them out in handfuls. The more he threw down, the more he seemed to hate the shop. 'It's only because of me the other reps keep coming.'

'Get out,' Frank shouted. 'Get out of here!'

Phil swerved to avoid the customer in the rain hood and lurched through the door. After that he fell into his car, revving the engine until it screamed. They heard the shriek of Phil's brakes as he headed for Castlegate.

'What have you done now?' Kit was so pale he looked sick.

Frank felt a deep burning inside him, an anger that made his head throb. 'Phil shouldn't even be driving.' He turned back to his shop.

And there, crouched on the floor and picking up album sleeves, was Ilse Brauchmann.

'I was just passing,' she said.

12

So Long, Farewell

WHO KNEW? WHO knew that beautiful women wore plastic rain macs? But of course they did. Even strangers with long necks and eyes like vinyl had to be practical when it came to British weather.

First she was apologetic. She should have come before. It had been difficult, though: 'I've been busy.' Presumably with her fiancé, though she had the grace not to say that. She hoped she hadn't inconvenienced anyone by leaving her bag a whole week? Two red circles sprang to her cheeks, looking remarkably like something Kit would make with scissors and crepe paper.

Frank stuck a cigarette in his mouth. He flicked so hard at the lighter, it nicked his thumb.

Ilse Brauchmann seemed nervy too. She said she would just collect her handbag and leave. Oh but she couldn't believe it when she'd spotted all those lovely posters in Unity Street. 'No one has ever made a poster for me before.' She kept her eyes fixed with almost mathematical precision on a point in the floor.

'I didn't make the posters,' said Frank. 'They were nothing to do with me.' He marched back to his turntable, stepping his great feet around album sleeves.

Kit retrieved her handbag from the counter and mopped it with the cuff of his jumper.

'We were afraid you'd gone,' he said.

'Oh?' She sent a surprised look over her shoulder. It landed right on Frank. 'No, I'm still here.'

'Is your fiancé here?' Kit continued.

She looked even more perplexed and said, 'Um.' A little hovery noise.

'Have you fainted any more?'

'Fainted? No.'

Before Kit could ask anything else, she produced from her coat pocket a small parcel wrapped in purple tissue paper. 'This is a token,' she said. 'To say thank you.'

'You don't need to give me a present,' interrupted Frank from his turntable. He was hot and trembling – it must be the row with Phil.

'It isn't for you. It's for your assistant manager.'

'Me?' said Kit. Pointing at himself for extra clarity.

'It's small. I mean, it's nothing.'

But Kit was already ripping open the paper. He pulled out something blue, and began running in joyful circles.

'Oh my God! Oh my God! Have you seen what this is, Frank?'

'It's a shirt,' explained Ilse Brauchmann. 'There is a blue tie as well. I could only find one with stripes. I hope you like it.'

'It's my own uniform, Frank! Like the shop assistants at Woolworths!'

On to the chest pocket she had stitched his name in a chain of neat red letters. *Kit. Assistant Manager. Welcome.* She had even given him a little pearl-stitched exclamation mark.

'You made this for me?' sang Kit. 'Oh my God! Oh my God!'

He galloped upstairs to try on his new shirt and tie. They could hear him, directly above, falling over boxes as he tried to find a mirror.

There was an awkward moment that morphed into another awkward one.

Ilse Brauchmann took off her plastic mac. She was wearing a slim plain skirt and a turtleneck sweater. Nothing to write home about, though she was so cold she kept her gloves on. Her dark hair was mostly pinned over the crown of her head in a chaos of curls and a few strands dropped loose at irregular lengths around her ears. She returned to the business of rescuing album sleeves, slowly, carefully, plucking them up with her long arms, one here, one there, and studying the titles. 'I'm sorry about what happened. Was he a rep?'

'It's not your fault.'

'And what happened to your window?'

'Kit sat in it.'

For a moment she did nothing, she just ogled. Then she did something completely sideways.

She laughed.

But not a normal laugh. It was a delicious creaky sound that seemed to shoot up without warning, and after all the tension with Phil it tackled Frank from behind and made him laugh too. A ballooning of happiness. Only, now that he had started with the laughter thing, he couldn't stop. He'd forgotten what it was like, just to laugh and laugh. And Ilse Brauchmann was apparently the same. 'Stop, stop,' she kept howling, nostrils wide, wiping her eyes, clutching her sides. 'What are we doing? This is crazy.' Even the way she said the word made it funny. Crazeeee.

Hooo hoo hoo.

Haw haw haw.

Then, 'I'm sorry. That's not funny.' She pulled on a solemn face and went back to being sensible. They both did. She picked up a few more record sleeves.

'*Mist*, this one's torn,' she said.

She walked in her slow way over to the counter – he noticed the swing of her hips as if she were following an invisible line – and opened the drawer to pull out the broken Sellotape dispenser. She just seemed to know where things should be. He couldn't help but watch, entranced, as she rubbed her gloved hands a moment, gave each finger a stretch, before resting the album sleeve on the counter. Drawing a length of tape, she lifted it to her mouth to bite it free, before sealing it carefully in place and smoothing both sides. She frowned as she took up the broken Sellotape dispenser and gave it her full attention. Her hands were round it like tools. She worked methodically and without fuss. He still had absolutely no idea what she needed – she was just as silent to him as before – but it was good, he thought, it was good just having her here. Even his shop seemed to like her. The blue of the Persian runner bounced out and became even bluer. Without warning, the world had snapped into sharper focus and become more interesting. Upstairs he could still hear Kit falling over boxes.

He said, 'What did you make of the Vivaldi?'

'Oh.' She widened her eyes and pursed her mouth, as if she had accidentally swallowed a cherry stone. 'I didn't listen yet.'

She held up the album cover for him to inspect. You could barely see the join; she had repaired it beautifully. Then she lifted the Sellotape dispenser as well. 'I fixed this. I hope you don't mind.' Opening the drawer, she slotted it carefully inside. 'Shall we have a quick look at that window?'

He followed her to the front of the shop, where she examined the piece of hardboard propped against the glass to keep it in place. She asked if he had nails and a small hammer, and when he produced his old bag of tools, she knelt and searched through it until she found a box of tacks. He stood beside her, in helpless and grateful wonder, as she popped six of them between her teeth and then nailed them in place, one by one, with quick, steady hits, securing the hardboard against the wooden frame. It was a shame he had no putty, she said. But at least the window would be safe for the moment.

In all the time she had been with him in the shop, they had barely spoken, and yet there were so many things he wanted to say to her. He felt irresistibly drawn to her great quietness; it was a silence so deep, the possibilities were endless.

So when she said, 'You do a lot to help other people. Don't you ever think about yourself?' he didn't slope off to his turntable, as he usually did if things got personal, he just thought carefully about her question.

He said, 'Not really. I like helping other people.'

She nodded.

Then she asked, 'Do you remember all your customers?'

'Yes.'

She looked at him and he looked at her and they smiled because there didn't seem to be much else to do.

Then she said, 'What would you do if you didn't have your music shop?'

He thought again and then he said, 'I'd have a music stall.'

They were silent.

'Why?' he asked. 'What about you?'

'What about me?' The happiness had gone from her face. She was all shining eyes.

'What do you do?'

'Oh. Me. I'm really not very interesting.'

She blinked with such sadness he had no idea how to keep his hands from reaching out to hold her.

But hang on, STOP RIGHT THERE, what was he doing? What was he thinking? She was engaged. Remember? She had someone else. Someone really good-looking, no doubt, and successful. A city boy. A hotshot. He could picture him. (Yes, really picture him, he thought. You know this kind of man. Smart, good haircut, tanned skin, expensive suit. He saw them more and more these days, driving smart cars that were so low off the ground he could only assume you had to roll to get inside them.) Look at yourself, he thought. Your battered suede jacket, your broken shoes. Your shop doesn't even have proper units.

She stooped to pick up another record sleeve from the floor. 'Do you know this one? Concerto for Two Violins in D Minor by J. S. Bach. Can you tell me something about it?'

Gazing at her, so beautiful and irregular, so still and unknown, so here and yet so temporary, something inside Frank gave a shift. It was like a ship sinking in his stomach. He wanted her to leave. He couldn't explain. He didn't even want to explain. What was there to explain, beyond the fact she was unavailable and he was a write-off? He was turning into someone he didn't even recognize. He needed her gone. Out. Now. He never wanted to see her again. He lurched back to his turntable.

'Actually I'm closed.'

'Closed?'

'Yes.' He reached for his door keys and got her cactus plant.

'I was trying to help, Frank.'

What was she doing *now*? Using his name? As if she were reaching a hand through his skin and squeezing his insides? And yet the way she said his name made it sound so whole and new in the world. If only she would say it again and again. Oh and one more time, please—

'Did I ask you to help me?'

'No.' She looked confused. Taken aback.

'I don't need it. I don't need help.'

She picked up her mac, her bag. Straightened her spine. 'Of course you don't.'

He wanted to rush to her side. He wanted to put his arms out to her and apologize. He wanted to say, *Who are you? How can I help?* Instead he watched her struggle to thread her long arms inside the sleeves, and then doing up her buttons, one by one, before pulling a hard knot in her tie belt. He watched her doing all this and there was a version of the scene, he somehow knew, it was out there somewhere, where Frank sat opposite Ilse Brauchmann and told her everything about the Concerto for Two Violins by J. S. Bach, but instead he stood behind his turntable, arms folded, hurt and angry and alone, and he let her leave without another word. They didn't even say goodbye.

'Look, Frank. Look at me.' Kit swung open the door to the flat and stood proud in his new blue shirt and tie. He had also wet his hair and smoothed it to one side. Seeing the empty shop, his face fell like a half-baked soufflé. 'Oh but where is Ilse Brauchmann? Did she say why she left her bag? Did she tell you why she fainted?'

'No,' said Frank. 'She didn't, and we'll never find out. We won't be seeing her again.'

13

Bach's Eyes

'Nothing is what it seems. Did I ever tell you about Bach's eyes, Frank?'

'No.'

'Would you like me to?'

'Yes, please.'

Peg was up a ladder with a sheet of wallpaper. She had paste in one hand and a Sobranie cocktail cigarette in the other. Peg had told Frank about Bach – she was often telling him about Bach – but so far she had not displayed any interest in home improvements. So here she was, a substantial woman on top of a small ladder. The best way to keep her up there was by letting her talk about something she understood.

'Bach was a genius,' she said, sploshing her bedroom wall happily with paste. 'He was the bee's knees. He could take a simple little tune and improvise. He'd put it here, he'd put it there, he'd put it back to front, upside down, and then bingo. He didn't even have to write it. This was all just going on in his head. He was jazz, Frank. He was jazz in fucking Baroque fucking Germany.'

She wobbled in excitement. The boy gripped her ladder for dear life.

'He had twenty kids. Did I say that before?'

Frank said yes. She often said that. Peg was thirty when she met Frank's *father – or rather, fathers – it stood to reason he had one, but she had no idea who it might be. She also had no intention of making the same mistake twice. Frank could never work out what she meant by that – especially since every-thing else about her life came in multiples. Boyfriends especially. She had lots of those, and mostly married ones. For a while he scanned them for similarities to himself, looking for little clues like eye colour or ear shape. He even took to smiling at them in meaningful ways before he went to bed, until one of them asked Peg if her son had some kind of remedial problem.*

But for now she was up a ladder. She was wearing a blue kimono with a pink turban. She was swearing like a trooper and talking Bach. She was also hanging wallpaper.

'In Bach's time, the point of music was to praise God. But he had suffered. He was an orphan by the time he was eleven. Then he had all those kids and over half of them died. His wife, she died young too. He knew about loss and despair. Just as he knew about getting pissed and into trouble. So his music is halfway between man and God. It's how man becomes divine. It's like tripping.'

Peg posted the end of the paste brush between her teeth, along with her cigarette, so that the brush seemed to fume of its own accord. She lifted the paper into place. It was an extravagance of grapes and flowers. They all seemed very blue. 'Is it straight?'

Frank cocked his head to the left. 'Yes.'

'It doesn't look straight.'

He couldn't imagine there was much of a difference between straight and tilted, as far as this wallpaper was concerned.

'Is it too much?'

'It's beautiful.'

'Terrible eyesight.'

'Me?'

'Bach. Cataracts. He had an operation, but the doctor – I mean, this man, Frank, he was not a surgeon, he was a con man. He performed operations in front of a crowd in the market square. Bach went blind as a bat and after that he had a stroke. He was dead in four months. And then of course Handel went to the same man for the same operation and he went blind too. It's tragic.'

Frank gazed up at her wallpaper – it was lopsided, there was no denying it. But he couldn't help feeling it was the happiest thing he had ever seen.

Later he switched on the Dansette and she played the Concerto for Two Violins in D minor. She explained how the music worked like a conversation. Sometimes the violins were telling the same story, and sometimes they were having an argument; first one led the way, then the other. They might be so close they were like a piece of braid, or so far apart they had to call for one another across the dark. This wasn't like Vivaldi's 'Four Seasons' when one instrument took centre stage and became (in Peg's words) a right fucking show-off. Bach's Concerto for Two Violins was about learning to be two halves of a whole.

As the record came to an end, Frank felt so happy he was sad, and so sad he was happy. He wondered if it was the same for other boys? No one at school mentioned Bach or cataracts. Mostly they flipped him with pencils and left small dead things in his school bag. Not that he told anyone.

Peg never got further than that one strip of wallpaper. A few months later she was seeing a man with a passion for DIY and he painted the entire room a useful shade of brown. It was everywhere. Brown walls. Brown doors. Brown cupboards and drawers. DIY Man topped it off with a nice brown carpet. It was like being inside a mushroom. Not a trippy one. Just a plain brown cap.

But when the sun hit it, you could still see those grapes. The big blue flowers.

DIY Man slapped on another coat of paint but it was the same; no matter how much brown he used, the vivid past would not go away.

Like music, said Peg. Even when it was over, it kept living inside you.

14

Bye, Bye, Baker (Baker Goodbye)

THE BAKERY WENT overnight. On Friday it had been business as usual. Cinnamon rolls in the window, the sweet warm smell of Polish bread, a blue light in the kitchen at the back. Saturday morning, the shop was locked and dark. Even at lunchtime, there was no sign of the baker. Frank, Kit, Maud and Father Anthony tried the door. They rapped on the glass; they shouted his name. Father Anthony went back to his gift shop and tried ringing. No answer.

'Do you think it would be a good idea if I broke in?' asked Kit.

Everyone agreed that it would be a very good idea if Kit did *not* break in. The safest thing all round would be for Kit to remain exactly where he was on the pavement, preferably without touching anything, or indeed moving, while Frank fetched a stepladder.

A van turned into Unity Street. It parked up right over the kerb, and three men in boots, jeans and bomber jackets swung out. They were carrying hacksaws, axes and crowbars. So everyone forgot about the stepladder. Or rather, in the face of bigger things, the idea politely lost itself.

The men had keys. They unlocked the baker's door and worked fast.

They dismantled and carried out the glass display counters, the serving counter, the tables and chairs.

'What are you doing?' Maud stepped in their path.

'What does it look like?'

'Our fucking job.'

'So fuck off. Fucking freak.'

And Maud, who might have been expected to eat men like that for breakfast, merely nodded and knelt like a child and tied a terribly careful bow on her Doc Martens.

For the rest of the morning the men worked. Sounds of drilling and hacking echoed on Unity Street. They took in a handcart and re-emerged with the baker's oven strapped to it like a sick person on a stretcher. They did the same with the fridge. Proof boxes. An old workbench. After that they brought out tea chests into which they'd thrown bowls, plates and glasses. They'd even hacked off electrical wire and gathered it in coils. Sheets of hardboard were nailed against the window and door, along with a printed sign. *Purchased by Fort Development. Trespassers will be prosecuted.* It was the same with the florist's, and an empty house across the street. The men erected wire fencing all around the old bombsite, along with more *Fort Development* signs. Finally they erected a billboard with a large image of a lot of white people drinking coffee and looking very happy, though quite what that had to do with an old bombsite, or even Unity Street, was hard to understand. It was mid-afternoon by the time they were finished.

'Where's Mr Novak?' asked Frank.

'Search me,' said one of the men. His neck was lined with fat. 'I guess he went home.'

'The bakery *was* home. And what's Fort Development?'

'The new landlord.'

Maud, Kit and Father Anthony gathered on the pavement, staring at the new boards on the bakery. They felt the loss of the shop and short of laying flowers they had no idea what else to do, but they needed to honour the moment somehow. Then Williams the Undertakers came out, the two brothers holding their hats. Still no one spoke. Kit carried out chairs and Maud fetched blankets and they sat in a line on the pavement, smoking and looking up at the parade they all loved so much, with its falling-down masonry and two boarded-up shops, like a rot growing from both sides, along with the newly fenced-in bombsite at the end.

'Why didn't Mr Novak tell us he needed help?' said Frank.

Something of day remained in the sky – a thin blue ribbon – and it was not too cold. The light was that dim kind, falling like a filter, so that everything on Unity Street looked both separate and also made of the same substance. Even the houses opposite were blue, and so was the pavement. Light shone from the four remaining shops on the parade, and their windows were yellow pictures in the dusk. A funeral parlour, a religious gift store, a music shop and a tattoo salon . . .

'All life is here,' said Father Anthony, as if reading Frank's thoughts and also answering them.

Old Mrs Roussos appeared with her chihuahua in one hand and a flask of tea in the other. The Williams brothers fetched biscuits. Kit offered his chair to Mrs Roussos. Maud brought another blanket.

'You're not going to sell up too?' asked the old lady. She looked shaken.

Everyone promised they had no intention of going. 'We were born in this shop,' said one of the Williams brothers. 'The only way we're leaving is in a coffin.' Frank asked if it would be a double coffin and at last people laughed.

'Would you say something for us, Father?' asked Mrs Roussos.

Father Anthony reminded her, as he often did, that he was no longer a priest but she merely made a *tsk tsk* noise, as if that kind of detail was irrelevant. So he pressed his palms together and lowered his head. 'Dear Lord. Please help us to understand what we don't know. It is our differences that make us richer. All will be well.'

Was that it? They bowed their heads to say something shuffly, halfway between 'All will be well' and the more traditional 'Amen'. Mrs Roussos began to weep and when Maud passed her a Kleenex the old lady took hold of the tattooist's hand. Then somehow Kit grabbed Frank's hand, Father Anthony reached out for the Williams brothers and here they all were on Unity Street, this small line of shopkeepers, clutching hold of one another in a chain, while in other parts of the city more small stores were probably being boarded up, and police sirens wailed.

More residents came out. They brought chairs and hot food – a curry, a dish of dumplings, garlic bread – and they told stories about the baker. A woman spoke about a time she had rung from work and he kept his shop open so that she could have a loaf. Another man said Mr Novak had stayed up all night once to make a birthday cake with a red iced bird for his daughter. They lingered in front of the bakery, sharing food and talking about the kind things he had done for them. Pete the barman carried out beers, Frank played music from his shop, and by the end it was more of an impromptu street party.

They just had to look after one another. They would be OK, so long as they stuck together.

15

I Will Survive

MOONLIGHT FILLED THE shop like water. Frank sat at his turntable, thinking about a customer he'd helped once. A little boy.

He used to come to the shop every Wednesday. He couldn't always reach the records, so he asked Frank once if he might have something to step on, such as a wooden box. There was something very earnest about this child. Blond hair; almost white. Eyes so blue they could pierce holes in you. He was seven or eight.

When Frank looked at him and listened, he met a kind of echoeyness, like a house that has no furniture. Frank introduced him to Haydn, then Glenn Miller, the O'Jays and ELO; the boy liked big, happy music to fill all those spaces inside him. He said little, but once he mentioned his mother didn't go out much and another time he said he had two big brothers and that his father worked away, so Frank got the impression his parents were separated.

'It's my fault,' he said another time.

'What's your fault?'

That was when the boy showed Frank his arms. The skin was covered in bruises, like terrible flowers. Who had done that? The boy wouldn't say. It was as though he needed Frank to know this was how life was for him; that was enough. He never bought anything, of course. Once or twice Frank tried to give him a record until the boy confessed he had no record player. It was the first time he cried; his tears were huge fat drops on his cheeks. Like lozenges.

'Are you going to ban me now?' he said.

No, Frank told him; 'You can come whenever you like. Even if it's the middle of the night. I am always here for you. You're a good kid. I want you to know that.'

And the boy did come back, for several years. Other kids got spots and oily hair but this boy seemed to shine, and Frank wondered whether it was because of what happened to him, whether something like that made a person stand out and be luminous, even when the thing that happened was a terrible one.

'You OK, chief?' Frank would say.

'I'm OK, chief.'

Then one week he just stopped coming. Frank asked a few people but no one knew anything about a child with blond-white hair who felt safe when he listened to big music. God knows, the world was probably full of them.

'But you made a safe place for him,' Father Anthony reassured him. 'You helped until he didn't need you any more and then he moved on.'

Sitting in the dark, Frank pressed his head in his hands. He wondered if the boy was genuinely happy, or if things had got so bad he couldn't even face music. Who knew where he was now? Who knew what he used in order to get by? It wasn't enough, caring from the sidelines. After all, Frank understood what it was like to be out of step with the world. He should have done more for that boy.

Hours moved slowly, and it always was the same: 'Do you think Ilse Brauchmann will come back?'

'No, Kit.'

'Do you think she has gone for good?'

'I do.'

The questions loosened Frank's resolve. Why, why had he let her go like that? Why was he so afraid, when all she had asked was for him to tell her about Bach? Even though he had tried to shake himself free of her, she seemed to keep holding on. Twice he took a walk to the end of the street, searching for a smart green coat, and wondering if she happened to be just passing.

The two closed shops were sprayed with fresh graffiti, and beards and horns were painted all over the happy faces on the billboard next to the bombsite. Then a representative called by from the council to report that there had been complaints about the falling masonry. He was a stoop-shouldered man, dressed in a suit the colour of a filing cabinet, and holding a clipboard. He informed the shopkeepers that until external repair work had been done, they would have to alert passers-by to the danger of falling masonry by cordoning off the pavement with plastic ribbon. They would also need to put up official council signs saying *Beware of falling masonry.*

'But how will people get to our shops?' asked Maud.

The representative from the council consulted his clipboard and said he would have to get back to her on that one.

So the shopkeepers cordoned off the pavement and put up their official signs.

The signs fell down.

On account of the falling masonry.

Kit designed an assortment of posters instead, and he also made it his business to check every morning on the length of plastic ribbon. He adjusted the slack so that it hung in perfect blue and white loops from one lamp post to another.

'Now it looks like the scene of a crime,' said Maud.

A cold wet fog dropped over the city and showed no intention of shifting. Sometimes you could barely see to the end of the street; when the sun burnt through, it was a blind white eye. A letter came in the post from Fort Development, asking if Frank would be interested in selling his shop. He rolled it into a cigar shape and stuck it in the bin. He felt an urge to kick the bin as well, but stopped himself.

That week there were several reported sightings of Ilse Brauchmann, or at least a woman in a green coat, made by regulars from England's Glory. The man with three teeth said he had spotted her going into a restaurant. The woman with curlers was convinced she had seen her in the chemist. But since none of them had actually met Ilse Brauchmann, it seemed unlikely. The last sighting was made by Kit. He described a woman descending the steps to a run-down basement flat.

'But why would a woman like her be going there?' asked Father Anthony.

'You pillock,' said Maud.

Kit conceded he might well have made a mistake with his sighting. He was on the number 11 bus and the fog was bad. Also – now he thought about it – the woman he spotted was wearing an old brown headscarf. So in terms of who Ilse Brauchmann was, and where she went, and even what she wanted, they all remained in the dark. The weekend came and went. Frank listened to the top forty on Sunday and sorted new chart singles on Monday morning. He seemed to have a cold coming. His head felt beaten and slow, as if it were dragging somewhere behind the rest of him.

'Frank,' said old Mrs Roussos, 'I have a tune in my head. It went like this . . .' Or someone else said, 'I'm having a bad time, Frank. I wonder if you can help . . . ?' He found his customers their records, same as always, he led them to the booth, but the thrill of getting it right was gone. It was just another thing he had to do, like putting out Mrs Roussos' bins, or washing off new graffiti. He watched himself going about his life like an oddly familiar stranger. If you took away the persona of Frank the shopkeeper – the big guy who kept helping people find music – who was the one behind?

The fact was, it was safer to stay uninvolved. He was perfectly fine with emotions, so long as they belonged to other people. Oh, he tried relationships after Peg's death, for a while he really tried, but he couldn't bear to get close. He didn't just feel abandoned by what she had done to him; he felt ransacked. He dated a waitress, a girl from the post office, a couple of older women. It was always the same. His need for love had become so great, there was no touching it. He lost confidence, he felt a fraud, or he got plain restless. And if a girlfriend so much as hinted at commitment, that was it, he freaked. Easier to disconnect from that part of life and turn his back on love altogether. Easier to find what he needed in music.

It wasn't until Tuesday, when a teenager asked for a copy of the new Michael Jackson, that Frank realized he had sold out. It dawned on him that the reason he'd sold out of *Bad* was because there'd been no visits from the reps. Not one since Phil; and that was a week ago. He had been so preoccupied he hadn't noticed.

'I already told you,' said Kit.

'When did you tell me?'

'Yesterday. But you were just staring out the window. I knew you weren't listening.'

Frank tried ringing one rep, but the line cut off as soon as he gave his name. The same thing happened the next time; he said who he was and the line went dead.

'Do you think they're avoiding you?' asked Kit.

'Why would they avoid me? They've known me for years.'

Finally a rep rang to explain he wouldn't be calling for a while and neither would the others. It wasn't just the CD thing – though that was difficult enough. Now it was the other stuff too.

'What other stuff?' Frank sat hunched over the phone at his turn-table. There were only two customers and he knew they weren't here to buy a record. One was an old woman, asleep in a booth, the other was a man from the end of the street who came now and again to inspect Frank's stock. He wasn't professional or anything. He just liked looking for scratches on records.

'I thought you were a good guy,' said the rep. 'We all did. But you shouldn't have upset Phil.'

'I didn't want to fake sales figures.'

'Everyone's doing it, Frank. He lost his job.'

'Phil?' Frank was so shaken he felt cold.

'He wants us to boycott your shop. You'd better deal direct with head office till this blows over.' The rep gave something that fell halfway between a laugh and a sneer. 'Jesus, man. Why couldn't you move with the times? When did you get to be such a coward?'

Another good question. And now that it had been posed, Frank thought about it all day. Should he have stopped Phil? Agreed to fake sales? Was that when he started being a coward? Or was it when Ilse Brauchmann asked if she could help and he told her to leave? And what about Mr Novak? Had Frank ever done anything to stop the people who sprayed his window? Some weeks he barely left Unity Street. How many more things were happening, if only he dared lift his head and look?

He tried to ring Phil and got his wife instead. She told him her husband was down the pub and they never wanted to hear from him again. He hadn't the heart to phone the other reps; if they needed to stick by Phil, he didn't want to compromise them. And anyway they were right. What was the point in driving all the way to his shop, when he wouldn't even take CDs? The only way to get new stock would be to do as the rep had told him; to ring record companies direct. He picked up the phone.

No, they told him, one after another, there could be no special deals. No more three-for-the-price-of-one; not if he was only taking vinyl. He would have to pay the full price if he refused CDs, and there would be penalty charges too if he wanted to return unsold stock. But how was he supposed to get hold of things like chart singles? he shouted. To which one of the A & R men laughed, 'I dunno, mate. Try Woolworths.'

So one day at the end of January, Frank emptied the till and threw on his jacket. Outside the air was so cold, his breath hung ahead of him like something he could touch. Frost had made white blanks of the car windows and trees offered their scrawny branches to the sky, as if they had given up all hope of seeing leaves again. The line of council plastic ribbon looped from one lamp post to another, with Kit's posters taped in each window.

BEWEAR OF FALING MASONRY.

In Articles of Faith, Father Anthony was dusting plastic Jesuses in the window, dressed in his coat and hat. When Frank came to the funeral directors', the Williams brothers darted out. They asked in unison what he thought.

'About what?'

One of them produced a carefully folded letter. It was good, thick creamy paper. Frank read as much as *Fort Development* and handed it back.

'They've offered to buy us out. And it's not peanuts, you know. No one else would want to buy us out.' The brothers exchanged a glance, as if they weren't sure which one of them should continue. 'Since Mr Novak went, we can't stop wondering who will go next.'

'That council man said someone could sue us if we don't make the external repairs. But we've got no cash.'

Frank said, 'The guy's just doing his job. No one's really going to sue. They're just trying to scare you. You know what we said? We have to look after each other. It's only if we begin to pull away from one another that the whole parade will fall apart.'

The brothers bowed their heads. One of them had a little egg stain on his lapel. They looked too small in their old-fashioned suits, like a pair of clowns from an end-of-pier show. Waiting and humble, no hair on their heads to speak of, just kneading their felt hats.

'You're right, Frank. We have to stick together.'

'Where are you off to, Frank?'

How could he admit things had got so bad he was intending to buy his stock on Castlegate? He thought again about Phil's business proposition. If Frank wanted to keep selling vinyl, he would just have to start faking catalogue numbers. After all, everyone else did it. At least he had the sales return machine.

As he passed Articles of Faith again, Father Anthony looked up at him from the window. He was playing Miles Davis. *Kind of Blue*.

He waved, as if welcoming Frank home.

16

The Boots of Miles

W<small>HEN</small> P<small>EG</small> <small>PLAYED</small> Kind of Blue, *Frank had no idea what hit him. It was 1959. The album had just come out, and he was eleven.*

As he listened, it was like doors opening, one after another. The notes started running when he thought they would go slow. They walked off to the side when he was sure they should go straight ahead. They grew fins and swam just as he had got used to them having legs. It was like knowing something and not knowing it at all.

'This is the record that will change history,' said Peg.

'Why?'

She blew a plume of smoke towards a tea-coloured patch on the ceiling. 'Because it takes music to a whole new place. Miles Davis booked all the best players but they had hardly any idea what they were going to play. He gave them outlines, told them to improvise, and they played as if the music was sitting right with them in the studio. One day everyone will have Kind of Blue. *Even the people who don't like jazz will have it.'*

How could she be certain?

'Because it's the dog's bollocks. That's why.'

The reason Peg loved the jazz musos was that she was like them. Show Peg a boundary, she crashed straight through it. She was forever leaving doors open, and there was a large gap in the garden wall where she had once rammed the Rover in reverse in order to drive forwards. One summer she took up amateur topiary, another she attempted French for beginners, but she couldn't stick with either of them. Rules bored her. Relationships were the same. It wasn't that she had no love to give, but rather that it troubled her to keep it in one place.

Peg called the jazz musos by their nicknames. Dizz, Trane, Count, The Prez. And she knew little things about them that a lover would know. Count Basie? He couldn't go to sleep without the light on. Lester Young? Another one who hated the dark. Duke Ellington was so afraid of finishing things, he never buttoned his shirt the whole way up. Dizzy Gillespie (Dizz), God, Frank, he was a joker.

'And Miles? You know the story about Miles? Such a peacock.'

'No, Peg.'

'There was this session musician once, who got a call. Could he do a gig with Miles Davis? So he turns up and he plays with Miles and honest to God, it's the best he's ever played. Only Miles keeps coming up to him. Pointing at the floor, like he wants him to turn down the volume. So he does, of course. But Miles keeps coming back. Keeps pointing at the floor and now he's looking really angry. "Miles," shouts the musician. "Just tell me what you want." And what do you think Miles says?'

'I don't know, Peg. I don't know.' He was already laughing.

'Miles points at the floor. "Check out my new fucking boots," he says.'

She loved that story. They both did.

Jazz was about the spaces between notes. It was about what happened when you listened to the thing inside you. The gaps and the cracks. Because that was where life really happened; when you were brave enough to free-fall.

17

Let's Get It On

'I HAD NO idea it could break, Frank.'

Kit stood behind the counter in his blue nylon shirt and tie, his name stitched in red letters across the chest pocket. He was also holding the sales return machine.

'I don't think Gallup had any idea it could break. What exactly did you do?'

'I unplugged it. To dust it.'

'That sounds harmless.' Though Frank wobbled on this last word.

'Then I dropped it.'

Frank flipped. 'It's a piece of machinery. It costs hundreds of pounds. I'm already in big enough trouble. How many times have I told you not to touch it?'

The question seemed to perplex Kit. He wriggled his mouth as if he were chewing a particularly sticky sweet.

'I don't mean you have to literally count,' said Frank. 'I mean, why the hell did you use it?'

'Couldn't you find Ilse Brauchmann?'

'Why would I find Ilse Brauchmann?'

'She fixed your pencil sharpener. She mended the Sellotape dispenser and the torn record sleeve. She sewed my name on my shirt and fixed the window.' He appeared to be on a roll.

Frank slunk back to his turntable with the sales return machine. He plugged it in, but there was no sign of life. Not even an electronic beep when he pressed the *Enter* button. Something caught his eye beneath his paperwork. A stalky thing, bearing a pink flower. It seemed to be growing out of Ilse Brauchmann's devastatingly spiky cactus plant.

'No. I am not going to find that woman. I'm too busy.'

Kit said nothing. He merely swung his head from one side of the shop to the other, with his hand to his eyes as if he were looking out to sea. He even went out and lifted a few crates of records.

'What are you doing now?'

'I'm searching for customers,' said Kit. 'It seems to me we've never been so quiet. But you go ahead, Frank. You keep being busy over there at your turntable.'

A saleswoman at Polydor repeated what everyone else had told him; there would be no special deals for vinyl, and there could be no replacement of the sales return machine either. They were only interested, she said, in dealing with proper shops that sold CDs.

'It's ridiculous,' Frank complained to Father Anthony that night. 'I've known these people years. And now they're treating me like I'm bankrupt.'

They were sitting inside the religious gift shop. Father Anthony had made tea and they perched either side of the wooden L-shaped counter. Despite the cold, Frank always felt comfortable in here, breathing in the smell of polish, feeling the thin old carpet beneath his feet, admiring the stark neat shelves of statues and figurines in poses of supplication and blessing, the books of prayer and religious poetry – their covers fading a little with years of sunlight – the boxes of gift cards and leather bookmarks. There was something so permanent about it.

'Has it ever occurred to you,' asked Father Anthony, 'that there is an irony?'

'What do you mean, an irony?'

'You ask your customers to trust you. You find them the music they need and of course that is not always the music they want—'

'Yes, yes.' Frank waved his hand impatiently, as if he were shooing things out of the way. 'I am helping them. It's what we do.'

'Helping someone is entirely different from being involved. Helping is all on your own terms.'

'So what are you saying?'

Father Anthony shrugged and smiled. 'You expect *other people* to change, Frank. But what about you? What are you so afraid of?'

The next afternoon Ilse Brauchmann came back.

It was raining again. She stood outside with her back to the window, holding an umbrella; she must have stepped right over the council ribbon. Frank bolted through the door and then remembered that something was missing. His jacket. Seeing her again his heart sprang to his mouth and he had to hold his face to stop the smile.

Green earrings studded her ears. He hadn't really noticed them before. Her ears. Maybe it was on account of her wet hair. Whatever it was, they were small and on the pointy side. She took short breaths, as if she had arrived in a hurry.

'It's me,' she said, in her broken accent.

'Well, yes. I can see that. Are you OK?'

'I was just passing.'

He checked to see if she had another dangerous plant in her hand but she had come cactus-free.

Frank pulled out a cigarette and flicked at his lighter, though the rain kept getting there first.

'Here,' she said.

She made a cup of her leather-gloved hand around the lighter and a small yellow flame sprang to life. Briefly their faces were lit with the same golden shine. For a while they stood side by side, not saying anything, just getting very wet beneath her umbrella. It seemed to be useful only in so far as it was channelling rainwater in a direct line over both of them.

'I thought you'd moved on.'

'No. I'm still here, Frank. I got a job.'

'You're staying?'

'For the time being.'

A car slowly moved the length of the street, churning up spray.

'I was rude,' he said.

'You were,' she said.

'How can I make it up to you?'

He tugged hard on his cigarette but his lungs didn't seem to have enough pull in them. He heard the rain, sirens far away, he heard the slush of traffic beyond Unity Street, and yet Ilse Brauchmann was still as silent as she had been that day, three weeks ago now, when she fainted outside the music shop.

She said, 'I played the Vivaldi.'

She paused. He paused. The universe held its breath.

101

'And?'

She reached for his cigarette. She held it poked out at arm's length, away from the rest of her body.

'I heard the things you told me. The birds and the storm and a dog barking. I heard a summer day. Thunder. I heard the wind. People slipping on ice, and then falling asleep by the fire.' All this she spoke to the street, with that cigarette dangling, as if it had dived from the sky and made a beeline for her hand. When she returned it, the filter held the bloom of a pink lipstick mouth. He had to suck it a little bit to one side.

'I could listen to the "Four Seasons" because you told me what you hear. So I wondered—' She stalled. 'I wondered if you would give me lessons?'

'Lessons?'

'We don't have to meet in your shop. We could meet in cafés. Or go for a walk. I want to hear you talk about music. I mean, I'm not asking for a date or anything.'

'A date? God, no!' He said it again, in case she'd got the wrong idea. 'God, no. As if. I mean, *God*—'

He laughed.

She laughed.

He guffawed.

She sent him an askew look.

'Excuse me. I'm not *that* bad.' The pingy circles were back in her cheeks. 'I'll pay. For my lessons. You can name your price. We could meet once a week. Besides . . .'

She twisted her head to glance inside the shop and gave a jump. Kit was right on the other side of the window, his face squidged into the glass above the hardboard; a sort of soft jelly-version of Kit. He waved his hand like a flipper.

She continued. 'Besides, it seems to me you need all the customers you can get. And you would be helping me.'

Helping her? How could he possibly do that? He had no idea what songs would please her. Frank scooped his hand through his hair but it was like a dishcloth. 'I can't give lessons about music. I run a shop. I sell records.'

She nodded, as if this was exactly the answer she expected. 'Of course. Isn't that what people call you English? A nation of shopkeepers? Well, I understand. I won't come again. I've made a fool of myself too many times.' She bowed her head. Tapped the wet pavement with the toe of her wet shoe. 'Stay in your shop, Frank. It's a good, safe place.'

She turned and went fast through the rain, clutching tight to her umbrella, as if it were some kind of handle steering her away from him. He watched her all the way to the end of the road until she rounded the corner and – snap – she was gone.

Where would she go? Past the big stores on Castlegate? Towards the precinct, the cathedral? The park? And then the derelict warehouses? Rushing on and on until she reached the docks – where weeds grew as high as your shoulders – and then the river and after that the sea?

Where do you come from, Ilse Brauchmann?

Who are you?

He had lost an opportunity. It was like missing a train, or something more important – something that would never come again. There was no accounting for the grief that suddenly filled him. An old drunk staggered from England's Glory. Finding the wall, he settled against it and slid all the way to the ground.

'Wait!' Frank called. 'Wait!'

His plimsolls were pounding the pavement, throwing up rain. His lungs pulled in deep, stabby breaths. He was running down Unity Street, past the parade, past the pub, towards the corner. He was breathing in the city.

Something happened that afternoon on Castlegate. Shoppers might have noticed a great big man, lumbering through the rain, no jacket, in pursuit of a smart young woman in a green coat and gloves. Had she stolen something? Forgotten something? Were they friends, lovers, what? Whatever the reason, they were both very wet. They stood opposite one another in the middle of the pavement.

'Frank?' she said. 'Frank?'

Now that he'd finally caught up with her, his body seemed to be on strike. He could barely breathe and he felt in dire need of a chair.

'I. Changed. My. Mind.'

Her face lit up. 'You did?'

All around them, the vast shopfronts shone through the black rain like ocean liners. Dolcis, Army & Navy, Tammy, Burton for Men, Woolworths. People rushed past, heads bowed, umbrellas open, bags of shopping in their hands. Ilse laughed. Frank laughed.

'So how are we going to do this?' he asked. 'I mean, I've never done this sort of thing before—'

'Me neither. This is a first for me too.'

'We could meet—'

'Yes?'

'Somewhere—'

'Yes—'

'That we both know—'

'Like—'

'The cathedral—'

'Yes—'

'And take it—'

'From there?'

'Yes—'

'When?'

'Next Monday?'

'Um—'

'Or not—'

'Tuesday?'

'What time?'

'I don't mind—'

'You say—'

'No. You—'

'Five thirty?'

'Five thirty?'

And that was how they planned their first lesson. In words of pretty much one syllable, and without the aid of full stops.

Tuesday. A week from now. Outside the cathedral, after closing time.

Frank bounced all the way home, flushed and giddy as a child.

18

The Messiah

'HALLELUJAH!' *SANG THE CHOIR.* 'Hallelujah!'

Frank and Peg lay side by side, listening to Handel on the Dansette. 'Isn't it marvellous?' she whispered. 'Isn't it the best?'

Afterwards he lit her a Sobranie as she told him about Handel. How he wanted to write music that ordinary people could understand. Unlike Vivaldi, he died a wealthy man, though like Bach he suffered from cataracts and had two botched eye operations. Three thousand people came to his funeral. She was very moved by that.

'But what about the Messiah, *Peg?'*

'Before the Messiah *things were a bit shit for Handel. He had no money and his last few works had been turkeys. Then Handel read the libretto for the* Messiah *and that was it. Bingo! He saw the light. He shut himself away and he wrote the whole thing in twenty-four days. I kid you not. He didn't even leave the house to get a sandwich. Finally his servant goes in and what does he find? Handel is holding the "Hallelujah Chorus" in his hand and crying. "I have seen heaven," he says.'*

'Did he? See heaven?'

'Maybe. Maybe he was just shit-hot at writing music.' Her mouth hitched upwards. She was winking beneath those giant sunglasses.

'He knew, you see. Handel just knew he had got something. It hit the button, Frank.'

The Messiah premiered in Dublin. It was a charity performance and so many tickets were sold the audience were asked to leave their swords and hoop skirts at home to make enough room. The hall was packed. Standing room only. It was a triumph; the first big fund-raiser. It was like George Harrison organizing Bangladesh, only Handel was doing it in 1742.

That was why Peg loved the Messiah best of all. Because it showed people they were not alone. No matter about their differences, the music lifted them up and lowered them down, only to raise them even higher. It worked like a spell.

Hallelujah. Hallelujah.

PAUSE.

HAL–LE–LU–JAH!

Peg had been dead fifteen years and it was still the one record he couldn't bear to play. It hurt too much. Even now.

SIDE B: FEBRUARY 1988

19

Help!

'Us?' said Kit. 'Us?'

It was past closing time on Unity Street and they were in England's Glory, all the shopkeepers from the parade, as well as the regulars, old Mrs Roussos, her chihuahua, the man who only liked Chopin, and another stick-thin young man who seemed to have been in the shop all day, though no one knew who he was or what he wanted, beyond tea and biscuits. Earlier someone had fed the jukebox with enough coins to play 'Eye Of The Tiger' ten times and then left in a hurry. Kit had tried to unplug the jukebox but given himself a small electric shock in the process – there was nothing anyone could do but wait for the song to end.

'You want *us* to help *you* to help *her*?' repeated Kit. He seemed to be having difficulty getting past his personal pronouns. 'But how?'

Frank messed up his hair. That was the tricky part – he had no idea. He had agreed to give Ilse Brauchmann a lesson about music. That had seemed a very good idea at the time. Now – faced with the practical question of what to find for her and what exactly to say about it – he realized he had no clue. He'd barely slept for worry. Beyond the fact she seemed to quite like green and had an aptitude for fixing things, he still knew nothing about her.

'She told you she has a job now,' said Father Anthony.

'She's from Germany,' added one of the Williams brothers.

'She's new here,' said the other.

'And she always wears gloves,' pointed out Kit. 'She didn't even take them off to write a cheque. Did she keep them on when she helped you fix the window?'

'Does it matter?'

'It's very strange.'

There followed an animated discussion about the mystery of Ilse Brauchmann's hands. Father Anthony said she just seemed a formal kind of person; the Williams brothers thought it might be a question of hygiene. The man who only liked Chopin said she probably had chilblains, the old men at the bar agreed on severe burns, while the man with three teeth threw in a curve ball and suggested they might be false.

'Oh my God!' shrieked Kit, so bound up in empathy he forgot how to draw the line between what they knew and what they didn't. 'Poor woman! That's awful!'

'She wears gloves because she's cold,' said Maud. 'It's freezing out there. She also has a fiancé in case we've all forgotten. I don't know why we're so desperate to push Frank into the arms of a woman who's getting married.'

Maud had a way of saying 'we' that made it sound less of a collective experience, and more like a hideous mistake.

'Of course she has a fiancé,' said Father Anthony. 'Of course we know that. We just want Frank to make a good job of his lesson. We're trying to help him.'

While the group renewed their previous debate about the true identity of the man she was engaged to marry – was he English, for instance? German? Had his career brought him here? Could he really be a film star? – Frank pinched the bridge of his nose between his fingers. Why had he agreed to talk to her about music? Open a small door and she had moved into his head, taken up residence and unpacked her things; not only that, she had also brought her fiancé, his fast car and all the other sophisticated young people she must surely know. Frank saw them sometimes, swarming into the new wine bars that were beginning to open on the other side of Castlegate, so confident of their place in the world they spoke very loudly as if no one else could hear or understand. Frank felt ill. He had thought it would be easier than this. If possible it was even worse than the prospect of listening to the *Messiah*, and he had no intention of doing that either. 'I have a few ideas,' he said weakly.

That was a good starting point, said Father Anthony.

'But if I tell you them, you'll laugh.'

Of course they wouldn't, said Father Anthony. They were his friends. Why didn't Frank try out his ideas on them? The old ex-priest put down his pineapple juice and plaited his long fingers into a steeple, the way he did when he wanted to listen carefully.

'So I was thinking I could write a sort of poem. I could tell her about music and all the things she is missing and then I could recite it.'

'Your poem?'

'Hm-mm.'

'Outside the cathedral?'

'Quite possibly.'

Everyone listened with a polite but quizzical expression, as if Frank had just grown an extra set of ears and no one knew how to break it to him. The Williams brothers reached for each other's hands.

'Have you written poetry about music before?' asked Father Anthony at last.

'No.'

'Have you written any poetry whatsoever?'

'Not really.'

The group nodded, and in the absence of something to say, they nodded some more. Kit blew into an empty crisp packet and sat on it. *Bang.* 'I see,' said Father Anthony.

'Or I was thinking I could learn something like the piano, and then I could play for her.'

'Seriously?'

'I don't know.'

'At five thirty on Tuesday?'

Maud doubled over towards the table, holding her chest, her shoulders heaving, and emitting tiny sobs.

'Is she hurt?' asked Frank.

'She's killing herself laughing,' said Kit.

She was not the only one. Glancing from one face to another, Frank realized the entire group was busy disposing of mirth in handkerchiefs, beers and crisp packets. Even Mrs Roussos' white chihuahua was doing a smiley thing with his teeth. Frank began to grin too, and then halfway into it he thought of Ilse Brauchmann and remembered what he had to do and felt sick with worry all over again.

'It's all right for you. I'm – way out of my depth here.'

It was Father Anthony who finally spoke. 'Frank, when I met you I was in a terrible mess. We all know that. You listened to me and then you found me jazz. You didn't write a poem. You didn't play it on the piano.

114

You didn't tell me everything there was to know. You just listened to me and then you got up and found the record I needed. She said she wants you to talk to her about music. So tell her what you hear when you listen. Be yourself.'

The others concurred. They mentioned the music Frank had found them. *You found me Aretha, you found me Bach, you found me Motown.* Be yourself, they agreed. But of course that was not so straightforward. They had no idea who he really was. No one did.

When he was about eight, Frank had called Peg 'Mother'. He was waiting for the school bus when she had turned the corner, luminous in a yellow kaftan. 'Hello, Mother!' She marched straight past. He was a laughing stock.

'I didn't realize you were talking to *me*,' she said later. 'I don't know why you're so upset.' But he was, he was very upset. It wasn't the laughter, he was used to that; but he had felt utterly abandoned. Cast adrift.

'Couldn't I call you that sometimes?' he had asked. 'Everyone else calls their mother "Mother".'

She pulled a face as if she had just eaten something off. 'What's wrong with calling me Peg? That's my name.'

He had suggested some alternatives. Mum? Mama? Mother Peg? ('What the fuck?' she said.) He explained he thought it might be nice.

'Why do we have to be the same as everyone else? If I call you Frank and you call me Peg, it shows everything is fair and equal between us. No strings attached.'

He had tried it, though, when she was out of earshot. 'Good night, Mother.' 'Thank you, Mother.' To his shame he discovered he rather liked it; and he wasn't convinced, when it came to mothering, that he wanted to be on fair and equal terms. Once in a while, it would have been comforting, he had thought, to be – well, looked after. Cooked a hot meal. Called 'Darling'.

To have strings, like everyone else.

The night before the first lesson, Frank pulled out armfuls of records. There was only one solution. Since he had no idea what music would please Ilse Brauchmann, he would have to do the next best thing. He would have to give her the music that pleased *him*. Bach, Joni, Miles, Bob . . . all those records he had learnt to love. He spread them on the floor all around him, and it was like a pleasure garden, he thought, a pleasure garden of fairground attractions – this one slow, this one fast, this one so wild it could turn you upside down. It was good looking at them. His friends. He fell asleep feeling very happy and sure of himself. Excited.

So what happened in the six-hour period while he was unconscious? When Frank woke, he was a different man. The moment he thought of the day ahead, his body began to pound. Not only that, he discovered his hair had put in an appearance as a halo. He tried dampening it with water and that only made things worse. Now it was a halo with spikes. He cooked eggs but hadn't the stomach for eating. When he went down to open the shop, his hands were shaking so much he dropped the keys.

'Oh my God. You look awful,' said Kit, bounding inside.

What Frank needed was a plan; some changes were required. If he didn't want to meet Ilse Brauchmann looking like a terrified shop assistant with bad hair, he needed to fix a few things. So he went to a proper barber. He asked if the man thought he could do anything with his fringe and the barber said with hair like Frank's, what you needed was a good-quality styling wax. Frank went to the chemist and bought a pot of Dax.

While he was there, he made the mistake of asking the assistant if she had any advice about aftershave. Her opinion was that a big man like Frank needed a big smell like Jovan Musk; it was dead sexy. Frank was about to explain that really he didn't need to smell sexy, he just wanted to smell normal, when she whipped out a tester bottle from beneath the counter and shot him with a scent so powerful it penetrated his nose with the force of paint stripper. It wasn't just sexy, it was obscene. All the way home, he tried to dodge the smell, but it seemed to have infiltrated his skin and bones. He took a shower and it was still with him. So now his hair was wet and no longer looked the way it had looked when the barber cut it; it was back to doing the halo thing, just a shorter version.

Frank made a stab at fixing his hair in the exact way the barber had shown him. It looked even worse. After that he tried on several jackets along with several pairs of shoes but ended up with his regular plimsolls and beaten-up suede jacket. He had an appointment at the bank before he met Ilse Brauchmann. On the way out he ran into both Kit and Maud.

'Oh my God, what's that foul smell?' said Maud.

And Kit said, 'What happened to your hair?'

'Does it look awful?'

'It looks. It looks.' Kit straightened his Ilse Brauchmann tie. He seemed to have run out of adjectives. 'It looks *neat*.'

'In a bad way?'

Maud said nothing; she just sucked her molars. Sometimes, Frank thought, you had to be grateful for small things.

'A loan?' repeated Henry. 'Why do you want a loan?' His office was heated to the point of tropical, and he swung slowly left and right on his chair. Frank was on the other side of the desk on the very small seat where he had sat fourteen years previously. Either the chair had got smaller, or Frank had got bigger. In either case, the only way to maintain a respectable position was to balance on one buttock. So, less of a chair, more of a perch. And the aftershave was still with him. If possible, it was inflating with the heat.

'I need to make some alterations to the shop.'

Frank checked the wall clock above Henry's head. One more hour, and he would be meeting Ilse Brauchmann. Just thinking that made him want to get up and pace about.

'So how much do you need?'

'How much do I what?'

'Are you all right, Frank? You seem very nervous.'

'I'm fine.' Frank reached for his fringe and remembered he hadn't got one. 'I need five thousand pounds.'

Henry widened his eyes before expelling a long breath, as if he had just bitten into an especially lively chilli. 'That much? Why?'

Pulling out a piece of paper, Frank ran through the alterations he needed to make. The list had been drawn up for him by Kit, so it also included spelling mistakes and a host of exclamation marks. Aside from the external repairs to the falling masonry, the entire shop would be refurbished with proper wooden display units. No more plastic boxes and crates. There would be an illuminated sign above the door, a lit-up window display (and also a new window), as well as a shrink-wrap machine. A shrink-wrap machine? Henry laughed. What in hell's name was that? There was still something of the public-school boy in Henry. When he laughed, it came out more like a guffaw, as if he had done something he shouldn't in the science lab. 'What's happened to you, Frank?'

'I accept that people want CDs. That's what's happened. People don't want their old records. They bring them to me every week. Some people don't even want money. They're just desperate for the space.'

'So you're finally going to stock them?'

'CDs? No way.' Frank grinned. 'I'm going to save vinyl. I'm going to make it even more *beautiful*.'

He explained. Once he had the new shrink-wrap machine, he would be able to sell his records individually heat-wrapped in cellophane, with the vinyl sealed inside the sleeve. Each one would come with its own label, handwritten and decorated by Kit, describing what exactly you needed to listen for. People would flock to the newly refurbished shop; it would be like one of those specialist stores you read about in the *NME*. That in turn would generate new business for the remaining shops on the parade. Unity Street would be back on the map.

'What's your balance at the moment?'

Frank said he wasn't sure. He wasn't in the red exactly, but he was probably heading (kind of) in that (sort of) general (pinkish) direction. He found himself wafting his hands a lot. 'Can I smoke in here?'

Henry called through to a clerk and while they waited for the balance on Frank's account, Henry answered Frank's enquiries about the family as if he were batting off shuttlecocks. 'Good! Fine! Yes!' On his desk, there were framed photographs of his wife and the boys, and one of Mandy before the kids; it was the only one, Frank noticed, where she looked happy in an abandoned way. For some time now, whenever he listened to Henry, he heard a strange lonely sound – like a minor chord tuned too fine. He had a hunch the couple were struggling.

The clerk laid a slip of paper on the desk and Henry sighed. 'It's not looking good, Frank. You have sixty-eight pence.'

'I thought perhaps I could get an overdraft,' said Frank vaguely. 'Lots of people have those, don't they?'

'The problem is that we've had instructions from head office to be very strict about overdrafts.'

'I thought this was supposed to be a boom time? I thought Maggie Thatcher wanted us all running our own businesses and looking after number one—'

'She does. But inflation's going up again. Head office is uneasy.'

'I can pay the money back. I just need a few months.'

'What are your books like? What kind of guarantee can you offer?'

Frank admitted he didn't actually keep any books at the moment. But he *would*. In future he definitely would. In terms of a guarantee, he was happy to offer his flat. Henry looked pained. 'You can't offer your flat, Frank. It's too risky.'

'This is an *investment*. Once I've made the improvements on the shop, I'll be competing with the big hitters on Castlegate. You watch, I'll be raking in the cash.' Frank took a glance at the clock. Five to five. His heart plunged. 'Look, I should go. I'm meeting someone—'

'A date?' Henry looked touchingly hopeful.

'No. A kind of – you know – lesson. I'm going to take her on a journey through music.' He said it quickly, hoping Henry wouldn't stop too long and examine the contents of that sentence. 'By the way, this is for you and Mandy.' He searched through the bag of records at his feet and pulled out an album.

'What's Shalamar?'

'Play it tonight when you get home. Side one, track one. "A Night To Remember". And make sure the boys are out of the way.'

The two friends looked as if they might hug but then the idea seemed to lose its way and instead they got infinitely more sensible and shook hands.

'So what do you think? Will I get my overdraft?'

'It's unlikely, but I'll do what I can.'

This time Frank did embrace his friend. He couldn't help it. It was a great big bear hug that almost floored Henry. Afterwards Henry straightened his cuffs and his tie and cleared his throat several times as if he were reassembling himself into a bank manager. Frank asked in passing what Henry knew about Fort Development and Henry said he'd never heard of them.

'They want to buy up Unity Street.'

'Why would they want to do that?'

'You're right.' He smiled and thanked Henry again. 'Trust me. You're going to love Shalamar,' he said.

The light was beginning to change, darkening. The air was as sharp as glass and a bitter wind had swept in, smelling of cheese and onion; at least it did something to counterbalance the Jovan Musk. Traders were already packing away stalls on Castlegate, shouting that it was your last chance to get bargains. Frank passed the clock tower – a gang of junkies crowded round a plastic bag – before taking a left turning down one of the cobbled alleyways that led to the cathedral. People had set out goods for sale here too – but these were single personal items placed carefully on a blanket; a paperback book, a plug, an ashtray, one walking boot. God help me, he thought.

Gulls swung to and fro, pale crosses against the sky. The cathedral was ahead, square and sure of itself. Frank tried to rehearse what exactly he would say to Ilse Brauchmann but he couldn't even remember how to speak. He stopped. Turned round.

He would run straight back to the shop.

But someone was shouting across the green. Were they in trouble? This person was waving his arms, and springing up and down—

'Kit?'

A few feet to his left, Maud stood scowling in her stripy tights and fun-fur jacket. Father Anthony – wearing a hat with earflaps – was peering over his broken spectacles at a bus timetable. His breath seeped from his mouth like white smoke.

Frank marched over. 'What are you all doing?'

'We're just out on a Tuesday night,' said Kit. He couldn't look Frank in the eye. 'It's a free country.'

Father Anthony said that, as it happened, he was very interested in the route of the number 11 – he had no idea it went through so many parts of the city. Maud offered no explanation whatsoever.

Kit bit his lip. 'Also, we wanted to check you are OK.'

'I am terrified.'

'Will you get the overdraft?'

'I doubt it.'

'You have the records for Ilse Brauchmann?'

'Yes.'

'Remember what you have to do.'

'What do I have to do?'

'You have to get a good look at her hands.'

122

'Right now I am struggling just to stand up.'

'OK. Well, *bonne chance*.'

'Thank you.'

'That's French.'

'I know.'

Kit looked as if he might like to recite more French, or perhaps further words of encouragement in other European languages, but at that point he trod in something compromising and had to scrape his shoe on the kerb.

'Remember. Just be yourself,' murmured Father Anthony, still studying the wonderful complexities of the number 11 route. 'Tell her what you feel when you listen. What are you going to talk about?'

'The "Moonlight" Sonata.'

20

Moonlight Sonata

'WHAT DO YOU know about sonatas and Beethoven, Frank?'

Frank repeated everything he knew. A sonata was traditionally made up of three sections. Fast. Slow. Fast.

'Bullseye,' said Peg.

It was Haydn and Mozart who really cracked the sonata, but it was Beethoven who reinvented it, just as he reinvented the symphony. Bach was king of the Baroque; Mozart and Haydn were kings of the Classical; Brahms, Chopin, Liszt and Berlioz were the great Romantics. Bruckner, Mahler and Wagner brought music into the twentieth century; Stravinsky and Schoenberg redefined harmony. But Beethoven was in a class of his own. He didn't write music to praise God. He didn't write it to earn a living. Beethoven wrote music because he had to.

'Yes yes yes!' Peg puffed out a whoosh of smoke that almost choked her, it was so happy. 'So the first thing to know about the "Moonlight" Sonata is that it has fuck all to do with the moon.'

'Nothing whatsoever?' Now that he was twelve, Frank found himself editing out Peg's swear words and replacing them with more maternal ones.

'It was a critic who gave it that name. When he heard the sonata, he said it

124

was like looking at the moon on a lake. Fuck knows why. I guess he was sitting by a lake. So after that everyone thought it was just a nice bit of music about the full moon and some water.' She held up the new album cover. It showed – surprise, surprise – a full moon and some water. 'I mean for fuck's sake,' said Peg.

'So it isn't about the moon?'

'No! It's a revolutionary piece. It's crazy. It's Beethoven taking the rules and snapping them in half. It's not fast, slow, fast. It's slow, fast, fuck off. It's anarchy!'

Peg told the story of the 'Moonlight' Sonata. Beethoven had fallen in love with one of his students. He was a complicated man. Moody. Abused as a kid. No idea about things like personal hygiene. He was always falling in love with his students but this one was a countess and she was seventeen.

'Then bam. A bombshell. Beethoven finds out two things. One: the countess is going to marry a count. Two: he – Beethoven, not the count – is going deaf. He is poleaxed. The man IS music. What will he be without it? So he pours all those feelings into his piano sonata and he dedicates it to Julia. It's like rocket fuel. I mean, a full moon. For fuck's sake.'

Peg lowered the stylus on to the vinyl. She settled herself on the floor. Tick, tick went the record—

'Aren't you going to join me?'

'I think I'll stay in my chair.'

Afterwards, Peg remained lying on the carpet, staring at the ceiling. She didn't say anything for a long time. She just blew smoke rings and sighed. When he listened to her, she seemed very sad.

'Peg? Do you think we should get something to eat?'

They fixed one of their regular suppers. A tin of mock turtle soup from Fortnum's, along with a box of Bath Olivers, followed by canned peaches and condensed milk. Peg's cookery revolved entirely round packets and tins.

It was only as Frank carried plates to the sink that she began to speak. 'I was fifteen when I fell in love. He was a friend of my father's. Had me once a week in the back of his car. God, I loved that man. We carried on for years. But did he leave his wife? His kids? Did he hell. Broke my fucking heart. If you learn one thing from me, make it this. Love is not nice. Stay away from it, Frank. Stay away.'

21

A Beautiful Pea-Green Coat

SHE WAS OUTSIDE the cathedral. You couldn't miss her. She stood waiting in her green coat beneath an old-fashioned street lamp; still and erect, and somehow illuminated to the point of brilliance, though maybe that was another of those details his head supplied. He had assumed a woman like Ilse Brauchmann would keep you waiting. The air went clean out of him. Would she notice if he walked straight past?

Clearly she would, because she waved.

Frank's face began to smile, all of its own accord, so he had to pretend he was glancing round and appreciating the loveliness of the night in general. The smile solidified. He couldn't actually get rid of it. He tried to make out he was remembering a particularly hilarious joke.

Her face fell. 'Is it me?'

'What?'

'Do I look funny?'

'Of course you don't.'

'I tried a straightening comb. It's a disaster.'

There *was* something very flat about her hair. She was right. It was looming round her face like a veil. But then again, Frank could hardly talk. You could probably smell him before you could see him, and his fringe was a wedge.

She didn't mention that. She just lifted her face to his, her eyes so solemn he failed to breathe again.

'I thought you had forgotten,' she said.

Forgotten?

How could he?

Would he ever?

She suggested they should go to a café nearby, called the Singing Teapot. It had ruched pink curtains, and a display of teapots in the window; none of them exactly singing but quite happy-looking none-theless, ranging from a plain old Brown Betty to a more extrovert thing, painted with flowers. There was no one else in the café. They chose a round table by the window and took off their coats. She kept her gloves on, though.

'I close at five thirty,' said a waitress, charging through a pair of saloon doors at the back, and pointing to a clock on the wall. She was a large young woman in her early twenties, kitted out in a black dress that was too small and a tiny lace cap.

Ilse Brauchmann lifted her eyes. It wasn't a smile, and neither was it a challenge; it was more a direct connection. 'Couldn't you just serve us? We don't need very much.'

The waitress pursed her mouth. She tugged at the hem of her dress. 'Go on, then,' she said.

However, there were some drawbacks. She could not, for instance, serve alcoholic beverages without food. Ilse replied that food would be lovely, and the waitress said it wouldn't, on account of the fact the cook had gone home. There was tea or squash. That was it, in terms of drinks. And food, in fact.

'Thank you, I'll take lemon squash,' said Ilse Brauchmann.

'We've got orange.'

'I'll take orange. With a cube of ice.'

'We don't do ice.'

Ilse Brauchmann smiled. No ice would be lovely. 'I suppose we should get on with our lesson,' she said, once the waitress had stormed back through her saloon doors and they were alone again. He asked if she had a notebook or a pen or anything like that, and she said she didn't. She was happy just to listen. She cupped her exquisite face in her gloved hands and blinked with those large eyes, as if clearing things out of the way in order to see him all the better.

'The thing, uh, about music—' Frank was shaking. Never mind Ilse Brauchmann's hands, his own were jelly; he thought it would be a good idea to sit on them. 'The thing about music is that sometimes we know it so well we, uh, we don't know it at all. My first lesson is about listening—'

'*Bon appétit*,' interrupted the waitress, slamming down a tray with their drinks and leaving.

But Frank was such a barrel of words and feelings, he felt unable to swallow. Also, his hands were still beneath his arse and unavailable for duty; there was no way he was going to tackle a tiny teacup. 'The "Moonlight" Sonata is by Beethoven. Do you, uh, know Beethoven?'

'Aren't they a rock band?'

Oh well, this was a disaster. He might as well give up. 'Beethoven was German. He was kind of the biggest thing ever in classical music. What's wrong? Why are you laughing?'

'I know who Beethoven was, Frank. That was a joke. I'm not *stupid*.'

She appeared to find her joke hilarious. She actually couldn't stop laughing. Then her laugh did something untoward, coming out as a hiccup. She shot her palm to her mouth. 'I'm sorry,' she said mutely. 'I will be sensible now. Go on, Frank. I'm listening.'

Time passed: but how, he had no idea. Whenever he looked at the clock, it had jumped forward. Slowly and with much clearing of his throat, Frank told Ilse Brauchmann what he felt about music. How it had been a part of his life since he was a boy, and so had vinyl. How it had been like stepping into a secret world through a cupboard. He had not intended to say any of this – he had spent years listening to other people – but now that he had started, one word seemed to pitch up after another. Every time he dared a glance in her direction, her eyes were locked on his. He could feel it without even looking – the depth of her gaze. It seemed to draw the words out of him.

He told her about Peg, the white house that she had inherited, all her married men, his exiled and irregular childhood. Not even Father Anthony knew these stories but the stillness with which Ilse listened was as great as the sea. It seemed without end. Besides, what did he have to be afraid of? She had no interest in him, she was engaged to someone else. At the end of the hour, she would hurry away from this café, she would get on with that very busy life of hers, she would be with her fiancé and forget all about the things Frank had told her.

She sat with her face tipped in one hand, listening. She didn't smile or frown or do anything except watch with her solemn black eyes.

Frank explained that as he grew older he had searched for music of his own on the radio – his mother rarely visited shops, they had most things delivered – and this was how he discovered the connecting threads between music and learnt to love not one genre, but all of them. Music was a part of him – he had been brought up that way. Really it was the only thing he knew. He had been a no-hoper at school.

Braving his tea, Frank discovered it was stone cold.

Nice, though.

The best tea he had ever drunk, in fact.

He had chosen her the 'Moonlight' Sonata, he said, because it was one of those very famous pieces that everyone liked and no one really heard. So he wanted to help her listen. What he was going to tell her was not the kind of thing she would ever find in a textbook. It was just how he felt when he played the record.

Ilse Brauchmann nodded.

He explained the whole story about Beethoven and his student Julia, just as Peg had once done. 'When I listen to the "Moonlight" Sonata, I see him sitting at his piano next to her. It's as if he's playing his own love letter, just waiting for a sign that she understands. The music starts softly. It's kind. Because here he is, this man who's old enough to be her father, this man who's always falling for the wrong woman, but *this* one, you see, she's so beautiful, and she's so above him. The music builds up and down, but it never runs away, it just waits for her. And the higher notes go *up, up*, and the lower ones repeat the pattern, saying *yes, yes*. It's like two voices, asking one another if they feel the same, without – you know – without using words. But then Beethoven does something else as well. He makes the higher notes lead the way, as if he – Beethoven – is now Julia, and she – Julia – is *him*. It's so intimate, what he's doing, he's practically having sex with her.'

'Sex?' Her face stretched wide. 'Beethoven?'

'Or at least good foreplay.'

131

Sex? Foreplay? Horrified, he heard the words that had come from his mouth. He reached for his tea, and got another mouthful of cold. It was probably best to keep talking.

'So we get to the second movement. And it's fast. It's happy. It's a bit of a surprise. You think, *Oh I get it. You're all right, Beethoven. This isn't hurting you. Good man.* But that's just a trick. Because then we get the third movement and it's like he's a different person. It's *wild*. Beethoven jumps off his stool and he leaps right on top of that piano. I mean he's inside the thing. He's ripping it up. It's *punk*. He takes everything that has come before and he kicks it sky high. Because Beethoven knows, you see. He knows that you don't find peace until you've been to hell and back. So what's he saying? Is he saying, *Don't believe the hype, life is shit*? Or is he actually saying, *Yes, it's shit but it fits inside a sonata.* It's up to you. But you will never find out unless you listen.'

In all this time she had barely moved. Was she even breathing? He felt exhausted. If the waitress had offered him a blanket, he would have lain down and slept – and yet by the same token, he felt so wired he had no idea how he would ever sleep again.

The Singing Teapot waitress bashed through her saloon doors carrying – not a blanket at all, but a Hoover. It was already six thirty. Fully dark outside.

Frank passed Ilse the bag of records. There was the 'Moonlight' Sonata, as well as *Kind of Blue*, along with another of his favourites, *Pet Sounds* by The Beach Boys. He asked her to listen. That was all she had to do. If she took the time, there was so much waiting for her that she didn't yet know. It would be like new spaces opening up, one after another.

At last Ilse Brauchmann spoke. Her accent broke the words into

132

separate syllables, making them seem larger and more complex in meaning. 'Thank you, Frank. That was an amazing lesson.'

She paid the bill, and passed Frank an envelope. Fifteen pounds. More cash than he made in a day. She rose to her feet and slipped on her green coat, all the time without looking at him, then she moved to the door. Thanking the waitress repeatedly for her kindness, Frank gambolled after Ilse Brauchmann in case he lost her all over again.

It was her idea that they should see the moon on the lake. 'I mean, I know the music is not about that, but still it would be nice to see it? *Ja*?' They had made their way along the cobbled alleyway from the café and crossed Castlegate. The gates to the park were unlocked. He didn't even think about it. He just said 'Yes!' – actually, he said '*Ja!*' – and followed.

The moon was low. Not really a full one; more like a half-sucked sweet. All along the path, the dark bare trees were strung with coloured lights, stretching ahead in loops of red and green and yellow. A slight wind soughed and rustled in the branches.

They passed the bandstand, closed up for winter, and left the main path to go down towards the lake. It was wonderfully quiet. Just the tiny purling of water against the shore, and the muffled city in the background. She led the way to the jetty and he followed until they stood at the very edge, with the dim water all around them. It rocked the line of pleasure boats tied up with rope and shaped like white swans. Now that his eyes were used to it, the dark was a smudge. Not fully black, but more a kind of velvety blue. The two of them stood side by side, watching the lake. Smoking. He felt curiously at ease.

'Wouldn't it be nice to go in a boat?' she murmured. Before he could object, she had knelt and untied one. 'Get in. Quick.'

Part-way between the boat and the jetty, three important things occurred to Frank.

One: he was very large.

Two: the boat was very small.

Three: he couldn't swim. It was another of those ordinary things that Peg had neglected to teach him. Point of fact, he was afraid of water.

As his right foot hit the boat, it – the boat – appeared to plummet downwards. Water came sloshing over the sides and it jerked away from the jetty. So now here he was, one plimsoll safely land-bound, the other already drenched in very cold water, while the gap between his two feet seemed to be growing at an alarming rate, with the rest of Frank stuck in the middle.

'Jump,' said Ilse Brauchmann.

Jump? Had she any idea who she was talking to? He said, 'Whoa!' That was all he could come up with.

Two firm hands pushed his shoulder and sent him flying into the boat. It was like landing in a plastic cup. The boat pitched high to the left, then high to the right. Water poured in – the bottom of the boat was a puddle. He held out his hand for Ilse but she was already stepping in, all by herself. The boat see-sawed violently. It was hardly an equal distribution of weight but at least he was less in danger now of tipping backwards and plunging head-first to his death at the bottom of a lake.

'How deep is this water?' he asked.

'Very deep, I guess.' Completely matter-of-fact, she was.

She slotted the oars into the rowlocks. Water seeped over her shoes but that didn't seem to bother her. He heard the muffled splash as the oars hit water, and the rhythmic creak of the boat.

'When did you learn to do this?' he said.

She glanced over her shoulder, guiding the boat towards the centre of the lake. 'Oh I never did. But it can't be difficult.'

His feet were so wet, his shoes felt stuck to his socks. And he was squashed inside what must be the rear end of a small plastic swan, with his knees jutting towards his chin. There was a lot about his situation that struck Frank as uncomfortable and potentially life-threatening. Nevertheless he felt childishly thrilled. As a boy he had stood looking down from the cliffs towards the beach below, while other kids played in the sea and their mothers sat with picnics and towels. He had longed to join them.

The moonlight lay in fractured pieces all across the water, and so did the reflections from the little coloured lights strung up in the trees. As the boat moved forward, the water parted and sealed.

Ilse Brauchmann pointed out the cathedral in the distance. She showed him the direction of his shop, Castlegate, and then the docks. She craned her neck backwards and told him the names of the stars, pointing at the different constellations so that he could find the pictures. Who knew there was an actual plough up there? Seven sisters? A boyfriend of Peg's had mentioned the Plough once and suggested Frank should go look; but without adding anything so helpful as instructions as to where he might find it. The oars hit the water, *swish, swish*. Ilse Brauchmann's hair was not flat any more. It was hoopy with curls. (*Hello, curls*.) Over on the jetty sat her green handbag and his bag of records; the sensible pieces of them waiting, like parents, on dry land.

She said, 'Poor Beethoven, huh?'

'Yes, poor Beethoven.'

'I guess he was really in love.'

'I guess.'

'Are you married?'

'Me? No.'

'I thought you and the tattooed woman were an item?'

Frank laughed so much he almost capsized himself. 'No. I kind of don't do all that stuff.'

'Are you gay?' The straightness with which she asked the question threatened another small drowning.

'No, I'm – I'm good on my own. But you're getting married. That's great.'

'Oh,' she said. Then, 'Hm.'

She rowed until they were right in the middle of the lake. It was like floating in a sea of ink, he thought, not in the past and not in the future, but a place of their own. The water rocked them gently. He couldn't even see her face any more, only the slender shape of her like a cut-out in the dark.

She said, 'When I was a child, I wanted to be famous. I wanted it so much. I even practised in the mirror. I really did, Frank. Being a famous person. I practised laughing and saying hello and even taking a bow. I couldn't bear the fact that life was just – you know – here and gone. All for nothing. But now I don't think that. I think that loving another person and being kind is about the best thing you can do. What is it they say? No man is an island.'

Afterwards she tied up the boat exactly where they had found it and he walked her back through the park. They still didn't speak. It was as if the two people who had sat in a café and then rowed in a pleasure boat and quietly talked about love were no longer the two people now heading back to their separate lives. Occasionally he thought she gave a sigh, as if she wanted to say something, but it was more than likely her feet were wet and extremely cold. Ice particles moved like flittery flies around the lamps. They reached the gates.

Stopped.

Waited.

'Well, goodbye,' she said to her nice shoes.

'Goodbye,' he said to his old plimsolls. 'You have your records?'

'Yes. Thank you.'

A silence. One so taut and complicated and beautiful that in another life he might have kissed her.

'A cab,' she said, spotting a free one across the street. 'See you next Tuesday!'

He watched her climb into the back seat and wave as the cab moved on. Being with her was the same as staring into the sun; he saw nothing and yet when he looked away, there she was, a raucous white light imprinted at the heart of everything. Yes. She was going to marry someone else. But he had never felt so happy.

22

A Night to Remember

'HELLO? IS ANYONE home? Hello?'

Henry stood calling at the door. The house was so silent he was afraid Mandy had finally gone and left him. They lived thirty minutes outside the city, on a modern estate with electric gates and leafy avenues that were named after English poets. 'Mandy? Boys?'

'The boys are upstairs,' Mandy's voice called back.

He found her in the kitchen. She seemed preoccupied with a tricky stain that only she could see; she kept rubbing at the worktop in small concentric circles.

Henry remained hovering at the doorway, useless and smiling in his socks. He hadn't touched his wife for over a year. He said, 'Frank came in today.'

She said, 'Oh.'

'He wants an overdraft.'

'Oh.'

'It's going to be difficult. He's taking a big risk.'

They spoke in the flat monotone they used these days in order to

138

remain on open road where nothing would jump out and surprise them. One wrong word and it was like trees coming down.

'Apparently he's branching into music lessons.'

'Oh,' she said again. 'Wow.'

Henry couldn't explain how it had happened. He couldn't pinpoint one particular moment. Long ago they had been very happy, they talked about everything, they could argue and make up and nothing seemed the worse for it, the world was still in one piece. But after the birth of the boys, a gap had begun to open, so small at first it was barely noticeable. Nothing terrible was said. Nothing terrible was done. And it wasn't that he had any desire for anyone else – he was too tired, and so was she. It was as though several signposts had been missed – easy instructions, that you thought you could do without – and now it was so vast, this space between them, he had no idea how he would ever reach her.

'By the way, Frank sent this.' Henry held out the record. For the first time she stopped doing things that didn't need doing, and she looked at him.

'What is it?'

'Shalamar. He said something about track one.'

'Put it on.'

'It's not really our sort of music, Mandy—'

She screwed up the cloth and threw it in the sink. 'Oh for God's sake, Henry. Put the record on.'

There was no light in the sitting room, save an orange glow from the street lamps, and it was cold too; they had stopped sitting down together around the same time they stopped touching. Henry switched on the sound system and eased the vinyl from its sleeve. Really he was a prog rock man. Emerson, Lake & Palmer. And Mandy – well, she was the bookish type. Always reading some romance from the library. He placed the record on the platter and cued the tone arm to track one.

It opened with a funky electric guitar that caused Henry's shoulders to make an involuntary lift and fall. Then came a small section on keyboard that reminded him of Phil Collins and instantly reassured him. (Phil Collins and a keyboard equalled a ballad.) No sooner had Henry thought this than a synthesized bass and drum arrived, accompanied by a waft of violins, and a stab of horns from the brass section. Then a young woman with a clear and strangely sweet voice sang, '*When you love someone it's nat'ral, not demanding.*' By now it wasn't only Henry's shoulders that were moving; it was his feet and arms too.

'Turn the volume up.'

He was shocked to turn and find Mandy watching at the doorway.

'What about the boys?'

'They never leave their bedrooms.'

Henry twisted the volume dial on his sound system, causing a pillar of red lights to spike upwards. Mandy sauntered around the three-piece suite, swinging her arms with the gesture of someone flapping her blouse to get air. He stayed swaying in the corner of the room, while she swayed in the middle. '. . . *to you, baby, I surrender. Get ready. Tonight*—'

'Dance with me,' she said.

'Me?' Henry pointed at his chest, totally baffled, as if he'd only just met himself.

'Who else have I got? Come on.'

So now Henry made his advance across the carpet, bobbing his head, and trying to clap in a carefree way, so that she might think clapping and bobbing were the sort of things that bank managers did all the time when they travelled from one side of a room to the other. The rhythm was a grasshopper – the moment he thought he had it, it snapped out of his hands. Henry didn't know this music, he had no idea how you were supposed to dance to it, but as Mandy began swirling round and round, and he hovered close by – not exactly in her way, but in her general vicinity – he discovered a happy movement that struck him as a little like digging, without actually employing a spade. Now that he listened, he felt there was something irrepressibly good about this song, as if everything would be all right. More than that. As if everything was about to *happen*. Henry put down his spade and began swinging a pair of imaginary tassels. Meanwhile Mandy had also moved on to something new. Hands clasped above her head, she rolled her hips as if she were riding a pony. A button on her blouse slipped loose and he saw the softness of her skin. Smelt the earthy sweetness of her.

He wasn't thinking any more. He was just dancing. Henry lunged past the three-piece suite and grabbed hold of his wife.

23

Silver Machine

'So, Frank?' 'Did she turn up?' 'Did she like the "Moonlight" Sonata?' 'Did she take off her gloves?' 'Are you going to give her any more lessons?'

That morning Kit's questions came so fast, Frank had to swing left and right in order to dodge a direct hit. He repeated the details over and over. ('Would you say her hands looked strange?' *No, Kit.* 'Big? Small?' *Average.* 'Would you say they looked real?' *Yes, Kit. They looked extremely real.* 'Did she say anything about her fiancé?' *Not much.*) When Father Anthony popped by, it was the same. The same with the Williams brothers, Mrs Roussos and Pete the barman. They all wanted to know what had happened. By the time Maud shoved open the door and stood with her arms folded, looking dangerous, Kit knew the story so well, Frank sat behind his turntable and left him to it.

'So?' said Maud.

'He told her about sex in Beethoven and then she took him on a pleasure boat. We still don't know the situation with her hands.'

Maud kicked something inanimate, and left.

For the rest of the day, Frank moved in a kind of stupor. He was sick with longing to see Ilse again and by the same token, he had no idea how he would face her, how he could keep going through this. It was like existing on turbo power. He felt a desperate need to lie down. And on Thursday there was more good news.

'Oh my God! Oh my God!' sang Kit. 'We've got it, Frank! You did it!'

Henry came up trumps. Confirmation of the overdraft arrived in the post, along with paperwork to sign, and a thank-you card from Mandy. ('*How did you know we needed Shalamar?*' she had written at the bottom, along with several kisses and some hearts. '*We love you, Frank!*' Henry had added a more conservative '*Jolly good record.*') Frank glanced briefly through the paperwork and ticked all the boxes marked for him to tick and crossed the ones he was supposed to cross.

'You're using your flat as a guarantee?' said Father Anthony. 'Are you sure about that?'

Frank reassured him it was just a formality. He signed his name and sealed the envelope.

There was also a letter from Fort Development, expressing further interest in purchasing the shop. Frank shoved it in the drawer, along with the invoices and household bills he hadn't yet dealt with.

There was much excitement. Kit could talk of little else. He stopped asking questions about Ilse Brauchmann's hands and carried all his enthusiasm to the refurbishment. It was going to be like a whole new shop, he kept repeating to customers. Meanwhile Frank scoured the pages of *Exchange & Mart*, searching for a suitable shrink-wrap machine because he would save money if he bought it second-hand. Kit watched in tense silence as he made the call. When he repeated the price – eight hundred pounds – Kit gave a gulp like the draining of a plug. After that,

Frank found a glazier in *Yellow Pages* and several builders to quote for the refit, and then the fun began. It was time to order new stock.

'You only want *vinyl*?' a member of the sales team would repeat, when he rang the record companies, one after another, to make his orders. Yes, Frank would repeat. He was interested in coloured vinyl, picture discs, singles, 12-inch and double albums. Yes, he would also take foreign imports, one-off pressings, acetates and limited editions. No, he did not want CDs. Not even freebies. He did not want cassette tapes either. But what about the exciting new titles, they asked, that were only available as CDs? Or what about the fact you could now get tracks on CD that were not available on vinyl? In March there would be the new Morrissey, Pixies, Talking Heads, a special Beatles compilation, not to mention *Now That's What I Call Music (11)*—

'Did you not hear me? I want records. Only records.'

'At full price?'

'Yes. At full price.'

Several people reminded him that the returns policies for vinyl were changing. There could be no swapping stock in and out any more. Charges would be made for the return of unsold records and some companies would not provide any credit whatsoever. It was not a lucrative way to run a business, they warned. But Frank was barely listening. No, he repeated, he would not under any circumstances stock CDs. He would buy his vinyl at top price and accept the risks. After all, he had the money in his account. He could buy whatever he liked.

Boxes of vinyl began to arrive the next morning. Rare original pressings, bootleg copies, white-label promotional labels, as well as entire box-set collections. Seven- and 12-inch singles in the shapes of hearts, birds and hats; limited-edition releases on coloured discs in blue, red, orange, yellow, white and even multicoloured splatter. Soundtrack records, popular favourites. World music, second-hand classics, demos. Rare mono recordings, limited-edition audiophile pressings. Independent companies, mainstream companies. Plain sleeves, picture sleeves. Albums with posters, fold-out flaps and signed covers.

Frank thought of Ilse Brauchmann all the time. Even when he tried not to, PING; there she was. He saw the way she had listened without even seeming to blink as he told her what he felt about music. He thought of sitting opposite her in that tiny boat in the middle of the water, and how the rest of the world had felt both full of miracle and not there at all. He wanted to talk about her, speak her extraordinary name, he wanted to let it out, this great feeling that seemed to swell inside him, and yet by the same token he wanted to hide in the booth and sleep for a hundred years. He made lists, he jotted down album titles, he paced the shop, muttering about music as if she were right beside him. He had no idea how he would come up with a second lesson.

Saturday was the day before Valentine's. It rained non-stop. A shower of hailstones came in the afternoon, so loud it was like sitting inside a percussion instrument. Kit made a big tissue-paper heart to go in the broken window, along with a new poster – LOTS OF NEW VINYL IN STOCK! COME IN! – while Frank sat at his turntable, playing love songs and requests. (Kit wanted The Carpenters, 'Please Mr Postman'; old Mrs Roussos and her chihuahua asked for Edith Piaf. The man who only liked Chopin dropped by to say he had met a nice woman through the dating agency. He wondered if there was some Aretha he could buy for her? 'Oh, I think you're ready for Marvin Gaye now,' said Frank.) The shop was full all day. They made their biggest sales in months.

Flushed with his success on the creative side, Kit remained at the counter with his colouring pens and drew designs for the refurbishment of the new shop. He stopped anyone who would listen – and quite a few who wouldn't – to explain the exciting new layout. There would be a high-tech modern counter to replace the old one, and special new display units. No more boxes, no more crates. The Persian runner would go straight in a skip; it was probably a fire hazard anyway. No need for the shelves behind the counter where Frank kept his vinyl stored in master bags; from now on, records would be individually labelled and sealed in cellophane within their sleeves. The new shrink-wrap machine would stand at the back of the shop. No one but Frank would be allowed to use it.

'It could do a lot of damage,' Kit told old Mrs Roussos. 'There have been some nasty accidents with shrink-wrap machines.'

'Goodness.' Mrs Roussos clutched tight to her little white dog, as if he was in danger of being heat-sealed as well. 'Is Frank sure this is a good idea?'

'Oh yes,' said Kit. 'No one else has one. Not even Woolworths. These days you have to stand up if you want to be counted.'

Frank was about to close late on Saturday when Maud showed up. She had dyed her Mohican a new shade (green?) and appeared both cross and bored. She paced the floor in her fun-fur coat until she stopped in front of him with her hand on her heart and said in a rush, 'I've got tickets for a film I just wondered if you wanted to come I mean I don't care if you don't I was just wondering I don't give a shit really.'

'You're asking if I want to see a film?'

'*She's Having a Baby.*'

'Who is?'

Maud smacked her head. 'It starts in half an hour.'

They missed the beginning and the film was not entirely Frank's cup of tea, though he quite liked the soundtrack. They sat in the back row, smoking and eating wine gums, surrounded by couples. Twice Maud prodded the two in front who were so busy necking they were an obstruction to her view. Afterwards Frank and Maud walked back along Castlegate and she made disparaging remarks about the big chain stores. 'Who would buy this crap?' she asked, time after time; if things went on like this, every city centre would morph into the same thing, and so would the people who shopped there. They passed a group of girls in pink sashes, vomiting into the gutter. 'Hen night,' said Maud. 'Shoot me if I get married.'

Frank laughed. Aside from himself, Maud was the most single person he knew.

Unity Street was so still and quiet, it was like arriving in a different land. Someone had smashed the bulb on a street lamp and it stood sombre in the dark. The rain had stopped but you could still hear it in the air, a dripping and creaking of water. A man walked a big dog on its lead, trying to get it to pee. Even England's Glory looked empty. Pausing outside her salon, Maud came out with another sentence that seemed to involve a hot drink, along with the fact she didn't give a shit but she was putting the kettle on.

'If you're inviting me in for a coffee,' said Frank, 'then yes, please.'

Maud's tattoo parlour was the opposite of the music shop; it was neat and sparsely furnished, verging on cold. She unlocked a door at the back of the shop, leading out to a small yard. Frank's eyes widened.

In the fourteen years he had known her, she had never so much as mentioned a garden. The yard was nothing like the one behind Frank's shop; more of a bin than a space. This was thick with hundreds of small evergreen leaves. Maud returned inside to flick a switch and a host of tiny white lights zipped to life. There were two plastic chairs either side of a table, along with a striped sunshade hung with wind chimes. She brought a bottle of whisky and glasses, and chucked him a blanket.

'I didn't know you were a gardener, Maud.'

'There's a lot you don't know about me, Frank.'

They stayed in her surprise garden, surrounded by leaves and lights, beneath a net of stars, drinking whisky. He talked about records, while Maud moved from one plant to another, easing dead foliage from her plastic containers and checking the wooden stakes that supported the smaller plants. She tied up the stems that had grown loose and added sand to a few pots that had got too wet.

'How long are you going to do this music lesson thing?' she asked.

'I don't know. It depends on her, I guess.'

'When's she getting married?'

'I don't know.'

'What does she do exactly?'

At the mere thought of Ilse Brauchmann, Frank's knees were jigging. 'I don't know that either.'

Maud said, 'Hmm.'

The lights were already off in Father Anthony's flat, and the Williams brothers'. She began to yawn.

Frank stood. 'I should head off.'

'You could always—' Maud shrugged as if she couldn't be bothered to say the rest. 'I don't care either way. I'm just saying, you know. I mean. We might as well.'

She stood in front of him, awkward and embarrassed, sucking her mouth, waiting for him to give her the cold shoulder. In any other circumstances Frank would have turned and fled, but this was Maud, and it occurred to him how much he cared for her. So he put out both arms and awkwardly drew her close until she tucked, somewhat angular, against his chest, the tip of her Mohican about level with his chin. They stayed a long time like that, Frank breathing softly, Maud with her neck stiff and her hands in fists. He thought of the tenderness with which this small warlike woman had moved from one plant pot to another, pulling out dead leaves and checking the soil. Normal people just want something to love and look after, he thought; that's all they want.

'You don't want to get involved with me,' he said. 'We're good like this, Maud.'

Breaking away, she snatched up their empty glasses. 'You're a tosser, Frank. Go home.'

The shrink-wrap machine arrived on Monday. (Only one day until Tuesday. Was this the reason Frank was so agitated? He couldn't sit still. He couldn't even eat.) The machine was silver and about the size of a freezer. Had he not checked the measurements? asked Father Anthony. Not only was the machine too big for the space, it was also so heavy four people were required to carry it into the shop. Five, if you included Kit, though he slammed the van door on his fingers and spent the rest of the morning with his hand wrapped in toilet paper. Since the refurbishment was not yet finished – actually, of course, it hadn't even begun – they parked the shrink-wrap machine just opposite the door to Frank's flat. It had a large blue hood and chassis to optimize airflow and heating performance. Since it was second-hand, the seller had also thrown in a free roll of PVC film and a first-aid kit.

Frank and his customers gathered around. Someone tried to lift the hood. Mrs Roussos held out her chihuahua so that he could get a proper look. ('Don't!' yelped Kit.) How did it work? Where, for instance, was the instruction manual?

'It doesn't have one,' said Frank vaguely. 'But I'm sure it must be very straightforward.'

He pressed the 'on' switch. The machine did a number of things that seemed remarkably complicated. First it made a buzz and gave out a smell of burning; then something deep inside began to flash and another thing began to whir. Frank peeled off a length of PVC and wrapped it loosely around a record. 'It probably goes like this,' he said. He dropped it quickly into the main unit via a narrowish slot – a bit like posting it.

The trouble was that no one could see inside the machine. Once a record was in it, it was in it; there was nothing anyone could do but hang around and wait. The machine made another whirring noise and became hot. Kit leapt backwards and stubbed his (good) hand on a booth, causing Mrs Roussos to shriek. Then the machine gave a clunk and fell silent.

'What is it doing now, Frank?' whispered one of the Williams brothers.

Just as Frank was about to lift the hood and check, the machine gave off another clunk and a series of thwapping noises. Ten seconds later everything stopped, and then a record plopped into the bucket on the other side. They rushed to look. Peered down.

'Oh dear,' said Kit.

'Is that it?' asked Mrs Roussos.

'This might take a bit of getting used to, Frank,' said Father Anthony.

The album was sealed. Definitely. Never had an album been more sealed. You couldn't argue with that. It had been sealed more times on one side than the other but this was early days, you couldn't expect to get it right first time. No, the only real drawback was that the record was no longer flat. It rose at the edges.

'What on earth has happened?' asked Father Anthony.

'It's warped,' said Maud. 'It's melted.'

'Will the record work, Frank?' asked Mrs Roussos.

When he tried to pick it out of the bucket, it was so hot it burnt his fingers. 'Only as a fruit bowl.'

Kit fell to much scratching of his hair. 'I can think of *one* person who could help,' he said.

24

Beata Viscera

'THE WAY TO HEAVEN is not through the clouds. It's in the joy with which you look at the world, despite your pain and your sorrow.'

Peg stood at the French windows, surveying the sea and the sky.

'And of course to sing,' she said. 'Well, that's very fine indeed.'

Frank slid the new record from the sleeve, just as Peg had once taught him. He wiped it with her terylene towel, following the groove, and then he checked the stylus for dust. 'Beata viscera' by Pérotin.

Peg told him all she knew. Pérotin was living in France around the end of the twelfth century. In those days music was mostly plainsong. It was a bit – how could she put this? Fucking plain. One voice. One tune. Sung by a monk. In a church. 'You get the picture?' Then came Notre Dame and music had to do something new. 'It had to grow some balls because one monk singing one little song wasn't going to get anyone excited in a cathedral that size. So what Pérotin did was he took two voices and he gave them two tunes. And then he took three voices. Four. Pérotin kind of started the whole harmony thing. If it wasn't for Pérotin, there wouldn't be—'

'Yes, yes,' he said. 'I get it. You don't need to go on.' Frank was sixteen now and he towered over Peg; he had shot upwards and sprouted a load more hair.

152

He also had musical tastes of his own and he got tired of her stories, just as he got tired of the different men who showed up. Dregs, some of them. Beneath her sunglasses he once spotted a black eye. He had suggested she needed a new hobby. Golf or something. ('Are you serious? I have slept with half the golf club,' she said.)

Despite Peg's warning about keeping away from love – or even in an effort to redress it – Frank was going steady with a girl at school. Deborah. She wore home-knitted sweaters with kittens on them, and her nipples – he had touched them twice – were like cherries. The thing Frank really liked about Deborah was that she was normal. She had two parents, for starters, and they lived in a semi-detached house with proper central heating. Her mother cooked meals every evening, which they ate at the dining-room table. Frank watched her sometimes, chopping onions, browning meat, and he felt warm to his toes. And they were nice people. Kind.

He thought again of Deborah's red nipples; inside his trousers he grew so tight he had to gasp for breath. He tried to think of ice cubes.

'Are you going to play that record?'

'Hang on a minute, Peg.'

He edged towards the Dansette, keeping his back to her and avoiding all sudden movement.

Tick, tick. Tick, tick.

Out of the silence that was bigger and emptier than silence, something came floating. A voice: slim and delicate, it moved on miraculous muscles as though time didn't exist. It swept him up like a bird. He could actually see it. A whole world at his feet. The white house, the sea, in the distance the town – oh God, here came that hot swelling in his groin.

Peg remained at the window. 'Yes. You're a man now, Frank. Ready to fly.'

25

Ain't It Funky Now

HE HARDLY DARED believe that she was here.

Ilse Brauchmann sat opposite him at their round table in the Singing Teapot. She was talking so fast her hair kept dropping out of its stacked-up curls. They hung like black ribbons, and none of them were quite the same length either.

'Oh my God, Frank!' and 'That bit where . . .' and 'You know?'

He had thought he was over the worst of his nerves but his insides were leaping. He had spent the whole night utterly miserable; convinced she would let him down. Now he couldn't even steal a glance at her without a happy grin suctioning itself to his face. He decided to focus on the button on her white blouse, third one down. It was a perfectly ordinary little button. Nothing could go amiss if he looked there.

The waitress had fetched tea and squash, and also provided a round of toast. '*Bon appétit.*' She perched on a stool at the back of the café, her lace cap on her head. There were no other customers.

Fortunately Ilse Brauchmann had plenty to say. Gulping down her orange squash, biting her way through toast, she recounted all the things she had noticed as she listened to the 'Moonlight' Sonata. 'Oh

154

God.' (Got.) 'That bit where Beethoven's sitting next to her on the piano stool and he's trying to say he loves her, and she's listening and maybe she's saying she likes him too. I couldn't keep still. I was practically shouting!'

Yes, she had found the things he had told her to listen for. She could SEE them; not just hear them. She LOVED *Pet Sounds*. She heard the barking dogs, bicycles, sleigh bells, bongos, tin cans, trains and cowbells. (Cowbells? Hang on, what cowbells? He had never found cowbells.) And 'Caroline, No'; oh my God, that was sad! She was waving her arms so much, the safe little button on her blouse was in danger of becoming not safe at all. 'Was he in love with Caroline, Frank? What is the story?'

Her eyes were shining. Her cheeks were blazing. The freckles above her nose appeared to dance with a life of their own.

'Well, "Caroline, No" is complicated,' he said to her small ordinary button. 'It could be one of the most profound songs about losing something you will ever hear. But Brian Wilson said it was just about his girlfriend coming home with a bad haircut. I guess the deepest things can be very simple.'

And the Miles Davis? What had she thought of that? He was stunned when she paused a moment to collect her thoughts – closing her eyes as if she was searching inside herself for something to say – and then told him:

'I know this will sound crazy, Frank, but it was like doors opening, one after another.'

'You *felt* that?'

'I don't know why.'

'But that's how I feel too.'

'You do?'

They laughed. What else? It was like hearing himself speak, but in the infinitely more beguiling form of a beautiful woman with vast eyes and a broken accent.

'So what are you going to tell me today?' she asked. She twisted her hands nervously.

'Last week we talked about listening. This week I want to show you how music can take you for a ride. What we have today is a singing monk, an operatic show-stopper, the father of funk and one of the biggest heavy metal bands in the history of rock.'

He laid the new records on the table. One, two, three, four. Sacred music by Pérotin, *Tosca* by Puccini, James Brown's *Ain't It Funky Now,* Parts 1 and 2 and *Led Zeppelin IV.*

'Oh my God, Frank. This sounds ama-zing.'

He went over some ground rules. For a start, she had to listen lying down. Could she do that? She gave one nod. Grab your headphones, he told her. Unplug the telephone. Do nothing but listen. 'Because this stuff is wild. Trust me.'

Ilse Brauchmann stopped twisting her hands and held them clasped.

'So first off, this one's the oldest, and it's like going for a trip in the sky.' He went on to explain everything Peg had told him about Pérotin, as well as plainsong and polyphony. He even told her about his first girl-friend, Deborah. How he walked her home every day after school and then sat in her house, just sort of waiting to be fed. How her father wore driving gloves and did things like clearing leaves on Sunday. How her mother wore a pinny to peel potatoes and called Frank 'Sonny boy' and made him sandwiches for his three-mile hike back to the white house.

'What happened to Deborah, Frank?'

'We were teenagers. She moved on.'

'Is that why you want to be alone?'

'No. It was a long time ago.'

'You could not see someone for twenty years and still love them. I really believe that.'

He laughed. In fact he laughed so much he had to pretend he had a cough. 'Are you speaking from experience?'

She laughed too. 'I'm only thirty, Frank. You will have to ask me again in twenty years.'

The lesson had taken a sideways turning he hadn't expected. She didn't seem to have expected it either because she got very busy mixing her drink with the straw. He thought he'd better talk about a record. He picked up the Pérotin.

'Once you've heard "Beata viscera" you'll never forget it. It's just a single human voice but it feels like stepping on to a bird's back. The moment it starts, you're flying. It takes you up, it swoops you down, and then it lifts you so high you're a pinprick in the sky. But if you close your eyes and really listen, it holds you safe the whole way. Until I heard "Beata viscera", I had no idea human beings could be so beautiful. Every time you see a bird, you'll think of this.'

He realized he was holding his arms out like giant wings. The Singing Teapot waitress watched from her stool with an expression that was either amused, or heartburn. Hard to say.

And Ilse Brauchmann? What was she doing? Her skin was so waxy-pale it had abandoned its freckles. She said nothing, she just stared.

Frank pushed the Pérotin to one side and pulled out the next one.

'Right. *Tosca*. This is a BIG love story. In a nutshell, it's about this beautiful singer and she loves this guy, but Scarpia, the chief of police, is a real nasty piece of work and he's in love with her too. So he arrests her lover and bribes Tosca to be his mistress, but she turns round and stabs him. It ends up with her lover being killed anyway and Tosca kind of leaping off a roof.'

He wondered if his résumé of one of Puccini's most famous operas had come out too fast because once again her face had the gobsmacked look of a photograph.

'So this is the last five minutes of Act One. OK? It's the opposite of "Beata viscera". It's not a ride to heaven, we're going to hell. And Puccini puts *everything* in this. He's got Scarpia telling us how much he wants Tosca, he's got a church service going on in the background, he's got bells, cannons, the lot. It's like the big showdown between God and man – and God barely gets a look-in. By the end, Scarpia's singing the Te Deum along with everyone else, and it's fucking scary, you see, because this is the moment you realize Scarpia has put himself *above* God. There's no hope left. The curtain falls, and trust me, you need a drink.'

Frank found he was standing up. When had that happened? Ilse was watching him, completely straight-faced. The waitress was also watching, completely amused-faced. Catching his eye, she attended to an itch beneath her little cap.

Frank sat down again. He put the *Tosca* record with the Pérotin. He made a mental note that in talking about James Brown he must a) remain seated, b) not flap his arms and c) not say 'fuck'.

But how? How could anyone sit still when they were talking about *Ain't It Funky Now*, Parts 1 and 2?

'This one's about groove. The beat repeats and repeats and repeats.

Then just when you're not looking, BAM! It's a sock in the jaw. It's Muhammad Ali doing rope-a-dope with George Foreman. Have you heard of Rumble in the Jungle?'

Her mouth pooched into a gooseberry shape. He took that as a no.

'It was the biggest boxing fight in history. Ali hadn't a chance. He offered himself like a human punchbag, and then just when Foreman was beginning to wilt he pulled out a right hand that sent Foreman to the floor. That's what James Brown does to you in *Ain't It Funky*.'

Ilse frowned. 'I don't like boxing.'

'That wasn't boxing. That was art.'

Frank realized that not only was he standing again, he was also being Muhammad Ali and George Foreman.

Was it possible she was on the verge of laughter? She lifted her hand and covered her mouth.

Frank resolved to speak slowly and sensibly about the last record. He thought it might help if he crossed his arms.

'Right. "Stairway To Heaven". This one kind of unravels in layers. I mean, it's all there, right from the beginning. It's big, and it knows it's big, but you're only allowed to have it piece by piece.'

He had a feeling that might sound sexual.

'It starts small. Single guitar. Robert Plant sings like he's remembering. After that, more layers keep adding. By the time Jimmy Page comes in with his guitar, the thing's flying. It's epic. You'd do anything for it not to stop. It's like a really good orgasm—'

Frank had to ram his hand in his mouth.

'What I am saying is that all these pieces know how to climax.' (Seriously? Did he just say that?) 'We recognize things when we hear them, even if we don't know exactly what they are. And when we hear them, they make the world feel *right*. But it's, um – it's six thirty. I guess you need to go.'

And what did Ilse Brauchmann do? As Frank packed her records into the bag? As he gave her 'Stairway To Heaven' that was like an orgasm? Or 'Beata viscera' that flew like a bird? James Brown who was like Muhammad Ali, and the show-stopper that was *Tosca*? Did she search for a pen and take notes? Ask further questions?

No. She remained wide-eyed. Stock still. Entranced.

Paying the bill, she passed Frank his envelope of cash in silence and made for the door.

Outside the two of them stood looking at nothing in particular, waiting to part. Frank wondered if Ilse might suggest another excursion to the park, or show him further constellations, but her face seemed lost in another horizon altogether. He walked her back towards the cathedral, telling her as they went about his plans for the shop, and the new shrink-wrap machine, until he too ran out of words, and there was only the click of her heels and the shuffle of his plimsolls echoing from the old buildings on either side of the alleyway.

At the cathedral they stopped. Looked towards the taxi rank. Failed to move.

He said, 'I guess your fiancé will be waiting.'

Ilse Brauchmann replied with a sigh. 'Frank, there's something I need to tell you.' She stopped. Sighed again. 'It's really important. There's something you need to know—'

It was the BIG MOMENT. It was like the last track of side A, before you flip to side B. It was the middle eight in a song, where a new chord comes in or the tempo shifts, to herald a change. For six weeks, the shopkeepers

160

on Unity Street had asked one another who Ilse Brauchmann was, and why she wanted to know about music. And yet as Frank watched her now, struggling to say something that was obviously difficult, chewing her mouth as if she were in pain, or – more significantly – afraid of inflicting pain *on Frank*, he made an executive decision.

It was fair to say they had travelled some kind of distance during the course of their two lessons – he hadn't just told her about records, he had told her about himself – and whatever the difficult and important thing was that she needed to tell him, he did not want to hear it and risk changing things. It had not been a part of his plan to open up to a woman and now that he had begun, the thought of never doing it again filled him with sadness. She expected nothing from him, and yet she absorbed everything he wanted to say. It suited him to believe he meant nothing to her. This was where he was happiest, after all. Floating way out, in the solitary depths of things. Disconnected.

So instead of allowing her to struggle onwards, instead of asking a tricky but illuminating question, like '*What* exactly? *What* do I need to know about you?' he cut the conversation dead.

'Don't.'

'What?'

'Don't tell me. I mean, I know you're engaged. You don't need to tell me anything else. I'm fine.' He gave a thumbs-up to show just exactly how fine he was.

'But, Frank—'

'No. It's fine. It's fine. It's fine.'

He looked across the road. A free cab drew up.

'So I'll see you next Tuesday?' he said quickly. 'Same time, same place. Lesson three?'

'But, Frank. You will hate me—'

'Hate you? How could I hate you? We talk about records. It's a business arrangement.'

Ha ha, he went. To show how easy and tremendously-without-difficulty this all was.

To his surprise, Ilse Brauchmann was not laughing. She gazed back at him with an expression of slow-spreading pain. Then – at last: a half smile. A nod. 'Yes, Frank. You're right. This is a business arrangement.'

As she fled with her bag of records, he shouted, 'Hey! Hey! I don't suppose you know anything about shrink-wrap machines?'

It was seven by the time Frank got back to Unity Street. A police car was parked outside Articles of Faith and a small crowd had gathered. Maud stood smoking hard with her hand on her hip, while the Williams brothers spoke with a policeman. Kit was washing down Father Anthony's shop window.

'Where have you been?' asked Maud.

'Giving a music lesson.'

Maud made a scoffing noise and screwed her boot over her cigarette. 'Kids spray-painted Father Anthony's windows. He was only upstairs in his flat. He's really shaken.' She spoke as if there was a direct, culpable link between Frank and the bad news.

'What did they write?'

'Stupid stuff like *Shitface* and *NF*.'

At the window, Kit made elaborate sweeping strokes with his sponge – whatever else the words had said was gone, although the glass seemed more on the grubby side than clear.

Afterwards, Frank and Father Anthony sat on the kerb smoking.

'It will be me next,' said the old ex-priest.

'What do you mean, it will be you next? What kind of silly talk is that?'

Frank patted the old man's shoulder. It was thinner than he remembered, like bone inside beige wool. 'You fetch me if this happens again.'

'Fort Development have sent a new letter. They've made another offer to buy us up. Have you read it?'

But Frank was barely listening. He was thinking of dark eyes and falling-down curls and a pea-green coat. He was thinking of records and further lessons and all the hundreds of things there were to say about music. 'It will be OK. There's no way we're going down now.'

26

I Say a Little Prayer

ONCE UPON A time there were two people who were in love. She was married. He was a priest. The end.

Inside his shop, Father Anthony read the letter from Fort Development again. '*We would like to take this opportunity to repeat our offer to buy your property, and to introduce you to a new set of apartments that will soon be undergoing construction in the docklands area. We are also in a position to offer highly competitive rates on endowment policies. Please accept our invitation to speak with one of our consultants at your earliest convenience.*'

He gazed at the shop he had run for twenty years, and saw it as a stranger might. The carpet was so thin, you could see straight through to the floorboards. He hadn't sold a bookmark in weeks, let alone a statue; he slept at night in his hat with earflaps, just to keep warm, and he survived pretty much on a diet of water and baked potatoes. And now here was a development company offering him decent money to sell up. He thought of the love he had left behind long ago, and the drink that had replaced it until Frank turned up and found him jazz. Abandoning Frank would be like walking away from your own son. He would miss him as much as the air itself. But he had no idea any more how he could keep going; and now there was the graffiti.

It was too cold to go upstairs. He sat at the counter, watching the messed-up window, then he tried to close his eyes. 'Give me a sign, Lord,' he said. 'It can be very small. I don't mind. Just tell me it's time to sell up.' He stayed very still, waiting.

Outside someone began trying to start a car, turning the engine over and over. *Chug chug chug.* It was all he could think about. When he looked again at the window he almost yelped: two teenage boys were peering straight back at him, one big, one small. Before he could reach for the telephone to call Frank, they had shoved open his door.

'But I'm closed,' he said.

'Your door's open,' a female voice said back.

So one was a girl. The one who most resembled a big teenage boy was a big teenage girl.

Father Anthony's heart began to flutter like a bird in a cage. They were dressed in coats and boots; the boy had a weaselly face, and the girl wore a football scarf. They stood side by side, barricading his path. He had no more than a few coins in the till, and there was barely anything of value upstairs, unless they were interested in poetry, and the odd cut-glass fruit bowl.

They didn't move, they just remained in his way, casting an occasional glance over at the shelves. They seemed to know what they were up to and were simply biding their time. It occurred to Father Anthony there were probably more of them outside; the light was going, he could only see the dark, the cold.

He managed to stand but his legs were trembling. He said, 'Please don't break anything.'

'Is your name Father Anthony?' asked the girl.

He nodded.

'You're a priest? Right? A proper one?'

'I *was* a priest. I tried my best to be proper. A proper priest and a proper human being.' His voice sounded rusted over. 'Do you – want to buy something?'

She said, 'Do you do weddings?'

'I beg your pardon?'

She said it again, only a bit slower, as if she thought he might be deaf or very stupid. 'Wed-dings. DO you DO them?'

'No, I'm, uh, retired. If a couple wants a priest to marry them, they go to their local church.'

'We tried that,' the boy said at last. 'He told us we needed a licence and shit.'

The girl winced as if she wished the boy hadn't gone and done a swear word. He lifted his arm and tucked it round her. There was something almost comical about the way he had to reach up to get her.

'You want to get married?'

'Can you do a BLESSING?' shouted the girl. She seemed convinced he was senile. 'If you can't do a WED-DING?'

Father Anthony had to do a mental rearrangement of the entire scene. So they were not here to mug him, or deface his shop, or steal the little he had. They just wanted to be together, they wanted to give a name to their love, and they were as nervous as he was. 'Yes,' he said. 'I would be honoured.'

'Do we have to kneel?'

'We can do it standing up.'

'Nah. I think it's more proper kneeling.'

166

There was no dirt to speak of on the old carpet, and no bumps either, but nevertheless Father Anthony smoothed it with his hands as if he were clearing puddle water. The two teenagers got down and knelt at his feet with their eyes screwed shut and their hands tucked beneath their chins like squirrels.

Father Anthony removed his hat and said, 'O Lord, please look down on this young couple and take great care of their love. All will be well.' There was a silence. Outside a dog walked past and cocked its leg on a street lamp.

'Is that it?' asked the girl.

'I haven't done this kind of thing for a while. I'm a bit out of practice.'

It took the couple a moment to get up. The boy insisted on helping the girl but she was heavier than he expected and he almost lost his balance. The girl blushed and made a business of arranging the tassels on her scarf and then thanked Father Anthony.

He stood watching as they walked hand in hand down Unity Street. He was filled with an old warm feeling that was like growing twelve feet tall. He thought of the woman he had loved all those years ago; her head on his shoulder for the last time. *It's right this way. It's right if I go.* Real love was a journey with many pitfalls and complications, and some- times the place you ended up was not the one you hoped for. But there. Better to have held her hand on a summer's day than nothing at all.

He looked up at the city sky, more orange than black and certainly without stars, and he began to laugh. 'Thank you for that one. Thank you.'

Ripping up the letter from Fort Development, he switched off the lights, put on his hat and climbed the stairs.

27

Heaven Knows I'm Miserable Now

'IT'S ME.'

Thursday morning, first thing. Ilse Brauchmann stood at the door of the music shop.

'I was just passing—' She gripped tight to her handbag with both hands, as if it were a small float and she was on the verge of hurling herself into deep water.

Frank and Kit stared.

'I thought I might take a look at your shrink-wrap machine.'

Frank and Kit stared some more.

'I have a couple of hours. Then I have to get back to my—'

What?

Hairdresser? Swimming coach? FIANCÉ?

'Work.'

Frank couldn't move. How could a man be this many adjectives, within the space of one small moment? He was so delighted, confused, excited, terrified, happy, sad, totally sure, totally uncertain, he merely stood behind his turntable like an actor who had forgotten not only his lines, or his part, but also which production he was in.

Fortunately Kit remembered all those things. 'Come in! Come in!' he sang, weaving past all the boxes of new stock to welcome her. He asked if he could help her find a record, or make her a coffee, but Ilse Brauchmann repeated she had little time, she just wondered if she could be of any help with the shrink-wrap machine. As Kit led her to the back of the shop, Frank waited for her to notice him and smile or wave or do whatever else two people who loved talking music should do, but she remained with her eyes glued downwards. Never had anyone shown such an interest in the faded weave of the Persian runner, and the putty-filled gaps between the floorboards. She didn't even glance up to say hello.

As Kit had predicted, she had a knack with the shrink-wrap machine. She took control of the situation in a way no one had done in the shop in years.

First, she stood looking at the thing in complete silence. She walked around it several times, then she stooped to peer inside, before studying the roll of PVC. She passed Kit her handbag and practised stretching a length of film over an album sleeve. She examined the mouth of the machine where you slotted the record, as well as the bucket at the other end where the newly wrapped album was supposed to land. She still said nothing.

Frank merely watched from his turntable, overwhelmed. He couldn't believe she had come back so soon. What had she made of Pérotin and James Brown? He was impatient to be alone with her and find out.

'Ach so,' Ilse Brauchmann murmured. 'Hm-mm. Aha. *Ich verstehe.*' She unbuttoned her coat and passed it to Kit. She was wearing a simple black dress. Next she opened her handbag and pulled out an apron. Looping the strap over her head, she tied it at the waist. She fetched two kirby grips out of her pocket to pin up some more of her hair.

'Shall I take your GLOVES?' asked Kit, doing his best to sound nonchalant, but sounding ominous instead.

She shook her head. 'No, thanks, Kit. I'm fine.'

'Are you SURE?'

'*Ja*, I'm sure.'

She switched on the machine and stood with her arms folded, waiting. She didn't do anything for a really long time.

Kit stopped worrying about her hands and worried about something else instead.

'Are you OK?' he asked. 'You're not going to faint or anything?'

'No. I'm just thinking.'

She stretched her arms above her head. Lowering them, she slowly pulled her fingers, one by one. She wiggled one hand, then the other. Rotated her wrists. Kit went back to worrying about her hands now and openly stared, transfixed, as if it was a piece of wonder she had anything on the end of her arms at all.

She picked up one record and wrapped it in cellophane, carefully smoothing it over the edges, but not too tight. She fitted it in the slot of the machine and pressed the green button. She stood waiting with her hands clasped together as the machine whizzed and thwapped. A minute later it emerged at the other end perfectly sealed. There was no mangled cellophane, no smell of burning, you couldn't even see the join. The album looked so shiny and perfect, Frank had to sit on the impulse to kiss it. How had she *done* that? When Kit led himself in a spontaneous round of applause, she shrugged with an embarrassed smile.

'It really isn't very complicated.'

Now was Frank's moment. He moved from behind his turntable and lingered close, not exactly in her way, but clearing his throat several times like a man with a cough who requires attention.

Kit passed her a new record for the machine. Frank listened to him explaining that the shop was going to have new units, and he listened to Ilse Brauchmann, agreeing how exciting this all was. Frank couldn't get a word in edgeways. Kit told her that each record would have its own special handmade label with listening tips, devised by Frank, and she said what a brilliant idea that was too, though she still didn't acknowledge the large man standing several feet to her right. In fact she seemed intent on looking everywhere but at him.

There was an ease between Kit and Ilse that made Frank feel oversized and superfluous. When he suggested Kit might like to go to Woolworths to buy labels for the records, Kit said he would go later. Ilse smoothed a length of PVC over a record, checking the fit.

'But you love going to Woolworths, Kit. You love buying stationery.'

'Yes, Frank, but right now I am extremely busy helping Ilse Brauchmann. Aren't I?'

'Yes,' she said, nipping the smallest glance at Frank's plimsolls. She didn't even have the grace to take in the whole shoe; only the end part, where his big toe made a bulge in the canvas. And neither did she mention the records Frank had found for her, or whether she had bothered to listen. Her manner towards him was so formal and cold, you'd think their two lessons in the Singing Teapot had never happened. Frank picked up some singles and made a neat pile of them. He had no idea where to put himself.

'Kit, I need those labels right now. I need to start writing up my listening tips.'

'Then why don't *you* go to Woolworths?' said Kit. Plain as day.

'Because I am busy.' Frank tucked his T-shirt into the waistband of his trousers. In the circumstances, he couldn't think of anything busier.

'We can manage without you. Can't we, Ilse Brauchmann?'

She didn't even have the decency to reply. She simply hummed. And not a proper hum. More like the closing of a door.

So what did Frank do? In a crazy, misjudged attempt to provoke her into – *what*? Feeling sorry for not appearing to notice him? *Missing* him? – he found himself declaring that he was off to buy labels. She merely shrugged, as if she didn't give a damn either way, and pressed the green button on the shrink-wrap machine. Frank walked slowly and deliberately to the front of the shop. He said again, without moving, that he was just off to BUY LABELS. In case ANYONE wanted to accompany him—

'Could you get some Pick 'n' Mix as well?' asked Kit.

Ilse Brauchmann passed a record into the slot and said nothing at all.

Frank had never walked so fast. There was a long queue for the till, so he abandoned the labels – the last place he wanted to be right now was Woolworths – but then he bumped into Mrs Roussos on the corner of Unity Street, who was having difficulty with her new microwave. By the time Frank had plugged it in, and then stopped to reassure the Williams brothers because they were worrying about another letter from Fort Development, forty minutes had passed. He flung open the door to his shop.

Empty. Just a pile of beautifully wrapped records beside his turntable, and Kit making a poster at the counter.

'Where is she?'

'Who?'

'Who do you think? Mother Teresa.'

'Mother Teresa was in our shop? When?' Kit looked all screwed up with confusion.

'No. Of course she wasn't. I mean Ilse—' He couldn't even manage her full name. 'The German woman.'

'Oh. She had to go.'

'Did she say when she'd be back?'

'Hm.' Kit thought very hard. He sucked his pen, he scratched his hair, and then he balanced on one leg. 'No.'

A steady flow of builders called by to quote for the refurbishment of the shop. They sucked their teeth and took sharp intakes of breath, as if the changes Frank was proposing were not only costly but also life-threatening. All he wanted, he kept repeating, were some essential repairs to the external masonry, and some new units.

The work was certainly going to be more complicated than Frank had assumed. It would require scaffolding, not to mention the hire of a skip and the removal of all the old plaster, in order to make a proper work-ing surface for the new stuff. It had seemed so much simpler when he had done the work himself with only the help of a book from the library and a few passers-by. But this, it turned out, was part of the difficulty. The shop was really a botch job. 'An accident waiting to happen,' one of them said. Even though the quotes were more than he had budgeted for, Frank made a down-payment and booked a builder and electrician to start as soon as they were available. If they worked part-time, there would be no need for the shop to close.

For the rest of the week, he tried his best not to wait for Ilse

Brauchmann. He ordered more vinyl. He listened to his customers and found the records they needed. He mangled several in the shrink-wrap machine, and also burnt his hand. But every time the shop door opened, his heart soared, only to fall flat. Had he offended her? Had she not liked the records he'd found? Maybe her fiancé had suggested someone else to give her music lessons. Someone with proper qualifications. He pictured another man telling her about Bach – without waving his arms, or referring to orgasms – and the thought made him wretched. If only he could replay their last scene. Why wasn't there an official manual about this kind of stuff, telling you what to do?

Word began to spread about Frank's new collection of vinyl. Even though it was not yet labelled, or indeed shrink-wrapped, a few collectors turned up, eager to rummage through his extensive stock before anyone else got there. They left with bags of records. One returned with a van. A journalist came to write a piece for the local paper and took Frank's photograph. (INDIE SHOOPKEEPER MAKES CRAZY BID TO SAVE VINYL. Beneath the heading, a photo of Frank with his eyes closed – he hadn't realized about the flash – and Kit, proud in his blue uniform.) A DJ was so delighted with Frank's selection of funk and 12-inch singles, he gave the shop several plugs on his late-night radio show. When Frank went down to unlock the door on Saturday morning, he was met by a queue of ten or more music fans and collectors. He saw a tweed coat, a bomber jacket, several anoraks and a knitted cardigan.

But a green coat?

Not a peep.

Tuesday the twenty-third of February. Half past five. The Singing Teapot café:

174

'I thought I had offended you.'

'I thought *I* had offended *you*. I came to help, Frank, and you didn't even say hello.'

'You didn't say hello to me.'

'But you're the shopkeeper. It's your *job* to say hello.'

It was only their third lesson. Sitting opposite one another at their regular table, they remained in their coats, as if they might leave at any moment. So here was Frank. Here was Ilse. And instead of ordering drinks and talking music, they were arguing about which of them had been the most unpleasant.

'You didn't even *look* at me, Frank.'

'You didn't look at *me*. You didn't even look at my plimsolls.'

'Did you want me to look at your plimsolls?'

'Excuse me.' The Singing Teapot waitress adjusted her teensy cap and placed two laminated place mats like a bridge between Ilse and Frank. She fetched two menus, two sets of cutlery, and napkins folded into fan shapes. Would they like their regular order? She had taken the liberty of getting in some lemon squash.

'I know the cook has gone home,' said Ilse Brauchmann, opening the menu. 'But the thought of all this food makes me so hungry.'

'I could do eggs?' suggested the waitress, scratching her ear and looking apprehensive.

'I'm not hungry,' said Frank.

Ilse Brauchmann flashed him a look. 'This nice girl is offering you an egg. The least you can do is eat it.'

'Thank you. I will have an egg.'

'Fried? Or boiled?'

'What?'

'You really don't need to sound so remarkably snappy,' said Ilse Brauchmann, sounding remarkably snappy.

Frank asked for a fried egg. Ilse ordered boiled. '*Bon appétit*,' said the waitress, so frazzled she forgot she had not yet cooked anything.

As soon as they were alone again, they were back to arguing. Ilse said she couldn't believe he would just march out of the shop when she had clearly gone to a lot of trouble to leave work and help him. But if she cared to remember, he pointed out, *she* was the one who had not said hello, or mentioned records, or even a thank you—

'I pay for my lessons. And it's good money too.'

'Do you think I need your money?'

She merely shrugged as if they both knew the answer to that one and she wasn't going to stoop so low as to voice it.

'And what about your fiancé?'

'What about him?' At last. A reaction. A mottled stab of red appeared in the skin just above Ilse Brauchmann's top button.

'What does he think about our music lessons?'

Ilse repositioned the ashtray, which was not, by any stretch of the imagination, out of place. She said nothing.

'Does he mind?'

'Why would he mind?'

'Does he even know?'

She gave an angry shake of her head. Her nostrils flared. 'Can you stop going on about Richard? Do you think the man cares whether or not I have music lessons?'

So he had a name. He was real. Frank didn't know why that hurt so much, but it did; only, it was a safe, familiar hurt. He could sit beside it, like a very old friend.

Here at last was the Singing Teapot waitress, smashing her way through the saloon doors with her rear quarters and bearing a tray. 'Excuse me.'

She arranged a pot of tea on the table, followed by extra hot water, a jug of milk, a bowl of sugar cubes, tongs, slices of lemon, packets of sweetener and one large glass of lemon squash, finished off with a foil umbrella, a straw and a plenitude of ice.

'*Bon appétit.*' She remained watching them and frowning, the way a child stares at a tower of toy blocks, willing it not to fall over. Then she hoofed it through her saloon doors.

Frank pretended to read the menu. He very much wanted to say something civil to Ilse Brauchmann but they seemed to have got themselves in a corner where only uncivil ones came out. And now they had started, there was – strangely – a kind of pleasure, or at least a relief, in saying the spiky things you shouldn't. 'So?' he asked of the Breakfasts page. 'Did you listen to the records?'

Ilse also picked up her menu. 'Yes,' she said, addressing High Tea.

'Did you lie down?'

'*Natürlich.*'

'Close your eyes?'

'*Jawohl.* Have you worked out how to use your shrink-wrap machine?'

In reply Frank made an airy noise that was not exactly negative, but not so big as a yes.

They continued to read their very interesting menus. *Beans on toast . . . scone with jam . . . ham sandwich with side portion of coleslaw.* Well, they could waste the whole hour if she wanted. It would still cost her fifteen quid.

177

Then, 'What music will we talk about today?' Her voice sounded childlike.

He lowered his menu. She lowered hers.

'Do you still want to?'

'Do you?'

Her eyes were coated with tears. There was something so brave and naked about the way she kept them fixed on his. It gave him a strange, unsettling feeling that it was in his power to really hurt her. He swallowed hard.

'Yes,' he said. 'I do.'

'Me too, Frank. I'm sorry I was angry.'

'It's me who should apologize.'

'And I like your plimsolls.'

'I like your shoes.'

'Well at least that's sorted. At least we know we have nice footwear.'

She reached for his hand. Strictly speaking, it was more a handshake than a handhold; not romantic, more in line with a business agreement. Nevertheless as his fingers caught the tips of her soft kid gloves, he allowed himself to imagine the delicate hands beneath. The slender fingers, the shells of her nails, her engagement ring—

'Eggs.'

Beside them, the waitress beamed proudly, as if she had not only cooked those eggs but also laid them. 'One fried. One boiled. *Bon appétit.*'

28

A Dress for Berlioz

'WE ARE WILD creatures,' said Peg, 'struggling to be civilized. Take Berlioz, for example. What do you know about him, Deborah?'

Deborah went the colour of her pink knitted jumper.

'Not very much, Peg.'

'How much?'

'Nothing actually.'

They were in the sitting room of the white house by the sea. Frank and Deborah had already gone the whole way – cherry nipples downwards – but this was the first time Peg had invited her for dinner. So far she had played Shostakovich and Bitches Brew. She had offered gin cocktails with an hors d'oeuvre selection of Fortnum's crackers and pineapple chunks. But there was no sign whatsoever of a good hot meal.

Deborah was in awe of Peg, and the white house too. 'She's amazing. So bohemian. And it's really cool the way you two live out here and call each other by your first names. As if you're just friends.' Frank didn't like to mention that the house was actually beginning to fall down. There were so many holes in the roof that when it rained, he slept beneath a tarpaulin.

'Let's not play Berlioz, Peg,' he said. 'Deb likes Mantovani and Herman's Hermits.'

'My parents like Mantovani. I don't mind what I listen to. I'm easy.'

'You don't mind?' repeated Peg. 'You're easy?' Her eyebrows were practically in her turban. You'd think Deborah had just confessed she walked the streets at night. 'What is Mantovani anyway?'

'It's kind of nice and swirly,' said Deborah.

'I've never heard of it.'

'You wouldn't like it, Peg. Listen, me and Deb are going upstairs for a while.' He was desperate to roll around with her. And something about the way she sat, all good and solid and reliable, made him grateful. She never asked questions like 'Have you heard this? Have you heard that?' Instead she asked if he was hungry, or if he'd had a nice day. For his seventeenth birthday she had knitted him a jumper to match hers – only instead of a pink kitten, he had a blue dog. ('What the fuck is that?' asked Peg.) Deborah was his ticket to normality.

But Peg was pulling out a record. Sensing an audience, she was not prepared to give up so easily. 'Let me tell you about Berlioz,' she said.

First off, he was French. ('I do know this,' said Frank.) He was a Romantic. ('Yup. I know that too.') Things were going well for Berlioz. At the age of twenty-seven, he won a music scholarship that took him to Rome but he'd only been away for a few months when he heard his girlfriend had met a new man. So what did he do?

'Golly,' said Deborah. 'I have no idea.'

'I do,' said Frank. 'It's not regular.'

Berlioz was beside himself. He took the first train back to Paris, along with a dress, a hat, a pistol and a bottle of strychnine. His plan was to burst in on his girlfriend and her new lover, disguised as a maid, or at least a maid in a hat, and blow out their brains. After that he would turn the gun on himself. The poison was just a back-up plan.

180

'Did he kill them?'

'No. Somewhere along the way, Berlioz lost the dress. Well, he had a lot to think about. Instead he threw himself into the Mediterranean.'

'Oh my God. He committed suicide?'

'No. He got fished out. Which is just as well because otherwise we wouldn't have his Symphonie fantastique with its famous use of the leitmotif.' Peg puffed on a Sobranie and adjusted the folds of her kaftan. 'Pineapple, anyone?'

Deborah's hand shot to her mouth. She retched but nothing came. 'Oh help,' she said, turning pale.

'Are you OK, Deb?'

'I'm pregnant.'

The room seemed to fall over. 'What?' said Frank.

'What?' said Peg. For once, she pulled off her sunglasses. Her eyes were small and blinking.

Deborah said it again. She was pregnant. Three months overdue. 'I've thought it all through. I want to keep the baby. Me and Frank can get married.'

29

Two Queens and a Duke

NOW THAT FRANK had held Ilse Brauchmann's hand – albeit briefly – he could think of little else, and it was also harder than he had anticipated to talk about music while eating a fried egg. Nevertheless the strange row with which they had started their lesson pushed their relationship into a new place. The argument had served as a kind of cleanser. Frank was reminded of the garden at the white house by the sea; how in the heat of summer it could look desolate, ransacked by heat and salt wind, but come rain, it was filled with new colour and smells, as if it had been given a whole fresh outfit.

Ilse said, 'God, Frank, I loved the records you found for me. All day at work, I have been looking forward to my lesson.'

In his mind he put her in an office with a large desk and a row of telephones. Fashion, he imagined. Or maybe she worked with her fiancé. He didn't need to know any more than that, which was just as well, because she said, 'James Brown! Oh my God! "Beata viscera"! And the Puccini! I couldn't even *breathe* . . . And "Stairway To Heaven". I love that! So what records do you have for me today?'

Music, Frank explained, said things that words couldn't. This was the theme of his third lesson. Unfortunately there was no room on the table to lay out all the albums – what with the plates, teapot and condiments, etc. – so he simply held them up, one by one, like signs. Today, he told her, she was going to meet punk, a weeping Queen, the Duke, and a man in a dress.

Ilse nodded with big, sparkling, astonished eyes. She was beginning to laugh and he hadn't even started.

'Music should come with a health warning. Put the right words with the right music and you get dynamite. What do you know about punk?'

'Nothing.'

'I want you to understand it. Because punk means something to me. OK?'

'OK, Frank.' Smile, smile, smile.

'So this is "God Save The Queen" by The Sex Pistols. The song came out in '77, the year of the Queen's silver jubilee, when the whole country was planning a street party. And what it says is the future's over. England's lost the plot. It makes a mockery of establishment and royalty, but it's also kind of witty in a really British way. Here was this group of four reprobates who could barely play. And they looked at everyone in their party hats, and they said the one thing no one was supposed to say. They said, *Fuck the Queen.*'

Ilse Brauchmann sat, stunned. She even forgot she had a boiled egg.

'The song got banned by the BBC and half the shops wouldn't sell it but I played it all summer. I considered it a public service. Not that I have anything against the Queen – I like her – but it was important there was a place where the unsayable could still be said. And fair do's to the Queen, I guess she agreed with me. She didn't chop off John Lydon's head or anything.'

Ha ha ha, went Ilse Brauchmann, all of a sudden laughing so raucously she had to make out she was yawning.

'"God Save The Queen" is one massive self-destruct button. John Lydon can't sing, he can't read music, and that's the whole point. The song isn't just anti-monarchy, it's anti-everything, including himself. But we need him. When the whole country's waving paper flags and eating finger sandwiches, you need someone to moon their arse. You see?'

Ilse nodded. Slowly.

Next he pulled out Dido's Lament, written by Purcell for his opera *Dido and Aeneas.*

'OK, so that was an explosion. This is an implosion. This is the saddest aria you will EVER hear. It's almost the end, and the one man Queen Dido ever loved has just left. He was her soulmate. He was the one. And now he's gone. She knows there's nothing left except to die. This is what it sounds like when a heart breaks.'

Ilse had reached for a toast soldier and was about to dip it in her egg, but stopped mid-air. She didn't say 'How?' because she still didn't seem to have the use of her voice, but he got the impression she would have, if she could.

'Oh God, it's so brilliant. Through the whole aria she's singing "Remember me, remember me" and it's all on the same note, until the very last time when her voice goes up. And it's *ah*.' He beat his chest. 'It breaks your heart because it's so desperate, that little change in the notes – and we get in that moment how ordinary we all are. Who will remember any of us? She's the Queen of Carthage and she knows it means nothing! *Ah.*' (Another beating of his chest.) 'She stops singing before the orchestra does, and that's the last punch really because the music has to go on without her, and it's so sad, God it's sad, it's so sad—' He had to stop because – to his horror – he was crying. She passed him a tissue. He said, 'Listen. Listen when you get home. Don't even take off your coat. Just lie on the floor with your headphones and listen.' He blew his nose extensively. 'I have a cold,' he said. Just in case she thought he was moved, or soft, or something.

Maybe Ilse Brauchmann had a cold too because she was also blowing her nose. He suggested that if she wanted to finish her egg, he could take a pause but she pushed the plate to one side and gazed at him with her chin in her hands. She was all listening eyes and flicky hair.

'Now we come to the Duke. Duke Ellington. And trust me, you will need him after Dido. He's so happy! So *glidey*! Track one, "Satin Doll". The instrumental version. This isn't an explosion and it isn't an implosion, it's just the biggest celebration. It's a track for every single instrument in the band. They all get to have a solo, and they all get to support each other. Duke Ellington used it as his last number and when you hear it you'll know why: it's like closing off the lights on the band, one by one, until you get to the very last *bom*. It's the happiest ever goodbye.'

Ilse laughed.

So what happened when he got to the fourth record, *Symphonie Fantastique* by Berlioz, and the story Peg once told about the man in disguise? He had begun to hope this was his best lesson so far – there was nothing he couldn't say to Ilse Brauchmann that didn't have her either howling with laughter, or on the verge of tears. Finally confident, and actually enjoying himself, he talked without one single 'um' or

185

'uh' about the absurd lengths Berlioz had gone to, in order to hide his true identity. He even described the dress and the hat – embellishing them with the kind of vivid detail that made them even more absurd and hilarious. He was so funny he made himself roar out loud; imagine this wild Romantic, striding through Paris in his dress, with a loaded gun and a hat. 'Who was he was *kidding*? It was *insane*. As if no one would spot him! How did he think he could get away with a disguise like that?'

Ilse struggled to her feet. Her face had a stricken, affronted look, as if he had leant right over the table and served a blow to her stomach.

'What's wrong? What are you doing?'

She grappled with the clasp on her purse but her hands were trembling so hard she couldn't open it.

'Ilse?'

'*Verdammt*,' she hissed.

'Please. Let me help.'

'I don't need it.'

Finally she managed; the purse fell open and she whammed a five-pound note on the table, along with his envelope of cash. She grabbed her coat. She didn't even bother with the records.

'I don't understand. What did I say?'

She fled to the door and glanced back once, only to reply, 'Don't you dare follow.' She made a strange wild pat at the air, stepped outside and was swallowed by the dark.

In silence, Frank replaced the records in their paper bag. He felt big and useless; he had no idea what he had said to upset her. The waitress watched from her stool in front of the saloon door, her mouth set in a grim line. By the look of things, she was prepared to keep up that expression for a very long time. Frank balanced his plate on top of Ilse Brauchmann's plate, and then had a go at folding the two used napkins. It was like clearing away the ghosts of things. If only he understood.

'Men,' said the waitress, in the same way you might look at a nasty cloud and say, '*Rain*'.

'But she told me. She told me not to follow.'

To which she rolled her eyes so hard they looked in danger of disappearing into the top of her head. 'Are you an idiot?'

He searched everywhere. Castlegate, the little cobbled alleyways, the cab rank. Now that he had made up his mind, he couldn't bear the idea of not finding her. The temperature had dropped suddenly – the cold was like pincers; it seemed to enter Frank's eyes and mouth and burn his insides. He had to dig his hands in his armpits in an effort to keep them warm and the air smelt particularly cheese-and-oniony. Above the city, the moon hung low, surrounded by a frizzy halo; there was something greenish about the dark, but it was possible he was back to being fanciful now.

He lumbered past workers going home from the food factory, traders packing up their market stalls, but never Ilse Brauchmann. He passed gangs of teenagers roaming the streets, a line of muffled bodies beneath cardboard, and young couples rushing from wine bars to the safety of their cars. From the brightly lit windows of Woolworths, there shone an entire wall-length display of CDs. He passed broken gutters, walls blackened by years of rain and car fumes, crumbling plaster, windows broken or closed with corrugated iron.

Graffiti and slogans. He even returned to the park and lumbered the entire path around the lake; pleasure boats rocking against the jetty, the water black as a seam of coal. But no Ilse Brauchmann. Once again, the woman had vanished.

By the time he was back at the cathedral, a first snow had begun. Tiny specks came slowly through the air, so weightless they seemed to be floating. Frank pushed on, scanning bus stops, pubs, restaurants. A larger flake fell on his sleeve and did not melt. Within very little time, the snow was coming more densely, as if the sky had a serious amount to offload and suddenly realized it needed to get on with the job. He returned to the Singing Teapot, wondering if by some chance Ilse Brauchmann had returned, but the café was empty, the main lights were off. The waitress stood at the window, her head craned up at the sky. Spotting Frank, she shook her head, suggesting she thought even less of him than she did of the unexpected change in the weather.

The snow was falling really hard now – pieces like kapok; entire cushion-loads of the stuff – and the ground was completely sealed. He could barely see up, and he could barely see ahead either. Across the street the wheels of a car spun over and over, failing to gain purchase. Joined by a few others, Frank helped to push it along its way.

'Where did this weather come from?' someone shouted.

'We'd better get home,' someone shouted back.

In a space of less than thirty minutes the city was smothered and silent. When Frank made a dash to the cathedral, it was only with the intention of warming himself a little before he went back into the snow to continue searching. Looking back on this moment, he wondered why it had not occurred to him that Ilse Brauchmann might already have left the city in a cab and be sitting in front of a fire beside her fiancé, but he was so full of trying to find her that fortunately none of those practical thoughts came to him. It is hard to look back on a moment when you are haring right through the centre of it.

If it was cold on the street, it was even colder inside the cathedral; a sort of preserved cold, like stepping inside a refrigerator and shutting the door. Tall stone columns soared upwards and fanned the nave ceiling. A businessman knelt beside his briefcase, an old lady sat with her head bowed, while two priests seemed to be flattening the carpet alongside the altar with their feet.

And there she was.

A pair of green shoulders. Alone in a pew.

Frank approached quietly, terrified of losing her again. Her eyes were swollen; her mouth was pale and puffy. Her leather gloves lay pulled off at her side and her handbag was wide open. She had a tube of cream that she was working into her fingers; pressing and rubbing it into the bare skin.

Frank sat at her side. He said nothing because he had no idea where to begin. It was Ilse who broke the silence.

'Were you making fun of me? Because I hide my hands?'

'Of course not. Why would I do that?'

'Don't you ever wonder who I am?' She spoke through gritted teeth, as if the words were hurting her mouth. With that she slammed her hands right in front of his nose. 'Look at them, Frank. Really look.'

'Yes. Yes, I am. I'm looking.' He wished she wouldn't do that. It was like watching her hurt herself. Also, she was quite loud. If she wasn't careful, she would have everyone else looking too. Fortunately they were so caught up in praying, they didn't seem to have heard this woman in her green coat, with her naked hands shoved in the air.

189

'You see? Berlioz was not the only person in the world who wore a stupid costume. You see? Look at my hands. Do you want to have a good laugh at me too?'

In size, they were really not so different from anyone else's, but it was the way they bulged at the middle joints like red buttons and had swollen up at the knuckles that shocked him. There was no bend in her middle fingers, though her thumbs were wrenched right over. They looked painful to wear, those hands.

'What happened?' His voice could barely find itself.

'Arthritis. It came on when I was in my early twenties. It will get worse and worse.'

She began to cry, but discreetly, as if she didn't want to disturb anyone else in the cathedral; after her outburst, it was this which moved him the most. That a beautiful woman could cry in a cathedral because her hands were ugly, and yet have the grace to do it quietly.

'But you're so clever with your hands—'

'Jesus, Frank. Anyone can fix a pencil sharpener. Anyone can bash some nails in a window frame.' She tugged a handkerchief from her sleeve and blew her nose.

He reached out. She recoiled but he kept his hand there, waiting in mid-air. The businessman left, the two priests retired to the vestry, and at last her hands came to his. He covered them with his own; the knuckles lay beneath his fingers like the backbones of a small animal. They were very hot.

'Do you get it now, Frank? Do you get it?'

She was not what she wanted to be. He understood. There was no need to say any more. Frank looked and looked at Ilse Brauchmann's swollen hands and he was so sorry – so caught up in his quiet, safe loving that hurt no one, least of all himself – he failed to spot the one thing she was desperate for him to see.

Outside the snow fell in joyous multitudes. Hiding everything.

SIDE C: SPRING 1988

30

I'm Not in Love

WELLCOME TO THE NEWLY REFURBISHT MUSIC SHOP!! read Kit's poster in the window. *NO CDS! NO TAPES!! WE ONLY SELL VINYL! EVERYONE WELLCOME TO COME IN!!!*

It was the tail end of March. Five weeks had passed since the freak snowfall that took the city by surprise. Days were warmer. Longer. Buildings shone in the sunlight, sometimes white as bone, sometimes copper, others as pink as a piece of rose quartz. In the early mornings, long thin clouds crossed the sky above the food factory like fizzy gold trimmings and coils of smoke melted into blue.

Spring had sprung. It was finally here. Trees waved their lovely new leaves. (*Look at us, Frank! Look!*) The bandstand in the park was repainted for the summer season, and the pleasure boats were untied from their moorings. Shops on Castlegate advertised summer stock; tables and umbrellas were set outside the wine bars. Woolworths had an entire window display of the new *Now 11* CD, and it wasn't even due for general release until April.

On Unity Street, windows were opened, blankets aired; washing hung on lines. Birds sang before it was light; Mrs Roussos said they were making a nest in her roof. The Italian family bought a swing seat for the garden. The two little girls with pink coats learnt to ride a bicycle. Another house was sold and boarded up with Fort Development signs, but there was no more graffiti. The billboard at the end that had showed all those happy people drinking coffee was replaced with another image of happy people pointing at brand-new houses. No one gave them beards or horns. When the company delivered a letter to every shop and house on Unity Street, inviting them to a public meeting in early May, there was no interest whatsoever.

In the middle of the parade, an illuminated sign flashed every night – THE MUSIC SHOP – though there was a small problem with the wiring and it had a tendency to fuse Frank's electrics. (The man who had installed it promised to fix it as soon as he had the new parts.) A colourful display of albums was arranged in the newly fitted window, each record individually sealed in cellophane, with a handwritten label of special listening tips. (Elgar, 'Sospiri'. *This is a short piece, composed in the months leading up to the First World War. You can hear the storm clouds gathering over Europe. Try this if you like The Walker Brothers!!*) The external masonry was still crumbling – Kit's posters hung from the lamp posts – but the length of plastic ribbon had snapped free and no one came back from the council to inspect it.

Inside the shop a set of new wooden units had been installed along the left-hand wall, and the table that had stood in the centre was replaced with a large free-standing unit. Display racks also ran along the right-hand wall, although they stopped very suddenly because the builder had run out of wood and was waiting for more. A high-tech counter stood just inside the door, with proper drawers and cupboards. The broken floorboards had been replaced with narrow new planks, but the Persian runner was still here; Frank couldn't bring himself to throw it away.

His turntable remained at the back of the shop, sandwiched between the two listening booths. Repeatedly the builder had complained that they looked like bedroom furniture. ('They *are* bedroom furniture,' said Kit.) But Frank would not even hear of replacing them. The shrink-wrap machine had its own special place just opposite the door to the flat, with a chair to sit on while you were waiting for it to do its thwapping and sealing. There was frequently a green coat hung over the back of it.

What had once been an eclectic mix of the shabby and the nailed-together was on the verge of becoming a smart and well-designed shop with thousands of records, ranging from 7-inch chart singles to rare collectable items. All that was required was for the builder to return and finish. He promised repeatedly that he would and also that he would hurry, which meant that he would keep going at the same erratic pace he had gone before. On three separate occasions, Kit, while searching for a record, got his jumper snarled on a nail and required rescuing. It had been unwise, Pete the barman said, to pay the builder up front.

Frank's fringe had grown back into the wild thing it had always been. He had also reached the limit of his overdraft. No, in truth, he had overshot it. He decided that instead of going back to see Henry, it would be better not to open any statements or letters from the bank. It was spring, after all. The warm weather and longer days would soon bring customers flocking to Unity Street. In the last week alone, Father Anthony had sold ten leather bookmarks and a paperweight, and a biker had asked Maud to tattoo his entire torso with hearts and flowers.

'This is your last chance, Frank,' one of the reps rang to warn him. 'Are you sure you don't want to change your mind and stock CDs? Are you sure you want to go it alone? I could call by. I've got some interesting things on CD. The guys miss you, Frank.'

Yes, Frank repeated. He was fully committed. He would only sell vinyl.

'There is NOTHING between us. We're just FRIENDS. She has a FIANCÉ.'

He said it every day. Each time an eyebrow was raised, a smile smiled, an askance look was sent in their direction.

Now that Ilse had shared the truth about her hands, his feelings for her had acquired a new ease. He was out of the washing machine of love, and happily hanging out to dry. He went to bed every night, he woke every morning, and there it was, his love, waiting for him, exactly as he had left it. Yes, Ilse Brauchmann had Richard; yes, she and Frank could never be together; but it suited him to love her like this. Steadily and faithfully. What had he been so frightened of? It gave him no trouble at all.

And now that Ilse had shared her secret with Frank, she too seemed more at ease. Sometimes he spotted her with her long arms caught around her shoulders like a lovely necklace, simply gazing and smiling at nothing in particular.

She came to the shop whenever she could. It might be for half an hour. It could be a whole afternoon. It depended on her work.

'I just thought I could put in a bit more time with that shrink-wrap machine,' she would say. If it was lunchtime, she brought sandwiches. Sometimes her hands were very sore; it could take a long time to warm them. Others, they looked so raw and swollen, it was hard to watch as she rubbed them with cream. But there were days too when she barely seemed aware of them at all. She stopped wearing her gloves.

'I knew your hands were real,' said Kit one afternoon.

Ilse looked utterly bewildered, but managed a smile.

'My mum has arthritis,' he said.

'Is she in pain?'

'No, she has dementia as well. Mostly she's trying to remember who people are. She doesn't even know my dad half the time.'

'How awful,' she murmured.

'I think she quite likes it,' said Kit.

It was the same for all the shopkeepers on Unity Street. Knowing Ilse Brauchmann's secret made her dearer to them. Bar Maud, they took her under their wing, in exactly the same way they had once done with Frank. Mrs Roussos gave her a tube of special cream. Father Anthony bought her a pair of summer gloves. When she happened to mention it was her birthday, the Williams brothers appeared, heads bowed, with a wreath of flowers. Frank bought a bottle of sparkling wine and everyone toasted her health while he played 'Birthday' from The Beatles' *White Album*. She couldn't stop laughing.

Lesson four. Lesson five. Lessons six, seven, eight. He introduced her to Haydn, Blondie, Brahms – Piano Concerto No. 1 – ('The music is a storm and then comes the piano and it's like walking into a sunlit glade'). Mozart, the boy wonder; Joni, Ella, Curtis Mayfield, Bob Marley, Chic (impossible to sit still), the Icelandic choir singing the sublime 'Heyr, Himna Smiður' ('Oh God, Frank,' she told him afterwards, 'it was like being held by a hundred hands'). The love songs of Reynaldo Hahn, including *A Chloris* ('musical time-travelling', he said); Shostakovich, more J.S., more Aretha.

When Frank and Ilse were alone in the Singing Teapot café, they talked music. Whatever records he gave her, she was desperate to hear, and once she had listened, she pointed out things that even he had not noticed. Their conversation was excited, happy, rushed. They had so much to say, their words toppled into each other. The waitress brought them their usual order of tea and squash with ice, but then she also began to produce hot dishes. One week she attempted lamb chops, the next it was steak pie. If another customer pushed open the door – and they rarely did – she was devastatingly rude. 'Closed,' she would yell, barely even looking up. But she seemed to have decided somewhere along the line that she liked being a waitress for Frank and Ilse, or at least that she was necessary to them in the same way that a small sprocket is necessary for the turning of a spool. He thought he even caught her listening sometimes from her place at the back of the café, her face red and sweaty with happiness.

They took to going back the long way after their lessons. The long way got even longer. They might go via the old docklands – Fort Development had erected fencing and signs there too now, though the site was still only wasteland and gulls – or they might visit the cathedral. They walked through the park and she talked about picnics in summer. Everything about the city had become beautiful to him and interesting. The small, plain brown houses, the clock tower where the junkies hung out, the derelict warehouses; even the cheese and onion smell when the wind blew in the wrong direction. Trees were bobbled in pink blossom, tiny ducklings swam on the lake as if they were being pulled on a string; the air was warm but not yet hot.

'How does it work, Frank?' she asked him once, as they walked past the bandstand to catch the sunset. 'How do you know what records people need?'

He admitted he had no idea. It had always been this way. Ever since he could remember.

'The cure is in the disease,' she said slowly, as if she were reading words from the pinked-up sky. 'Is there anything you *can't* listen to, Frank?'

'The "Hallelujah Chorus" in the *Messiah*.'

She laughed but even saying it gave him a sick, hollowish feeling in his stomach. 'I'm serious,' he said. 'It was Peg's favourite. I never want to hear it again. I think I would fall apart.'

In the shop, their relationship was entirely different. They barely spoke. For Frank, it was enough to be in the same place; Ilse at the shrink-wrap machine, him at his turntable. It was Kit who began to voice the questions Frank chose not to ask.

'So where do you live, Ilse Brauchmann?'

'Not far away.'

'Rented?'

'*Ja.*'

'Is it nice?'

'I guess.'

'Big?'

'So-so.'

'With your fiancé, Ilse Brauchmann?'

'You don't have to call me Ilse Brauchmann. You could just call me Ilse. It sounds like you don't know me.'

Kit sprang from one foot to the other; a sign of embarrassment and also of an imminent confession. He explained that he was learning German. He had borrowed a book from the library, along with a record. The problem was, there were scratches on the record. The needle slid all the way from lesson one to lesson six; from basic introductions, to 'In the hospital'. So far he could say hello, good evening, *'Ich heiße Kit,'* things like that, and he could also say he was expecting a baby in January.

Over the weeks, he asked other questions too. Questions that Maud, Father Anthony, the Williams brothers and even Mrs Roussos asked, whenever they met in England's Glory. Questions that Frank shrugged off and insisted were irrelevant; there was no need to pry, what he and Ilse shared was music, he didn't need to know any more. Questions that Ilse – when asked – seemed pleased to hear.

Grateful for.

In fact she was ready to answer Kit's questions at the drop of a hat.

So how long had she been in England? *She arrived in January.* Why was her English so good? *She learnt it at school.* What had she done before she arrived in the city? *Oh, not very much.* Did she like England? *Yes.* Why did she come? *To do something different with her life.* Did she have any brothers or sisters? *She would have liked to have them but she didn't.* What did her parents do? *Her father was a general handyman, her mother stayed at home.* What was her favourite colour? *Purple.* Purple? *No, that was a joke. It was green.* (HA HA HA, went Kit. 'That's so funny.') What was her job? *Guess.* A teacher? *No.* A doctor? *No.* A film star?

She laughed. 'I'm a cleaner.'

The idea of her with a Hoover was so wildly funny that Kit ended up with a nasty round of hiccups, and she had to go upstairs and fetch a glass of water.

'So when is your wedding?'

'My wedding?'

Gone was the laughter. She stopped messing around and looked directly over to Frank. He reached for his headphones, but no matter how hard he tried to lose himself to music, her voice still found him. She spoke slowly now, in that careful way she had, as if she were following words that had been laid out for her like stones on a path.

'I don't know, Kit. It's complicated. My father has poor health. I miss my mother too. I might need to go home.'

'So where is your fiancé?'

'He is, uh, travelling.'

'Travelling?'

'Aha.'

'He doesn't live with you?'

'Not exactly.'

'So why do you want Frank to give you music lessons?'

'Oh dear, the cellophane's torn.' She pulled a record from the shrink-wrap machine. She fixed a fresh length of PVC and put it through again; this time it came out perfectly. She fetched her green coat and, without another word of explanation, she left.

It was over three months since Ilse Brauchmann had fainted outside the music shop. Frank did not ask why it had happened, he did not ask where she lived or where she worked. He did not ask where her fiancé was, or what he did for a living, or even when they planned to get married. He knew about her hands, and for him that was enough. Besides, he loved her. He would always love her. He had moved beyond detail.

Lessons nine, ten, eleven, twelve. He gave her *Veedon Fleece* by Van

Morrison, Nick Drake, *Five Leaves Left*, The Stones, The Ramones, Bob, Schubert, Prefab Sprout, *The New Favourites of Brinsley Schwarz*, Graham Parker, Steely Dan, *Can't Buy a Thrill*, more J. S., more Aretha.

And when he listened?

It was always the same. He heard nothing but her silence.

31

Theme from Shaft

First there was the hi-hat ride pattern on cymbals, then *wah wah wah* went the guitar. After that, a full minute of piano, flute, punchy horn, funky bass, tambourine and heroic orchestral strings. It built and built like a river of water pressing towards the sea, until – *Shaft!* – at last here was Isaac Hayes with his smooth silky bass voice, sailing into the song like the coolest dude on a great big yacht. Loyal to his friends, lethal to his enemies, tender with his women—

Kit swaggered up and down the rows of vinyl, loyal to his friends, lethal to his enemies, tender with his women.

Shaft!

He picked up Aretha and put her next to Albinoni.

Can ya dig it?

He walked over to the shrink-wrap machine and plipped the 'On' switch. The shrink-wrap machine gave a whir and an increasingly nasty smell of burnt plastic. Kit yelped and switched off the machine and went back to being lethal to his enemies.

Shaft!

There were moments in Kit's life when he liked to pretend that he was very famous. He'd be fetching his mother's pills or waking his dad – and all of a sudden he would imagine a film camera zooming in over his shoulder. He could hear Isaac Hayes and then the deep voice of an actor saying, '*Kit fetches his mum's pills. Kit wakes his dad.*' His life seemed to have more purpose when he thought of the film cameras and Isaac Hayes.

On the whole, Kit was aware that things were happening in the world, and they seemed not to involve Kit. However hard he tried, he didn't seem to be a part. He wondered when it would start. *How can I help you today?* he would ask in the music shop, just like Frank, only instead of spilling everything, customers would take a sideways step and make a dash for the door. So he made funny noises to remind people he was here and that he was not a threat to anyone, he was fun. It had started as a joke but somehow it had got more serious and now he didn't even know he was doing it half the time. His hands shook because it made him nervous, this waiting to feel he was a part of things. It got so bad sometimes, the shaking, he had to pretend he was cold. Or he had to jump on the spot and do a funny voice and now it was even worse because everyone was looking at him as if he was even weirder when all he was doing was trying to be like Frank.

Father Anthony had told him listening was different for everyone. You had to find it in your own way. It was a bit like praying, he said.

Kit wasn't very good at that either.

He had no idea how Frank heard the song inside people. Sometimes Kit listened so hard his ears felt stretched, and he still couldn't get any-thing. When he listened to his parents, he heard the television. When he listened to Father Anthony, he heard old-man breathing. When he listened to the Williams brothers, he didn't hear anything, he just smelt

206

hair pomade. And when he listened to Maud, he generally heard her asking what the fuck he was staring at.

He was so busy wondering all these things, and being Shaft, the complicated man, he failed to notice a new customer slipping in the door.

'Hello, Kit.'

It was her. It was Ilse Brauchmann.

She laughed. 'Are you OK? I was just looking for Frank.'

Kit fled to the turntable and lifted the stylus too fast so that he dropped it and caused a nasty bump to the *sex-machine-to-all-the-chicks*.

'He's gone to buy new labels. I'm minding the shop.'

'Do you need any help?'

She took off her coat and her gloves. Her hands looked red and sore.

'No, I am fine. I am not supposed to touch anything while Frank's out.'

She laughed as if he was really funny, which was nice, of course, except for the fact he wasn't. He was being dead serious.

That was another thing Kit wondered. When he would stop breaking things.

She was watching him. He was afraid she would ask about Shaft or the strange burning smell that was still wafting from the shrink-wrap machine, so instead he made a wild grab at the nearest subject to hand.

'How is your fiancé today?'

She blushed. Then she sighed. She sighed so hard it was a wonder she had any air left in her.

'Oh dear God,' she murmured. '*Ich wünschte, ich hätte es nicht gesagt.*'

He had no earthly idea what she was talking about – his German

207

lessons had not progressed beyond useful introductions, and my day at the hospital – but how beautiful she looked, the sleeves of her coat pushed partway up her arms, a strand of hair dangling loose. He gazed at her and even as he gazed, Kit knew something else, something about Ilse Brauchmann that was bigger than words. It was soft. Melodious. He felt a flush of adrenalin and then the giddiness of a fall. It was like being nothing.

'Kit?' she said. 'Are you all right?'

He got it. He could hear the song inside her and it was the saddest, loneliest violin.

She was in love with Frank. That was her secret.

32

Raindrop

It was coming gently; not the winter sort that gets into your clothes and chills your bones, but a steady curtain of rain, plashing on the rooftops and cobbled stones. It was so warm that everything would dry again as soon as it stopped, and there would be that sweet, fresh smell in the city of leaves and grass, even when you couldn't actually see them.

'Tell me again,' said Ilse Brauchmann at their table in the Singing Teapot. 'It's such a good story.'

So Frank told her the story of Chopin and the Prelude No. 15 in D flat major for a second time, and as he did, she sat with her face cupped in her hands, watching the rain at the window. He told her about Chopin going to Majorca with his lover because he was ill and needed sun; he told her about the miserable weather they met there, and the monastery where they rented a cell that looked over the olive groves, and how Chopin waited weeks for the arrival of his piano, feeling more and more lonely. He explained that for him, Prelude No. 15 was another of those pieces of music that told a story – when he listened he saw rain falling on rooftops, and olive groves, and a little garden with lemon trees; he heard the kind of rain that comes soft at first, *pitter patter*, and then so insistently it is everywhere you look, and in everything you hear, until once again it is nothing except one small drop following another, right up to the last one that lands so surely and so kindly it is hard to imagine anything falling ever again. But it was a love song too, he said. 'At least I think so.'

'Why, Frank?'

'Because it's about waiting. It's about staying in one little dark place.'

'Would you wait for the person you loved?'

'Yes,' he said. 'Would you?'

'Yes,' she said. 'I would.'

And all the time they spoke, the rain fell, just like the Chopin prelude, hitting the window in beads that ran the length of the glass and then disappeared.

Afterwards they walked to the park and down to the lake. There was barely anyone else. She paid the boatman, and Frank untied a pleasure boat in the shape of a swan. He stepped into the boat without losing his balance this time and held out his hand for Ilse and she stepped in too. She leant back as she sat, and he leant forward, so that their weight was perfectly distributed in the little boat; then he took one oar, she took the other, and together they rowed the boat to the middle of the water, without a single word passing between them. The water was blue-grey with the day's reflection and trees, and dimpled as far as they could see with the falling rain. They sat for a long time, just watching the rain and smiling, her with one oar, him with the other. By now their hair was so wet it stuck to their heads like plastic, and the shoulders of her coat were more black than green, but they stayed out there in the middle of the lake, until the cloud shifted and the evening sun came out, and everything around them, every leaf, every blade of grass, every rooftop in the distance, shone like a piece of jewellery.

'Do you remember?' she asked.

'Yes,' he said.

He laughed.

She laughed.

'Wouldn't it be good,' she said, 'if it was like this for ever?'

33

Get Up, Stand Up

Fuck you. Go home. NF.

One Tuesday morning in early May, there was more graffiti. The people of Unity Street opened their curtains, and it was everywhere. Big slogans daubed on the pavements, walls, the billboard by the bombsite, as well as the shop windows. They had even sprayed *Irish Scum* on Father Anthony's door, and swastikas outside several houses. A neighbour said he'd heard a noise and rushed out, but saw nothing apart from a gang of kids in hoodies running in the direction of Castlegate. It could have been anyone. The shopkeepers called an emergency meeting in England's Glory.

So here they all were: the Williams brothers, Mrs Roussos and her chihuahua, Frank, Kit, Maud and Father Anthony. The regular line of old men were up at the bar, the man with three teeth sang about a dog, while the woman with curlers smoked an imaginary cigarette. Frank had been out all day, washing off the graffiti. He was very tired. Besides, he hadn't seen Ilse for three days. He assumed she was busy with her fiancé, but he couldn't sit still.

'Who are these kids?' asked Mrs Roussos. 'Why do they do this to our street?'

212

Father Anthony shrugged. This was what happened, he said, when the rich got richer and the poor got poorer. It wasn't just Unity Street; it was happening all over the city. The more people lost, the more they would fight against one another; this was human nature, he said.

'Maggie should bring back conscription,' said Pete the barman. 'That would sort these kids out. She should bring back corporal punishment as well.'

'Oh great,' said Maud. 'Pack them off to war and then hang them 'cos they're all fucked up. That's really going to put the world straight.'

'It's got so bad,' said one of the Williams brothers, 'we daren't go out at night.'

'Do you think we should all invest in iron shutters, Frank?'

'None of us can afford iron shutters,' pointed out Maud. 'I can't afford the central heating.'

'They might try to break in next time. They might have knives and things.'

Kit suggested they should fit a series of alarms in each shop so that they could contact one another if there was an emergency. Maud pointed out they already had such a system, and it was called a telephone. Meanwhile Pete the barman said what about setting up a vigilante group? They could take matters into their own hands, patrol Unity Street at night, keep an eye on things. They wouldn't do any serious damage, but they could carry baseball bats, maybe wear some kind of uniform. He asked if there were any volunteers?

The shopkeepers stared at him as if he had just dropped through a hole in the ceiling.

The Williams brothers held hands. Mrs Roussos pointed out this

213

was Unity Street, not Harlem, while Father Anthony began to laugh. Kit alone shot up his arm. 'I could volunteer, Pete!'

After that, the barman went pretty quiet about the vigilante thing. 'But who would put *Irish Scum* on Father Anthony's door? He comes from Kent.'

'It's a common mistake,' said Father Anthony. 'People assume all priests are Irish.'

'Jesus was Irish,' said Kit.

He seemed to have landed the conversation in an altogether different landscape. There was nothing to do but wait for the air to clear and then start off on a fresh one.

'Let's face it,' said Maud. 'Unity Street has gone down the toilet. Someone should pull the chain and have done with it. That florist was right to get out.'

'If the florist had stayed put, we wouldn't be in this mess,' said Pete the barman. 'Once one person goes, there's no stopping. It's like a pack of cards. We should have seen it coming when the baker went.'

Frank was impatient. 'I don't know why you're all talking as if every-thing is over. I have staked my *flat* on the refurbishment. Give it a few weeks, we'll have loads of new customers. Besides, we're important. We offer things people can't buy on Castlegate. We give our customers a chance to find something that they might actually *need*. We're a community—'

The shopkeepers stared at him bravely. Silently. Politely.

'Anyway, I should head off,' he said.

'Head off?' barked Maud. 'Where exactly do you think you're going?'

Sometimes Frank got the feeling that Maud was removing floor-boards, even while he was balancing on them.

'It's nearly half five. I'm giving a music lesson—'

Maud watched with a face like a bee sting. 'But it's the meeting with Fort Development. It starts here in an hour.'

'I thought no one was interested?'

'After what happened last night,' said one of the Williams brothers, 'people feel differently. We're scared, Frank. We need to hear what they have to say.'

'You'll have to cancel your lesson,' said Maud.

'She's expecting me.'

'Ring her.'

Frank did his best to appear airy and self-possessed but his voice lost all control of itself, and just came out squeaky. 'Matter of fact, I don't have her number.'

'I thought you and Greensleeves were *friends*.' Maud raised her eyebrows so high it was hard to remember what she looked like with them at a normal level. Then she muttered something that appeared to be entirely for the benefit of herself. 'Why's she so mysterious? What's she trying to hide?'

At this point Kit began to squeal as if he had been gagged. He held tight to his seat and went alarmingly red, presumably with the effort of keeping himself silent. 'Mm mm mm,' he went.

It was very nearly half past five. Inconclusive and bewildering as this conversation was, Frank now had four minutes to cover a distance that took him nine on a day with a strong wind behind him, fifteen on a more gentle one. He explained that all he was going to do was run to the café and tell Ilse what was going on. He would be back by six thirty.

Running was not something that came entirely naturally to Frank.

There was a lot of him to shift. No matter how fast he went, legs chugging, arms swinging like pistons, the pavement slapping the undersides of his plimsolls, he didn't seem to be going as fast as normal people did when they made the exact same movements. Several times, he was overtaken by joggers in the new Lycra gear. He limped past the row of market stalls – a trader had set up selling cheap CDs, and people crowded round it like children. Drunken voices sang down an alley; police sirens wailed. All he needed was to check Ilse Brauchmann was OK, and explain about the meeting.

When you witness a person before they have spotted you, it allows you to observe them in a pure way, without the extra complications of yourself. As Frank hurtled down the little cobbled alleyway that led to the Singing Teapot, head reeling, eyes swimmy, breath heaving, as he finally reached the glass door with the *Closed* sign already at the window, he saw Ilse Brauchmann as if for the first time. She was waiting at their table by the window, one knee over the other, her chin resting in the V of her hands. Even if he hadn't been running for nine minutes, he would still have felt winded.

The moment she caught sight of him, she sprang to her feet. 'I was worried you weren't coming—'

It took a while to breathe normally again. He explained about the new graffiti and the meeting with Fort Development, while the waitress laid the table. She proudly informed them she had been planning their meal all day.

'Look, I am really sorry,' Frank told her, 'but tonight I can't.'

'But she has bad news,' replied the waitress. 'And this dish takes no time.'

Even though he fully intended to be five minutes, ten at the most,

216

something happened in the café. Time didn't so much jump as give up altogether. It was like being with Ilse on the lake – the outside world was a distant shore of lights, and the two of them existed in a place entirely of their own, untouched and untouchable.

She said, 'My father's taken a turn for the worse. My mother wants me to go home.' Enormous tears clung to her enormous eyes.

'When?'

'I hope to stay here for another few weeks.'

'You'd come back?'

'I don't know.'

'But what about—?'

'What?'

'Our music lessons. The shrink-wrap machine.' He laughed to show that was a joke but she only sighed.

'I don't know, Frank. It depends—'

Here she was interrupted. The saloon doors whammed open, and with them a violent hissing accompanied by a cloud of smoke. It swallowed the café in seconds.

'Sizzling hot plate!' shouted the cloud of smoke, sounding uncannily like the waitress. Even Ilse Brauchmann seemed to have vanished.

'Is it meant to do this?' Frank yelled.

The cloud shouted back that the recipe hadn't specified. It also shouted, '*Bon appétit!*'

It required only a glass of water to put out the sizzling dish – whatever it was, it was charred to the point of disintegration – but now here he was, with a wet hot plate, the woman he loved talking about leaving, a distressed waitress with a potentially lethal passion for amateur cookery, while on the other side of Castlegate Fort Development would

217

be setting up their banners and posters and repeating their offer to buy Unity Street. Frank glanced at the clock and said the first thing that came into his head.

'Run.'

'Run?' repeated both Ilse and the waitress. 'Us?'

'Yes,' he shouted. 'Now.'

Maud was smoking outside England's Glory. She looked both tense and frightened. She wasn't so much inhaling her cigarette as chewing it. 'What the hell kept you?' She raked Ilse up and down. 'It's packed. You'd better *do* something, Frank. And who's the chick with the cap?'

'I'm a waitress.' (Said the waitress.)

Inside the bar, the crowd was so thick no one could move and there was a high buzz of conversation. Frank had no idea how such a down-at-heel cul-de-sac had suddenly produced all these outfits he had never seen before; everyone was dressed as if they were off to a cocktail party. There were men in velvet jackets, women in dresses, students with combed hair, and several dogs on leads. The woman in curlers had covered them with a silk headscarf. Even the man with three teeth had borrowed a tie.

Everyone was talking about the graffiti in the night, and how there was no respect any more. Tables had been pushed aside and chairs were arranged in lines. The windows were white as blinds and Pete was clearly having his best night since the Royal Wedding. At the front, a table had been set up with a large screen for a slide presentation. There were big banners with the Fort Development logo, as well as the large posters showing all those happy people drinking coffee and pointing at brand-new houses.

Frank tried to push through the crowd but did not get far. The Williams brothers had seats on the front row; Father Anthony was sharing a chair with Kit, and old Mrs Roussos sat a little apart because her chihuahua had taken a dislike to a poodle on the other side of the room and was snarling. The line of old men at the bar offered their stools to Ilse and the waitress.

So Fort Development was not simply a van full of men in bomber jackets who turned up to empty premises and boarded them up, it was also a team of men with matching grey suits and differing degrees of facial hair – one had a beard, another was bald but holding a clipboard, another had a moustache and a baton, the last was growing sideburns. They walked to the table at the front with their heads bowed, and because it was very warm they removed their jackets to hang them over the backs of their chairs. Then one of them – the one with the most hair, in fact – stood and asked for everyone to listen. He sounded nervous and it took a good few minutes for people to realize the meeting had started. First off, he wanted to thank everyone for the amazing turnout. Really they'd only been expecting a few people. They felt humble. (He made a humble prayer shape.) The meeting would be quick, he said apologetically. This was just Fort Development wanting to say hello. (The man with sideburns waved his hand. *Hello.*) There'd be time for free drinks at the bar afterwards, courtesy of Fort Development.

Pete gave a shout from the bar. 'We're only *here* for the *beer.*' People laughed.

Fort Development wanted to begin by explaining who they were. They were a development company ('Boo!' shouted a student with his dreadlocks tied into a hairband) but they were one with a difference; they were interested in *people*. They focused on improvements in

219

inner-city housing. They would like to give an example – here the man with a baton clicked a switch and images flashed as if by magic on the screen behind them of a) a housing estate, b) a woman smiling in a housing estate, c) a fitted avocado bathroom in a housing estate, and d) an upside-down group of men in a housing estate.

'Sorry,' said Baton Man. 'I put the slide in the wrong way round.'

The crowd politely tipped their heads to one side to get the general picture.

Now it was Clipboard Man's turn to speak. He behaved like one of the crowd; a jolly geezer. He said he too had grown up in a street like this. He too had played on a bombsite, and fetched groceries from the shop on the corner. He knew how hard this was for the locals.

People nodded and said, 'Hear hear.' Kit was nodding so much he looked in danger of giving himself whiplash.

Clipboard Man explained that there was no future in Unity Street. The council had it earmarked for demolition. A few people expressed their shock – this was the first they'd heard of it – but he quickly moved on. Fort Development were offering above the market rate for their houses and shops.

The Williams brothers put up their hands and rose simultaneously to their feet. They spoke falteringly about the generations of their family that had lived in the parade on Unity Street. People listened. Yes, they agreed, the two old men were right. People loved this street. Some had been here since they were children. Then a woman representing the homeless also stood and spoke about the housing crisis in the city. It was a small street, but there were flats here, bedsits, rooms to let. You couldn't throw all these people out. She talked earnestly about teenage prostitution, and drug abuse. Then another man stood and told a funny

220

story about the six children he and his wife had proudly raised in their terraced house, even though they only had two bedrooms. The man with three teeth broke into a ballad. It wasn't really about a street, it was about a train, but he had a nice voice, and only three teeth, of course, so everyone listened anyway.

Then Clipboard Man asked for another slide, which showed a close-up of a broken piece of masonry.

There would be an accident soon, he said. And if it was your house from which the offending masonry dropped, well. He shrugged. Good luck with that. Because you would be liable for damages.

The Williams brothers exchanged a nervous look and sat back down.

Now it was the turn of Sideburns. He asked for a moment more of everyone's time.

Clearly this was a great community. No one was denying that. But there were other great communities in the city. Had anyone actually heard about the new development down by the docklands? Those properties would be real investments. Fort Development weren't just offering to buy out the house owners on Unity Street – they could help with mortgages at the most beneficial rates. Right now they were practically giving them away.

The fact was, he had heard about what had been going on in Unity Street, and he had to admit he was alarmed. If he was a resident, he'd be worried about walking the street late at night. And now there had been the mugging—

'Mugging?' said Frank. 'What mugging?'

He was not the only one. A few people exchanged confused glances.

The speaker apologized. He hadn't meant to mention the mugging. Apparently the police were still conducting inquiries.

Despite his reassurances, people seemed uneasy. Pete shook his head behind the bar, as if this was the final straw.

'The fact is, this is *1988*. It's not 1948. These days we have *choice*. You don't have to take what you're given. You can get more.'

At this point Baton Man flicked his remote-control switch and vast images flashed all around of the happy white people drinking their coffee, to the accompaniment of David Bowie singing 'Ch-ch-changes'.

He started his own round of applause which Kit, by now completely baffled as to who was good at this meeting and who was not, also took up. Soon most of the people in the room were clapping.

Frank felt something with a sharp edge in his lower back and realized it was Maud's fingernail.

She hissed, 'Say something!'

He caught sight of Ilse Brauchmann watching him with a look of alarm.

He shouted, 'We're a community.'

No one heard.

'Louder,' hissed Maud.

He waved his arms. He said it again, 'Hey! We're a community.'

A few people on the back row turned and glanced at him, as if he were some kind of embarrassing disturbance.

Frank didn't even know what he was going to say. He just thought how it was for him when he talked music with Ilse Brauchmann; he spoke slowly and from the heart. 'Shops are like vinyl,' he began. 'You have to take great care of them. And communities are the same . . .'

Afterwards it bewildered Frank that he had no exact recollection of the words he used or where they had been hiding all those years. He remembered that people swivelled round to see who was speaking and that he spent a good while in fact not speaking, or at least not coming out with full sentences. He said something about life not always being easy. He said something else about it not being perfect. He likened community to being part of a huge broken-up family – which was especially confounding given his singular and unorthodox child-hood. He gazed across the crowded pub at those dark, wide eyes that were filled with such immense stillness and quiet he thought a man would never see to the bottom of them, and he kept talking.

'When I came here fourteen years ago, I had nothing. I was really lost. I found this street and yes, it was crap, it was falling down, and really ordinary, and someone even had a goat.' ('Oh, that was me!' inter-rupted a woman at the front. Amused laughter.) 'But you were kind to me. When I was trying to put my shop together, people called in every day to help. I didn't ask for that. You just turned up. And that's the thing about Unity Street. That's the glue that sticks us together. Yes, we've got problems, but over the years we have always made it work by listening to one another and helping. If we throw all this away just because we are afraid, or because we have an idea that life could be uncomplicated, I have an awful feeling it's a terrible mistake.' He might have also said something like 'You have to be careful what you lose,' but he wasn't entirely sure any more what he was trying to say, because his voice was wobbling with a mixture of emotion and fear, and his tongue had gone and appended itself to the roof of his mouth, and he was so hot he probably looked the colour of a panic button. If he'd said all that he hoped he had said – i.e. the above – he was bloody lucky.

Afterwards Kit led another round of enthusiastic applause. A few people gave Frank a wide berth but Mrs Roussos sobbed so much she could only cling to his shoulders, with her little dog pressed somewhere in the middle. Father Anthony shook him by the hand, and said he had never felt so proud. 'Did I make sense?' Frank asked; to which the old priest assured him that even if he had dried up a few times, they got the gist of what he was hoping to say. Residents came up to Frank to pat his shoulder. Good on him, they agreed. He had their full support. They would never leave Unity Street, they were a community, they loved this street and they would stick together. Even Maud managed a full-blown smile.

Everyone enjoyed Fort Development's free beer. A few people stayed to chat things through with the team of men in grey – Kit had a conversation with Clipboard about how to use a slide projector – but the general view was that the night belonged to Unity Street, and so did the future.

Afterwards Frank and Ilse Brauchmann walked the waitress back to her café. There was a sweetness in the air; the smell of a city that has been lived in all day. The leaves blew a little in the trees and the cathedral stood square and kind against the twilit sky. He felt exhausted but happy.

The two women went arm in arm, laughing as they talked about the evening. At the door of the café, the waitress said she would just clear up the remains of the sizzling dish before she went home.

'I fancy trying something European next week,' she told them.

Ilse Brauchmann didn't say anything more about her father, or going back to Germany. She just hugged the waitress and promised she was looking forward to it.

Then she turned to Frank and leaned up to break one kiss on his cheek.

'You were brilliant tonight,' she said. 'Not an island at all.'

*

The following afternoon, Williams the undertakers came to the music shop. They asked if they might have a quiet word?

The brothers removed their hats and studied the labels inside, as if they weren't entirely sure which was theirs.

'We went to see the people at Fort. The new houses will have proper heating, and that. And they are a good investment, you see.'

The other one said, 'You heard what they told us about the muggings. Everyone's talking about them—'

'But that wasn't *real*. There haven't been any muggings on Unity Street. You know that.'

The brothers nibbled their mouths and shook their heads. 'We can't do it any more, Frank. It's time for us to go.'

And they did. Not overnight, like Mr Novak the Polish baker, and not in a double coffin either, as Frank had predicted, but in a local minicab with a pair of furry dice hanging from the rear-view mirror. They were going to stay with their sister in Scotland for a while. It was years since they'd had a holiday.

The shop was locked but there was no vigil this time. No line of chairs, or plates of food; no stories of all the kind things the brothers had done. One woman said she was glad to see the back of the undertakers. It wasn't nice, she said, having that kind of business on your doorstep. And someone else said he wasn't being funny or anything but he'd seen those two old men holding hands.

How quickly and easily people seemed to accept the loss of the shop; it paved the way for more loss to follow.

The building would soon be boarded with Fort Development signs, and so would the house across the street with the Italian flag at the window. There was further graffiti. *Sharon is a cunt!* GO HOME. But also, *I love Princess Diana!!!!* and *This way to the music shop!!!*

('I did those two,' said Kit.)

The tattoo parlour, Articles of Faith and Frank's shop: only three left.

34

Protest Song

'SOUTHERN TREES BEAR *a strange fruit,' sang Billie Holiday from the Dansette.*
'Blood on the leaves and blood at the root . . .'

Tick, tick. Tick, tick.

The record came to an end and for once in her life, Peg said nothing.

'I don't know what came over you,' Frank managed at last. 'You've wrecked
my life.'

'She couldn't have that baby. How could she have a baby? She's seventeen.'

'We were going to get married.'

'Don't be so ridiculous. She wears ankle socks.'

He had no idea if she was even being serious. 'Did you talk her into it?'

'I explained the pitfalls.'

'Of marriage?'

'Of kids.'

'Jesus, Peg.'

Deborah had been to a special clinic. Frank didn't know she was going.
She just rang afterwards and told him there was no baby. Her voice was slurry.
'I don' wanna seeee you any morrr.'

He cycled to the street where she lived and knocked at the door. 'Deborah!

Deb!' he shouted until her mother answered. 'Go away! Go away! Haven't you and your wretched mother done enough damage?' Frank wrote letters, but they were all returned. He felt desolate.

He listened to a lot of protest music after that. Bob Dylan, Joan Baez, Woody Guthrie, Curtis Mayfield. If it didn't have a political message, he wasn't interested. He flunked his school exams and talked about joining the army, though he was only saying that to wind up Peg. Instead he got a job in a pub, with a room of his own on the top floor.

That summer Frank started sleeping with the landlord's wife. She had a bosom like a bolster and nestling against it he could forget Deborah for a while, and the baby they never had. He got three cracked ribs for his trouble, along with the promise that if he showed his sweet face again, he would end up on the pig farm.

Nineteen years old and he was back at home, listening to records and Peg.

'What kind of life would that have been?' she asked once. 'Married with a kid?'

Normal, he thought. It might have been normal.

35

Don't Believe a Word

SAY NO TO FORT DEVELOPMENT! read Kit's posters. UNITE FOR UNITY STREET! They were on every lamp post and every window. He even designed leaflets.

Frank had given it his best shot at the meeting, and it hadn't been enough. He spent almost every waking hour handing out Kit's flyers. He posted them through doors, he approached anyone who was foolish enough to catch his eye, he explained over and over about the campaign to save the houses and shops on Unity Street. Kit made a petition, which he took from one door to another, collecting signatures.

'What about the muggings?' people asked.

'There haven't been any muggings.'

But now that the idea had been planted, it took on a life of its own. Pete advised his customers to carry rape alarms. A man reported being followed by kids with knives. The more the residents of Unity Street talked about the muggings, the more certain they were that they had happened. By the end of May, several more houses had been sold to Fort Development.

Ilse and Frank continued to meet for their music lessons in the

Singing Teapot. She mentioned once that her father had a cold but when he asked if she was still planning to go back, she turned away and said, 'I don't know, Frank. I don't seem to know very much any more.' Another time she mentioned how tired he looked, and instead of talking he rested his head on the table and dozed, while she sat opposite him quietly watching the window. It could only have been ten minutes but it felt like the most replenishing sleep he'd had for weeks. In the shop new boxes of vinyl continued to arrive, waiting for her beside the shrink-wrap machine.

The council man called again and said there had been more complaints about the falling masonry. He insisted that unless the shopkeepers addressed the problem, the council would look into forcibly closing them. So out came the plastic ribbon, which Kit carefully looped from one street lamp to another.

One afternoon in June, Maud was helping herself to Frank's milk while he was out leafleting. Mistaking her for an assistant, a customer asked if she knew where Frank kept his Vivaldi. Maud replied that she was buggered if she knew how the shop worked. It was a law unto itself. Nevertheless she helped him search and eventually she remembered the afternoon Frank had talked about concept albums and the 'Four Seasons'. It wasn't exactly a day she was going to forget. There it was, a new copy slipped between 'The Look Of Love' and At Folsom Prison.

'Can you tell me anything about it?' asked the customer.

'Nope.' She flipped it over and scanned the sleeve notes on the back.

Something dropped through Maud like a weight falling through air. She had to grip hold of the counter to steady herself. She took the money for the record and filled out the sales book but her hands were shaking so hard she could barely write a straight line.

'See you again,' said the customer. 'Thanks for the help.'

She didn't even reply. She marched upstairs where she found Kit sorting through a new delivery. 'Frank's really gone out on a limb here,' he said. 'Who's going to buy this stuff?'

But Maud had no time for worrying about vinyl. She planted her feet squarely. 'Tell me again about that basement flat where you saw Ilse Brauchmann.'

No one could take it in. The shopkeepers sat in their circle in England's Glory; the old men stared from the bar. The woman in curlers gave up smoking altogether.

Pete the barman produced a plate of pickled eggs but they hadn't the wherewithal to eat. Not even Kit.

'She's a musician,' repeated Maud.

Confusion.

'A violinist.'

More confusion.

'She made records. The Berlin Philharmonic, for fuck's sake.'

They continued to stare at Maud with mouths open like fledglings. Kit's was so wide, he looked in danger of catching something.

'She played on the "Four Seasons". Look.'

One by one they passed round the record sleeve. Kit said he could only see a picture of some nice trees.

'Look on the other side, you pillock. It's her photo.'

There she was. A black-and-white young woman with enormous, frightened eyes and her hair half up, half down. And yet no matter how many times Maud said it, no matter how many times they stared at the record sleeve, and no matter how many times Maud pointed at Ilse Brauchmann's name next to '*first violinist*', Frank couldn't take it in.

Ilse Brauchmann was a musician?

She played first violin?

She made records?

The room began to swing so wide, he felt sick.

'I told you!' said Kit. 'I told you she looked famous! I said that right at the start!'

Frank was barely present, and neither was his head. People spoke and he heard bits of sentences, odd words, but he couldn't keep up. It was like repeatedly falling down holes. Getting up, only to trip into another one.

Maud explained all over again how she had taken the bus to the back-street described by Kit and there, sure enough, was Ilse Brauchmann's name beside a bell, in an old block of flats. Maud had asked a neighbour. Apparently she kept herself to herself. Played her music too loud but if you banged on the wall she turned it down. Hers was the bedsit down in the basement. The woman thought she had a job as a cleaner.

Frank's head stopped swinging and decided it would like to split open.

Father Anthony rose and stood next to him and touched him on the shoulder. 'You all right?' he murmured. His voice sounded swimmy.

'So why did she lie?' asked Pete the barman.

Everyone looked at Frank, hoping he would know the answer. But he couldn't think. He was like a building that has been swung at by a crane and ball. He yawned and one yawn wasn't nearly enough; they kept coming again and again.

Kit said something about Ilse's arthritis and another voice said of course, of course. Then people began to talk about Frank and music lessons and he didn't want to know any of it, he just wanted to curl up in a very dark place and listen to records. But what about her fiancé? someone else asked. Where was he in all this?

'Oh God!' Kit's arm shot high into the air. 'I think I know this one!'

Before Kit could say any more, the room slopped right over. Something acidic leapt to Frank's throat. He picked up his jacket and lumbered to the door.

'Frank? Do you want to talk?' called Father Antony.

'No,' he said. 'This time I really don't. Please let me be alone.'

That night he lay staring at the ceiling, studying shapes he could only just about make out in the dark. Was it minutes that passed? Hours? He had no idea. He couldn't see how he would ever get up again. Everything moved round like the spokes of a wheel to which he had been strapped. He raked over their meetings, trying to understand. The pictures in the 'Four Seasons'? James Brown as Muhammad Ali? What had possessed him? He tossed from one side of the bed to the next. Wherever he moved, the shock went with him.

Of course she made no music when he listened. The woman he had permitted himself to fall in love with didn't exist. She was a musician. She played on records.

After the death of Peg, he'd had to be so careful with his thoughts. He might be doing something very straightforward, like putting on a pair of socks, and out of nowhere the truth would rise up in front of him. He had tried to be angry for what she had done but he was so wounded he couldn't find it in himself to feel anything but the pain.

It was like losing something vital that he could not do without, while also realizing that it had never been his in the first place. So he taught himself to deal with the facts one by one. *All right, she's dead. I have to start again.* But then he got to the next part, her final abandonment, and it was like meeting a flood. He couldn't get round it. He couldn't even have it out with her. Everything they had done together, all the music they shared, it had meant nothing. *He* meant nothing. How else to explain what she had done?

So there he lay, thinking of Ilse Brauchmann and thinking of Peg, and everything began to merge, and he couldn't tell the difference any more between the way he had felt fifteen years ago, and the way he felt now. When he slept it was brief, but he clung to unconsciousness, hoping it would never be light again.

The next time Frank woke, he found he was still dressed and sunshine was slanting through the window. He wondered why everything seemed so flat and empty, and then he remembered. He had lost the thing he thought he had. Once again he had tried to love and been betrayed. The Ilse he loved didn't exist. The *woman* he loved didn't exist.

When he heard Kit knocking on the door of the shop he went down in a towel and opened up. Kit watched Frank as if he were afraid he might combust. He said quietly, 'It's Tuesday. It's your music lesson today.'

'I can't do it. I can't face her.'

Everything had worked until Ilse Brauchmann fell into his life.

36

Requiem

Tick, tick, went the record. Mozart's Requiem. Peg said nothing. She just blew out smoke and listened, a look of fear on her face.

In the last few years of her life, she became more spiritual. It would be an exaggeration to say she found God – Peg wouldn't find God if he leapt out of a cupboard, shouting 'Boo!' – but she talked about the fact her parents were dead by her age, and she developed an interest in things other than sex.

She listened to sacred choral music. She also took up painting by numbers and random acts of philanthropy.

Peg sent cheques to a few local charities and hung the walls of the old billiard room with her artwork. Botticelli's Venus, as well as some shepherdesses in the style of Gainsborough. As a result of her kindness to a care home she was invited to a Christmas ball for benefactors, where she was treated like royalty. She didn't sleep with anyone – most of them were on Zimmer frames – but she came home ecstatic. The following day she sent a cheque to a home for orphans in Africa.

She talked a lot about Handel's funeral as well as Beethoven's; all those people who showed up to pay their respects. She talked about Vivaldi too, and no music at the end. It could get her really wound up. She played the

Mozart Requiem, Rachmaninov's Vespers, Fauré, Schubert, Brahms, Verdi, Cherubini. The 'Hallelujah Chorus', of course. She loved that.

So it went on. Frank and Peg rubbing along, the white house getting more decrepit, the weekly delivery of groceries and records.

Until the evening he saw a blue light flashing up the drive, and a police car arrived.

'I'm afraid there has been a terrible accident.'

37

The True Story of Ilse Brauchmann

'I HAVEN'T A CLUE what's going on,' said the red face in front of him. 'But if you don't come and sort it out, I'm going to deep-fry your balls.'

Frank wondered what it was with the women of this city that when it came to threats, they seemed to involve such malicious intent towards a man's private parts. She was wearing a small black dress, but her head was missing something. A stiff white cap—

The Singing Teapot waitress.

What was she doing in front of his turntable? And why was she pointing at him with a wooden spoon?

'I just talked to the nice woman next door,' she said.

'Do you mean Maud?'

'She told me to dish it to you straight.'

Suddenly Frank felt both weak and afraid. He reached for a smoke.

'That poor lady is waiting in my café. She won't eat. She won't drink her squash. She's just sitting there, waiting for you. She looks *ill.*'

'It's best if you keep out of this.'

The waitress slammed both hands on the edge of his turntable, narrowly missing the potted cactus. It seemed to have sprouted another immense pink flower. She bent close.

'It's Tuesday. It's past six o'clock. You are *here*. She is *there*. I have bought the ingredients for the Weekly Special out of my own pocket. So get to my café.'

As he mutely followed her to the door, he felt Kit's eyes boring through him.

'What shall I do while you're gone, Frank?'

'I have no idea. Why don't you try getting something right for once?'

But really he was talking to himself.

'You're a musician.'

Frank and Ilse sat opposite one another at their regular table in the window of the Singing Teapot. She looked ill – the waitress was right – her body seemed folded in on itself, but his head was throbbing and his skin was freezing, and he was under no doubt that he looked even worse than she did. The album sleeve of the 'Four Seasons' lay between them. 'A violinist,' he said.

She gave a sigh without sound. 'Frank—'

'Why didn't you tell me?'

Sunlight caught the upper halves of the old buildings opposite. The sky was still very blue; like looking up at something lovely from the depths of a hole. It seemed a long time since they'd talked about the 'Moonlight' Sonata, or even the night it snowed and she showed him her hands.

The waitress appeared from the kitchen, sweating hard, and laid the table. She made a business of straightening their knives and forks, as if they were children and incapable of taking care of themselves.

'I can't eat,' said Frank.

'Me neither,' said Ilse.

The waitress ignored them and brought two plates from the kitchen, bearing them like gifts.

'*Tartiflette*. It's an Alpine dish. Ketchup?' She produced an extremely large plastic tomato. '*Bon appétit*.'

At least eating was something to do that was not talking. The waitress watched from her stool until they had finished. There was no noise but the obedient clink and scrape of knife and fork. Outside a man laughed and it was a distant sound, as if once again Ilse and Frank had slipped free of their moorings and were drifting in a space of their own.

When they were finished, the waitress gathered up their plates and crept back to her stool.

Frank looked at Ilse.

Ilse looked at Frank.

Eyes like vinyl.

'Can we start again?'

She told her story.

So Maud was right – Ilse Brauchmann was a violinist. But Ilse had been telling the truth when she told Frank she didn't listen to music any more. Kit too was right: she had to give up on music when her arthritis set in. She gave up playing and she gave up listening. She turned her back on the thing she loved.

The first time Ilse held a violin she was six. It was her teacher who noticed that if she wanted something, the child often sang for it. So the teacher introduced her to the only instrument she had to offer.

As she told this part of the story, Ilse Brauchmann's neck stretched up and tilted back like a swan's. She opened her arms and her eyes shone, as if her body was preparing to welcome the violin for the first time. It looked the most natural thing in the world. Of course she was a violinist.

She described how the teacher had put the bow in her hand and shown her what to do. In the time it took to draw the bow across four strings, Ilse knew. It was as if her future had turned up, all dressed and ready to go. She would be a violinist. And she laughed as she said that. 'I was so happy, Frank.'

The teacher was delighted. This little girl was a prodigy! She actually used that word; everything she showed Ilse how to play, she could do. The teacher showed her scales, arpeggios, runs, pizzicato; she got them right at the drop of a hat. 'Everyone was so pleased. Look, they kept saying. Look what this child can do! The music was inside me. I didn't even have to try.'

Within no time, Ilse had outgrown her teacher. Her parents were not well off but they paid for a tutor. At Christmas there was a concert and while other children were squeaking on recorders and bashing drums, there was little Ilse Brauchmann – with her dark, serious eyes – playing her violin.

So she went through school, practising every morning, every lunch-time, every evening, until she was old enough to go to music college. She was with other students who played music; there was no doubt in anyone's mind about their futures. She went from college to an orchestra – she was one of the few who got a job straight away. She recorded the 'Four Seasons' when she was only twenty. It was the high point of her life. There was talk of a tour.

And then it had begun; the thing with her hands.

At first it was just a little tremble, like a muzzy electric current, and sometimes her fingers locked, for no good reason. Then it got worse.

She started to lose control. She hid the problem, she gave excuses, but she began to make mistakes. Little things at first, but they got to be stupid mistakes that even a child wouldn't make. Her fingers might go stiff on the struts. Or she would feel a shock of pain and suddenly jerk the bow. She was relegated from first violinist to second, then third, then fourth.

Ilse looked down at her hands and Frank sat waiting for more. This great big man; he was nothing but liquid.

'My knuckles began to swell. It was *awful*. My fingers completely locked. Some days I couldn't move them. The pain woke me at night and it was worse after rain. The conductor took me aside. He told me they were letting me go. I was beside myself. I begged. I wept. I shouted. What will I do? I said. This is my life. He said, 'You could play for ballet classes.'

She touched her mouth with her fingertips, forbidding herself to cry. Frank reached out but she kept still and so his arm remained, beached, on the table.

'I wanted to be great. I didn't want to be—' She struggled to find the word. She even looked for it under the ashtray. '*Normal.*'

It was fair to say she got very low after that. She took a job waitressing and that was when she met Richard. He had no interest in music, especially not classical, and so long as she didn't have to look at what she had lost from her life, so long as she remained in hiding, she could just about bear it. Then – things got complicated and she left for England.

241

'Is that when you came to the music shop?'

She spoke the rest of the story very slowly, with a soft note of wonder in her voice, as if she were discovering things while she said them, and realizing how precious they were.

'I can picture it now. A cold, dark day in January. I had just arrived. I knew no one. Then I saw it, this little shop, on a run-down street. I went closer. I read the poster in the window. I saw all those records, the coloured lamps, people looking for music. It was so beautiful. I thought – Stand here for a minute. See if you can do it.'

'So why did you faint?' His fingers began tearing up the paper napkin. In fact now he looked, Frank discovered that he had already torn up several. There was a little pile of torn-up napkin all around him, as if he were making some kind of nest.

'It was too much. But the next thing I knew, you were there. You told me to stay with you. And there was something so kind about the way you said it.'

The waitress passed Frank a fresh pile of paper napkins. '*Bon appétit.*' He felt a need to keep tearing things.

Ilse said, 'After that, I tried to stay away. But I couldn't stop thinking about the way you told me everything would be OK. So I brought the plant as a thank-you. I didn't intend to stay but then Mrs Roussos interrupted, and you asked if I wanted a record—'

'You asked for the "Four Seasons".'

'It was the first record that came into my head. I didn't want to *buy* the thing—' Here came the blush in her cheeks. He realized he had become inordinately fond of those two red circles.

Briefly he remembered the group of shopkeepers sitting around the little table in England's Glory, trying to decide what to do with her

242

handbag. In his mind's eye, it was like seeing tiny people. Children.

'So did you listen to the record?'

'I couldn't face it. I stayed away from the shop. Then I saw Kit's posters. About my bag. I made him a shirt to say thank you. But you threw me out. That was unkind, Frank. I almost left that night.'

'What stopped you?'

'The "Four Seasons".' She took his cigarette and it dangled between her fingers. No one else smoked a cigarette like Ilse Brauchmann.

'I bought a really cheap record player and I listened. I felt – for the first time in years – the magic. I thought, maybe I could do it again. With this man's help, I could have my life back. Because you didn't talk about the technique of music. You told me how it *felt* when you listened. I got a job as a cleaner. A few offices. Nothing fancy. I asked you to give me lessons. And I didn't ask it as a favour. I gave you good money.'

'You said cash was no problem.'

'That *was* a lie. I tried to tell the truth about who I was – but you wouldn't let me. This was a business arrangement, you said.'

He hung his head. She was right. He remembered now. The way she had stood in front of him after their second lesson, twisting her hands. *Frank, there's something you need to know. You will hate me.* 'I have been so happy here, Frank. It has been like breathing again. Every record you gave me has been a little bit more like breathing.'

'What did Richard make of all this?'

He lit a fresh cigarette and passed it to her but she didn't take it and neither did he, so it sat in the ashtray between them, smoking all by itself.

She said, 'Are you serious?'

Even the waitress shot to her feet. 'Are you serious, Frank?'

It was like hearing stereo when you've got very comfortable with mono.

'What?' he said. 'What's going on?'

Ilse Brauchmann's eyes stacked with tears. 'Ohh,' she murmured. '*Was werde ich tun?*'

It was the waitress who filled the space between them, and also the silence. 'She doesn't have a fiancé, you great buffoon. What do you think she's doing here all by herself? They split up. He's back in Germany where she left him. Or travelling. Or doing whatever it is that he does. How could she be with a man who doesn't like music? She just didn't want you to think she was desperate. The truth's been staring you in the face the whole flipping time. She fell in love with you from the start.'

What followed was a PAUSE. Time stopped. The ground went whoooooosh. Frank was free-falling. Empty. Sick. He couldn't feel his feet any more. Come to think of it, he couldn't find his head. He wasn't sure how much more he could take.

Frank looked at Ilse.

Ilse looked at Frank.

Tears poured from her eyes. 'It's true, Frank. I love you.'

He stared at Ilse Brauchmann, as she gazed back at him across their little table, smiling and crying, and he wanted to be a man who said *I love you too.*

But he wasn't. He never had been. He didn't even know the shape of the words.

It was as dangerous as taking a running leap from a cliff. Supposing he said, *Yes, I love you too*, and she laughed? Or supposing they went back to the music shop, and spent a night together, and then she woke in the morning and said, *Actually, Frank, I'll see you around*. Because, given the lessons life had taught him, this was what would follow, as sure as night followed day, as sure as side A went on to side B. But this time it would be more pain than he could bear. He looked at Ilse Brauchmann and all he could see was the empty white house by the sea.

So he said, 'No.' He said, 'I can't.'

'What?' said the waitress, beginning to laugh.

Even Ilse Brauchmann's face had found a smile. They thought he was mucking about. They thought they were home and dry. 'You *can't*? Can't *what*, Frank?'

'I can't do this.' He was on his feet. Or rather, his legs. His legs had made a decision to go home. He staggered into the next table.

'What are you doing?'

'I'm a mess. You can't love *me*.'

She stared up at him as if she had not seen him before.

'Really,' he said. 'I mean it. Don't. Love. Me.'

She began to make strange tiny sounds. 'Ah ah ah.' Expulsions of air that came irregularly and were barely audible. As if she was stabbing herself with a needle, very sharp and deep. 'You *bloody* man.'

And the way she said it was how it always was with Ilse Brauchmann, her broken accent exposing the words for what they truly meant so that he heard them as if they had been forged for the very first time. She was right. He was no more than one massive, gaping, unhealed wound. He stumbled to the door. Swung it open. Felt the warm air.

'Wait!' shouted the waitress, charging forward. 'Wait!'

'No, it's over,' said Ilse Brauchmann. 'Let him go. I'm finished with England.' She had the tired voice of someone who sees no way out.

But even as Frank lumbered from the café, he was awaiting something, some divine intervention, the alley to close, the sun to carry him back. He pulled and pulled with his mouth but couldn't get enough breath in his lungs. Ahead, two lovers stood necking in a doorway.

He began to run. Slower at first, and then harder and harder.

It seemed he had no shape left, nothing you could hold and say, *This is Frank*. He was unstrung. He told himself to keep moving, not to think. If he kept moving, he might just stay in one piece. He lost his footing and stumbled past the people selling off their possessions on blankets; he almost sent a woman flying as she turned the corner. Behind him, the cathedral stood solid against the sky and a flock of pigeons scattered upwards.

Run, Frank. Run.

Shutters were coming down on Castlegate. Traders shouted at customers to get their bargains before it was too late. The sky was a hollow extending outwards and outwards to infinity.

Frank weaved past tables on the street, where couples sat drinking wine and taking in the beautiful evening. He passed the clock tower where junkies hung out, and old men on a bench, sharing cans of Special Brew. He took the turning towards the park.

The warmth had brought people out in crowds. They lay on the grass, they shared picnics, they rode bicycles, they scampered after balls, dogs, hoops. A group of deckchairs were set out for an evening concert in the bandstand, and a Mr Whippy ice-cream van was doing a roaring trade in cones with flakes. On the lake, the pleasure boats were all out, children splashed in the shallows, a man threw bread for the ducks, sunlight hit the water like fallen stars. All these normal people. Out doing regular, normal things.

She loves me.

She TOLD ME she loves me.

He had managed in one short time to say all the wrong things to the right woman, precisely because she was right. He was so afraid of having what he most wanted that he had tried to destroy it, once and for all.

She loved you from the start.

He felt his heart and chest swell against the restraint of sinews and cartilage; his ribs seemed to crack open. He had no idea how he would survive the rest of his life without Ilse Brauchmann.

But it was not over. There was time to start again. A picture of the music shop came to him, a little golden at the edges but never mind, he was allowed to be romantic now; Frank at his turntable, Kit drawing posters, Ilse at the shrink-wrap machine. He would offer her everything. His shop, his records. He would lay it all at her small neat feet.

Run, Frank, run.

Park gates. Oof oof. (Mind the road.) Castlegate. Market stalls. Oof oof. Come on, Frank. Turn the corner. Alleyway. Cobbled stones.

By the time he reached the Singing Teapot café, it was closed for the night. He thumped at the door, but the waitress did not appear. The lights were out and chairs were stacked on the tables.

Cathedral? Try the cathedral.

Two priests were studying the new carpet, but there was no sign of the woman he loved.

He started asking strangers. Passers-by. Have you seen her? Huge eyes? Hair kind of up, kind of down? About this height? Funny mouth. She's beautiful, no one like her—

247

He lumbered after a woman with a green scarf, only to discover she was blonde.

Maud. Maud knew where she lived. It was not too late. He must go back to Unity Street. He must get her address. He could be with Ilse within the hour. He would apologize. Confess he loved her. He would go to Germany with her, if she wanted. Yes. He needed to see more of the world. He could do that—

If only his body would move faster, but running had become more onerous. His legs were mush; his knee joints kept slipping. His face was so hot his head was jumping, and he constantly had to wipe the sweat from his eyes. It was as much as he could do to keep breathing. Alleyway. Castlegate. If he carried on like this he might have a stroke before he found Ilse Brauchmann—

'Excuse me, sir? Do you have a moment?' Four women in little box hats descended on him, asking if he would care to sample a new scent.

Down to the right. Across the road – he was almost there.

As Frank took the corner of Unity Street, he saw black clouds and smelt something bitter.

Maud was coming towards him, her mouth agape, her face grimy. Behind her there were flames, wreaths of smoke, flakes falling through the air like black snow. The noise was extraordinary. People ran with buckets of water, yelling at one another. Blackened boxes lay strewn down the street and yet another person seemed to have landed on the pavement.

'Frank! Frank! Where have you *been*?'

The music shop was on fire.

38

Hallelujah

I*T WAS THE handbrake, the policewoman told him. The handbrake.*

She had to keep repeating it because he was shaking so hard, he couldn't hear the words. They wouldn't seem to stick to the part of his brain where words went to make sense.

Peg had pulled over on the cliff edge to watch the sunset.

Hit the earth like a falling planet.

The policewoman drove him to the hospital where Peg lay corpse-still, laced up to machinery, an array of bottles suspended above her head. The blue respirator tube poked from her mouth. He kept waiting for it to blow smoke.

He remained beside her. Every day, every night. He had no idea where else to put himself. He fetched drinks from the vending machine, and failed to lift them to his mouth. It was as though his body had forgotten how to be a body. And presumably Peg's had forgotten too, because three weeks later she died. A nurse gave him Peg's clothes in a bag, along with a tissue to blow his nose.

Then came the news.

'Charity?'

'Yes,' the lawyer repeated. 'Charity.' He read out the list again. A sanctuary for women, a children's home, a musicians' trust, the local church, the local hospital, a society for the protection of endangered butterflies. It went on and on.

'In the white house?'

'I beg your pardon?'

'These people will be living with me in the white house?'

Patiently the lawyer explained all over again. In her will, Peg had made a provision leaving her extensive record collection to Frank. But everything else – his home, in fact – she had left to charity. Hundreds of people would benefit from her estate.

'But what about me?'

'I beg your pardon?'

'I'm her son.'

The lawyer apologized. He couldn't answer that. It was certainly an unusual arrangement but the will was bona fide. It would take a while for all the paper-work to be settled; until then Frank was welcome to stay. 'To be honest,' the lawyer said, 'the place will be sold for redevelopment.' Apparently she had also requested the 'Hallelujah Chorus' at her cremation.

When the day came, Frank dressed in his only black jacket and spent the morning in the pub. By the time he got to the crematorium, it was packed. Standing room only. The funeral director spoke in rhyming couplets about God and gardens and Peg being a flower. She seemed an utter stranger. He announced the 'Hallelujah Chorus', and the music hit Frank like a wallop to his insides. When it got to the final pause before the end, it was too much. He felt overcome. He had to stagger out for air.

There were pictures a few days later in the paper. CROWDS MOURN THE LOSS OF LOCAL BENEFACTRESS.

Peg didn't get a turnout of three thousand, like Handel. She didn't get a state funeral like Beethoven. But at least she had music at the end. At least there was a crowd. She did better than Vivaldi.

It took a year to complete the paperwork. Frank stayed in the white house. He drove into town and did odd jobs – sweeping leaves, cleaning windows – to scrape enough cash together to buy a flat. He stopped looking after himself. Smoked a fair bit of weed. Any relationships he tried failed. Usually he couldn't even get it up.

Then one morning he noticed a woman down on the beach. She was plump, nothing special to look at, but there was something engaging about her. She sat with towels and a picnic while her little boy threw stones at the waves.

'You don't recognize me, do you?'

'Deb?'

He hadn't seen her for seven years.

She made a space beside her and he sat. She offered him a jam sandwich, cut into a triangle. She waved at her boy and told him not to go too close to the water.

'How old is he?'

'Three now.'

'Are you—?'

'Happy? Yes. I am. I'm really happy, Frank.'

He took a bite of his sandwich. It was sweet and soft in his mouth. Despite the wind on the beach and the cold, suddenly he felt wrapped up and safe, as if someone had put a coat on him and done up the buttons. The feeling was entirely new to him and now that he had it, he was desperate not to let go.

'Mummy!' yelled her little boy.

'Look at you!' she shouted back. 'Aren't you the clever one?' She blew him a kiss. 'Aren't you my best?' It was tender and easy.

She turned back to Frank. 'I heard about Peg's accident. I'm really sorry. I know how much you loved her.'

His throat felt full of stones. There was no accounting for the loneliness that yawned open inside him. He said, 'Yes, well. It turned out I wasn't enough.'

It was supposed to be a joke at his own expense but neither of them laughed. Such a great big man and he felt barren.

'I am sorry, Deb,' he said. 'I think I let you down.' He couldn't eat any more sandwich. He could only look.

She reached out her hand. 'Let's face it, Frank. With a mother like Peg, you were never going to be ordinary. You were never going to love like the rest of us. It's probably in your genes.'

It was supposed to be another joke, but this one keeled over, same as the first.

He thought of the sweater she had knitted, the way she once stroked his hair. All those normal things. The distance between him and the rest of the world was immeasurable. Above him, a single gull sailed on the wind.

That night he packed his van.

Gone first thing.

39

Two Swans

IT WAS LIKE being dispossessed all over again. Years ago, he had lost the white house by the sea, but compared to this, it was nothing.

The heat met him like a slap. Tongues of flame darted from the counter, the central unit and those to the left. The old Persian runner was a river of fire. He began to retch almost as soon as he was inside. His eyes felt scraped.

All around him there were shelves blazing, boxes of vinyl like incinerators. The fire had practically run out of things to do. Water and broken glass swished at his feet. Then at the far end a knuckle of flame punched through the door of one of the listening booths and as it went up, dry as a match, the varnish blistered and the mother-of-pearl birds cracked open, and the whole thing was swallowed. Above it, the ceiling opened with a groan, sending out an orange rain of sparks. The second booth went up in flames, followed by his turntable. Frank tried to rescue the nearest crate of vinyl, stooping to grab it with his hands; it leapt alight even as he touched it. That for some reason was the thing that confounded him, not the pain, but the familiar box of records, one he had so carefully arranged and loved for all those years, now apparently intent on wounding him. Father Anthony pulled him roughly by the arm and the next thing he knew he was coughing his guts up on the pavement.

Frank's injuries were minor. A few small burns and cuts to his hands. But Kit, who had been working the shrink-wrap machine when it burst into flames, was taken to hospital.

He cried as they lifted him on to a stretcher. 'Frank, I'm so sorry. I'm so sorry. I didn't mean it. I was trying to get something right for once . . .' Tears squeezed from his eyes and made tracks down his dirty face. 'Will you ring my mum? She needs to take her pills. Dad will be asleep, you see.'

It was the smell that people remembered. For months to come, they would complain. Not just the smell when you passed the derelict shop, with its caved-in roof and smashed windows, but another one, a ghost of a smell, a bitterness, that seemed to have infiltrated the walls and windows of Unity Street, and crept inside drawers and cupboards. When the wind blew, a fine grey coating of dust covered everything. You couldn't even hang out your washing any more, one woman said. It was worse than the stench of cheese and onion.

In September, several more families moved out. There were boarded-up houses either side of Mrs Roussos, though kids pulled down the fencing surrounding the old bombsite and once again it became a playground. England's Glory served its last pint and pickled egg in October. Father Anthony's gift shop closed a week later. He put a sign in the window: *Thank you to all my customers for the years of pleasure you have given me.* Beside it, he left a folded paper bird.

But Maud was wrong about one thing. She was not finished in the summer, as she had predicted that day in January when the air was kind of blue, and Ilse Brauchmann came. There was fog in November, rain and wind in December, a day or two of snow. By the end of the year, Unity Street was a line of boarded-up homes and shops. Fort Development tried repeatedly to buy out the tattoo artist but she wouldn't budge, and neither would old Mrs Roussos. By '89, they were the only ones left. Kit's posters still hung at some of the empty windows. SAY NO TO FORT DEVELOPMENT!!

Maud saw Frank from time to time. Despite the irreparable damage to his shop, he kept trading. At first, he set up a table outside on the pavement, selling off what had been saved from the fire; at that point he was still trying to pay back his overdraft. Collectors drove over to see if he had anything worthwhile, but mostly people just dropped by to hang out with him and talk music. When he sold the shop to Fort Development, it was for a pittance. And he had no insurance, of course – he'd failed to send off the renewal. His friend Henry tried to talk him into applying for another loan but Frank was having none of it. Maud suggested he should live with her, but he shrugged and smiled and told her he needed a break from Unity Street. She met him another time drinking tinnies outside the clock tower and repeated her offer. He looked more tired now. Fragile.

'I'll come over later,' he said.

She cleaned out the spare room. She switched on the fairy lights in her little garden. She made a casserole and set out glasses. Paper napkins.

She waited all night and the bastard didn't show up.

She tipped the meal into the bin, dish and all, followed by the stupid napkins.

Next time she caught sight of him, it was about a year after the fire, and he was selling records down the alleyway by the cathedral, where people laid out their personal possessions on a blanket. He had a line of 7-inch singles, nothing else. He was with quite a few men and women, though none of them looked especially steady on their feet. One had a big quiff. She had a feeling she recognized him from years back; who-ever he was, he was hugging Frank a lot and falling over a lot and she didn't much like him. She wouldn't have said Frank seemed especially unhappy and if she was honest, she felt angry. He didn't spot her.

The last time Maud saw Frank it was November. She was going to meet a friend when she noticed him, this great big man, alone in the park on a bench by the lake. He was wearing the old suede jacket she knew, but it was more torn at the shoulder. She sat with him for a while. Asked once again if she could do anything to help.

He smiled. 'I'm OK. Thanks.'

So she talked about the first time he found her a record. How she'd asked for heavy metal and instead he'd played her Adagio for Strings. She described being in the little dark booth, like hiding in a cupboard when she was a kid; the music pouring through her veins like water, bringing her back to life. 'It was magic,' she said. 'You made real magic, Frank.'

He laughed as if they were talking about someone he had never met, but thought he might quite like if he did.

Mid-afternoon and it was getting dark. The ghost of a mist hung above the lake; two pleasure boats drifted side by side, like swans.

She said, 'Frank? I'm cold. I'm going now. Do you wanna come?'

He didn't answer. He just sat gazing at the two empty boats.

She left him to it.

SIDE D: 2009

40

The Four Seasons

2009. THE INTERNATIONAL year of astronomy, natural fibres, reconciliation and the gorilla. Also, as it happens, the two hundred and fiftieth anniversary of Handel's death. There are mobile phones, iPods. There is Facebook, YouTube, Napster, iTunes, Friends Reunited. Sales of digital music have overtaken CDs. Woolworths has gone. So have Tower Records, Our Price and hundreds of small independent record shops. Like vinyl before it, like cassette tapes too, the CD is on its last legs.

And yet music is everywhere. Supermarkets, shopping malls, subways. Pubs, restaurants, lifts, hospitals. Phone the bank, and she gets an orchestral rendition of 'Yesterday' as she waits for a connection. Even her dentist plays music. Bach once; the *Goldberg Variations* while he gave her a filling. Whenever she takes the bus, all she can hear is the thud of music from the headphones on the person next to her.

In a small suburb of Munich, Ilse Brauchmann shops in Lidl. There is not much she wants, just a loaf of bread, a few slices of ham, as well as something for tomorrow. It always surprises her, how empty her shopping baskets are next to everyone else's great big trolleys, how few things she seems to need. She is dressed in a green coat, green-and-white scarf, swingy trousers and nice shoes. Her hair is chin-length, silver strands threaded through the black, but these days she wears it in a bone comb that was her mother's. It still has a tendency to dangle or flick without warning.

It's a cold autumn day. The sky is a wedge of cloud that doesn't want to shift. She exchanges greetings with a few locals. They know about her working life (violin teacher). They know she has no children of her own but many godchildren whom she frequently drops everything to look after. People know she is happy, not badly off. (They don't need to ask that question. She is well dressed, even for a trip to Lidl.) Her own apartment, it turned out, was worth a fortune when she put it on the market. The once-poor quarter had turned into a very desirable one.

People like it when she tells them things, in small portions, and they think they know her, but they do not, they cannot possibly understand all the decisions she has made, the choices that have turned her into the woman they see today. The things she has left. The people she has loved. And there have been many. Several long-term relationships, lots more short-haul ones. Holiday romances. Flirtations. One-night flings. An affair that overstayed its welcome. Oh, the tall dark-haired men in great big jackets! They were her undoing.

The supermarket is so vast it weaves her into a daze. She keeps forgetting why she's here. So instead of the delicatessen, she finds herself in a long aisle staring at dental products. Toothbrushes, mouthwashes, specialist toothpaste, floss tape and picks. That's when she hears it. The 'Four Seasons'. The concerto called Spring.

It's thin over the system, but Ilse freezes. She feels desperate to hear the birds. She is barely breathing, she wants it so much. At the same

260

time a particularly large young man with wild brown hair thunders past, grabs any old tube of toothpaste, and then crashes straight into her.

Ilse has never been overweight. Not even when she returned suddenly to Germany in June '88 and indulged in what her mother called a period of comfort eating. Not even when her father died in hospital in '89 and that summer she went on holiday with her mother to Italy, where they ate pasta and attended concerts in churches every night. Yes, she gained a little extra ring of flesh around her tummy in her forties, some wing-like flappy bits she would prefer not to have at the tops of her arms, but she still fits a size ten; she has certainly never floored another human being. Nevertheless, on bumping into her, this great big young man shrieks, jumps backwards, trips over his own feet, and keels over.

'What happened? Are you OK?'

She is on her knees without noticing herself going down. He lies very still. A floored giant. Arms at his sides. Great big trainers poked upwards.

And what does she do? Hearing Vivaldi in the middle of Lidl? Beside toothpaste, both the special whitening and also striped fluoride varieties? Staring into the face of a young man with hair so wild you could lose things in there?

She bursts into tears.

'Oh my God,' he says. 'I'm sorry. Did I hurt you?'

The young man seems to have sat up.

'No, I'm fine. You just – I am fine. I really am.'

She offers her hand to help him but he mistakes this as a need for assistance and scrambles to his knees, then back to full height. Stooping over her, he puts out his palm and guides her to her feet.

She remembers a lake, twenty-one years ago. Moonlight on the water, like a hundred pins, swinging this way and that. Meanwhile Vivaldi's birds swoop between the shelves of Lidl—

'Are you OK now?' he asks.

'Yes.' She does her best to pull her face in order. 'You?'

'Yeah, I'm fine.' He laughs. 'See you, then.'

She watches him shambling towards the end of the aisle.

This still happens occasionally, even after all this time. She spots Frank inside a doorway, waiting for the right opportunity to step out and say, *Well there you are, hello!* Now and then she sees him lumber down an alley or turn a street corner, or maybe he is just a tall, broad-shouldered figure drinking tea in a café. She might be staring at a window, and there he is, his mirror-reflection shining beside hers. Or she crosses a road and suddenly believes – no, she *knows* – he is cross-ing one too. Sometimes he has a wife, sometimes he has kids, once he was driving the car behind hers, another time he was across a crowded room at a party, simply gazing at her with such great hope it took her breath away. If she approaches, he withdraws – it is not him, of course, it is some other man – leaving her with nothing but the vacant space inside her. Frank is a ghost that is permanently waiting, if not directly in her eyeline, then just on the periphery. Not that she has ever told anyone. Why would she? He is her skin and bone, he is her secret. He always was.

After all, she is not the only person who carries her heart in a suitcase. Several girlfriends – marriages on the rocks, children off to university – have discovered that what they need is not in the present, and not in the future either, but left behind somewhere in the past. A few friends use Friends Reunited to link up with old mates from college. Others use

Facebook. One has recently started dating her first boyfriend, whom she hadn't seen since they were teenagers. Another is thinking about moving back to her hometown.

'*Guten Tag.*'

The girl at the till is kind. Ilse has been living in her mother's apartment for less than a year but she always waits in this girl's queue, even if it's longer than the others. She can't be more than eighteen and she has a ring through her nose that makes Ilse sad for some reason, but she never fails to say something nice as she scans her customers' groceries, little encouraging things like 'Oh, that looks delicious,' or 'I think I might buy that too,' so that people feel good about the way they live their lives and the things they choose from supermarket shelves in order to fill them.

Ilse tries to pack her shopping into bags but her hands are stiff today – the weather doesn't help – and she's busy thinking of Frank, and she makes a complete mess of the job.

'It's the time of year,' says the till girl. 'It's always bad for people at this time of year.' She glances at Ilse's shopping. 'You're on your own? That's right?'

'I came back a year ago to nurse my mother. She died four months ago.'

'That's sad.'

'It is. I miss her.' Though the worst part was holding the hand of a woman who looked in her eyes and had no idea who she was. It was like a living death, infinitely longer and more bewildering than the moment her mother simply gazed at her and then stopped breathing. Nevertheless she wishes it was as easy as that, that she could just say she missed her mother, and that would be the end of it. Truth is, she has never felt so lonely. Whole days can pass without her uttering so much as a word. Not that her mother had said anything recently that would prompt a conversation, apart from the odd moan, the odd delightful and unexplained trickle of laughter – but at least there were the nurses to talk to, or someone else also visiting a relative. Now she is parentless, she feels strangely exposed and heroic. As if she has been called to step next into the firing line.

But the nice girl is still talking. 'Do you have a dog?'

'A what?'

'A dog can help.'

Ilse says no, she doesn't have a dog. She packs one onion in her bag as well as a half-litre of milk. She covers them with a lettuce.

'Some people like you have a dog. It keeps them active.'

'I'm fifty-one,' says Ilse.

'Yes,' says the girl; she doesn't seem to have heard. She is talking about a Pekinese or a poodle. Better still, these days you can get a cross-breed. A Pekinese that is also a poodle. They are nice, those little dogs. They sit on your lap. You can buy them outfits on the internet, little jackets and hats and things. You can carry them in your handbag to the park. That way you can meet other people who also have little dogs. It's good to get out. All this from a sweet young girl with a ring through her nose. She doesn't look as if she's stepped outside in months, let alone visited a park with a tiny cross-breed in her handbag.

'But I don't want to go to the park,' says Ilse. 'I don't want a dog.' She spots him again, the very large young man she floored earlier. He is at the next till, digging through his pockets for loose change in order to pay for his toothpaste. Spotting her, he grins and waves before he lollops off to the entrance where a young woman in a miniskirt is waiting. Ilse guesses he tells his girlfriend about the accident because she reaches up and touches his hair and kisses his forehead. It's such a small gesture, but infinitely tender, infinitely familiar. The girl would find him even in a crowd, even with a blindfold on her.

'Shall I put your cold meats in a separate bag?'

The girl is waiting for Ilse to reply. Other people are waiting too – a couple behind her, dressed in Mr and Mrs quilted jackets, as well as an old man slowly packing his own little bag of groceries at the next till. So is this her future, then? Single baskets, a bit of lettuce, and meals for one?

'I have to go back.'

'Go back?' says the girl. 'Have you lost something?' She presses her buzzer for assistance.

'England,' Ilse Brauchmann announces to the queue. 'I have to go back *now*.'

Once she has made the decision, it seems simple. So ordinary and straightforward, she can't believe it has taken her twenty-one years. But she still forgets. These days you can do anything. You can have a thought – angry, needy, ecstatic, blasphemous, no matter what – and it can be out there within a second; you don't even have to think about your thought. You can simply have it and be done. Next thought, please.

She buys her air ticket online. She checks in, chooses her seat and prints off her boarding pass. She throws things in a wheelie suitcase – now she has made her decision, she is impatient to be gone. Enough for four nights and English rain. She emails several friends, telling them not to worry, she has to go away for a few days. She flicks through her diary and contacts all her pupils for the week, explaining the same thing, and adding her most sincere apologies. She knocks on the doors of both neighbours but there is no answer. Instead she leaves them each a note – *I have been called away on business.* She signs her name, *Ilse Brauchmann*, and then adds that she is her mother's daughter in case they have forgotten.

By six o'clock, she is on a plane to England. Half past nine, she is in a hire car. Ring road after ring road. Warehouses like hangars. A landfill site the size of a hill. Clouds of gulls. Vast glass towers rising in the docklands area.

She recognizes none of it.

'Is it a special occasion?' asks the woman at reception.

'*Bitte?*'

The receptionist explains again. Not in German or indeed any other European language. Just a little bit louder and slower, as if Ilse is not standing immediately in front of the desk, but beside the decorative wall of water that falls endlessly on the other side of the hotel atrium.

Now that she is here, Ilse's English is taking a little while to wake up. Also, she can't help wondering if Frank will just appear. As if by magic. Her heart leaps about like a thing with strings. It's enough to make anyone forget their vocabulary.

The receptionist asks for a third time if she is here for a special occasion.

'What kind of special occasion?'

The receptionist consults the screen of her computer. She wears a blue neck-scarf to show that she is not just an ordinary member of the public who has wandered in off the street, but a fully paid and extremely helpful member of staff.

She runs through the options.

Is Ilse celebrating a) a birthday, b) a wedding anniversary, or c) a honeymoon? Or is she here in d) a business capacity? Ilse apologizes; she is just here to find someone. Would it make any difference to the price, she asks, if she were here for any of the other reasons? Again the receptionist consults her computer.

There is a) the birthday package – free helium balloon – there is b) and c) a wedding package – petals and a half-bottle of Prosecco. There is also d) a business and spa treatment package, particularly aimed at women of a certain age. No balloon; no petals either. But you do get the half-bottle, which you can exchange for a full bottle of fizzy water, as well as complimentary use of the gym.

Ilse asks for a double room with a view, please. Four nights.

Would she like an upgrade?

Why would she want an upgrade?

It's a quiet time of year. The receptionist can offer a very nice executive suite with two double beds and a seating area, offering a panoramic view. Ilse takes it. She hasn't had a holiday in years.

From her window she can almost see the whole city. Thousands of tiny lights tremble and flash and move at her feet. The sky tonight is just an empty old thing that vaguely glows orange; it's got nothing on the humans.

Her suite is the size of her mother's apartment. The two beds are so vast she could lie on them widthways and still not flop over the edge. The separate seating area might house a family, and the bathroom has facilities to shower, bath and also – should she feel the need – press a pair of trousers. She hangs her clothes in the wardrobe, unpacks her toiletries; they barely graze the space. When she checks her phone, there are already two excited texts from girlfriends. *'Where are you?'* *'What's going on, IB?'* Afterwards she orders a late dinner in the restaurant – tables of single diners, mostly men. But, faced with food, even a bowl of soup, she can't eat.

There's a familiar smell she can't put her finger on. It's only as she enters the glass-fronted lift that she gets it.

Cheese and onion.

41

Unity Street

NINE O'CLOCK IN the morning; Ilse Brauchmann parks on Unity Street. She's so nervous she hits the kerb.

So here she is, standing once more beside the parade of shops where she found herself long ago, gazing at Frank for the first time with her hands cupped to the window. She had only been in England for three days. She could barely afford a hot meal and she was staying in a hostel where people shouted all night. She knew, the moment she spotted him, that her life was about to be overturned. No wonder she passed out.

The shops are all boarded up – the old bakery, the florist, Articles of Faith (it has dropped some letters. It's now 'tiles of Fat'), the undertakers and the tattoo parlour. Even the big pub on the corner is shuttered. Graffiti everywhere, peeling paint and broken windows; though it's likely squatters live above Maud's old place because there are sheets of cardboard at the window, and a milk carton on the ledge. It's the empty music shop that leaves her reeling. The external brickwork is relatively intact but blackened and charred all over, the stain of soot exploding around the windows. It's impossible to see inside. Where there was glass there are only boards. A buddleia has decided it would be nice to grow out of what is left of the roof. A *fire*? Two pigeons emerge with a great clattering of wings from an upstairs window. When did this happen?

And what about Fort Development? The parade has *For Sale* signs nailed all over it. The old bombsite at the end has been tarmacked but it still looks like a bombsite; buddleia pushes through, lifting the tarmac like so much dead skin, along with mounds of rubbish and old household junk, and notices warning NO FLY TIPPING.

NF POWER. GO HOME. EAT DA RICH.

She shivers.

Despite the abandoned parade on one side, the terraced houses on Unity Street have done themselves up a bit. Some have loft extensions and they all wear satellite dishes like hard hats. Front gardens – small as they are – have been landscaped with a shrub or two, a strip of gravel for extra parking. Someone has erected a plastic gazebo, someone else has parked a motor home. For the first time in many years, she thinks about Mrs Roussos and wonders what happened to her. Her house has matching blue blinds now, pulled down halfway, like a set of sleepy, made-up eyes. From an upstairs window, a line of soft toys seem to be admiring the view.

Ilse asks in a newsagent's around the corner if the owner knew a man called Frank who ran a music shop. The owner says he doesn't. Does he know anything about a fire on Unity Street? He doesn't. A large woman with a shopping basket containing nothing but packets of biscuits says she heard something once about a load of vinyl going up in flames, but not about a record shop. They suggest she should try the 24-hour cash and carry. So Ilse tries the cash and carry and the young man at the till – fifteen if he's a day – says he had no idea there was once a record shop

270

round here – 'What, it sold like actual records? That must have been *sick*.' So there we go. That is the end of that line of enquiry.

Now that she is away from the docklands development, she sees how poor and grey this city still is. Other places in the world have got smarter and moved on, but there is a forgottenness here. Bar the small pockets of gentrification, everything is pretty much the same as it was in 1988. A man asleep in a doorway in broad daylight. A group of junkies. Three young men with muzzled dogs. A girl passed out on a bench. You wouldn't want to be out on your own at night.

She returns to Unity Street. Knocks on a few doors. Her head is beginning to hurt, right between the eyes, like a nail being twisted. She asks several passers-by – a man walking his dog, two boys with so many piercings they look upholstered. No one knew there was a music shop here, and they certainly never heard of a guy called Frank. A man says he heard there was a fire here once, and someone had to go to hospital. So does anyone know who owns these shops? 'People used to say the council were gonna knock that street down,' says another woman. 'They were gonna build a massive car park. But then the developer went bust. Loads of people lost their savings. You could buy those houses for nothing.'

Ilse asks if anyone is in touch with a tattooist called Maud? She would be about fifty now. No one has heard of her either. When Ilse asks about the religious gift shop, a man downright laughs. Maybe try online, he tells her, if you want to get weird shit like that. She makes her way back to Castlegate, asking people as she passes. It's the same each time. No one has heard of Frank or a music shop. Her face hurts with all the smiling she's had to put it through.

She realizes it must be lunchtime. She buys a sandwich but she still can't eat. She sits on a bench on Castlegate, beside a small temporary merry-go-round.

Not even her close friends know the truth about her six months in England. They knew at the time about Richard, of course, and the broken engagement – several told her she was a fool. They had no idea about her love for an English man who talked to her once a week about music. When he rejected her, it was more than she could bear; it hurt far too much to tell it. Besides, if you don't say something for long enough, it begins to seal over. A part of yourself that only exists in storage. You could probably leave it all your life. Boxed away. Just as she had once done with music.

That afternoon Ilse searches the entire city by foot. Castlegate, alleyways, pedestrianized areas, residential streets, the cathedral. The 2008 recession has taken its toll. Many shop windows are empty. FINAL REDUCTIONS. CLOSING DOWN! EVERYTHING MUST GO! WE WOULD LIKE TO THANK OUR CUSTOMERS. Where there was once a Woolworths, there is an empty warehouse selling cut-price pine furniture. A big bookshop has closed. So has a women's boutique. There is no butcher on the corner, no fruit and veg shop, no fishmonger. Not that she has thought of these places in twenty-one years, but now they are gone, she feels the loss of them as if they have been taken from her by stealth. They have been replaced mostly with charity shops, pawnshops and mobile phone outlets. *Bargain Booze. USA Chicken.*

It is the park that hits hardest. The bandstand is surrounded by fencing and pictures of a nasty dog. (KEEP OUT.) All around it, the grass is littered with butts and cans and needles. There is no sign of the pleasure boats on the lake. The water is clogged with old rubbish – a mattress, black carrier bags floating like bodies, bottles, car parts.

She sits alone on a broken bench, looking and looking. People talk about a stone in your throat, but this is like swallowing them one after another. When she finally makes her way back through the park, the dusk is already making flat, dangerous shapes of the bare trees.

There were coloured lights here once.

Back at the hotel, the person staying in the next room has the television so loud, Ilse can hear every word. She washes and undresses with a strange apathy. Now that she is here again, a sort of dullness steals through her, and the part of her that began the journey excited, keyed to a high pitch, exists no longer. She barely has the strength or inclination to take off her shoes.

What did she imagine would happen? That she could hurry back and everything would be the same? How could she have been so naïve? Or so full of hope? A day has gone, and what has she found? That no one knows anything about Frank or any of the other shops on the parade. That things change and move on, and often – it would seem – get worse. Over twenty-one years she has grown used to missing Frank. It's a thing she carries about with her, so familiar, so worn to fit the shape of her, it's like a little strap around her wrist; she can go months without noticing it. Now she feels his absence with a kind of hollowing panic that makes her weak. She should pack up in the morning. Go home. Do something useful with her life before it's too late—

Home? Where is that now? Her mother's apartment? She pictures a glass shelf in an old mahogany cabinet, lined with little porcelain boys and girls that her mother spent a lifetime collecting – shepherdesses in skirts and their amours in frock coats. So is this what life is? The steady amassing of little things, trinkets, small prettinesses, that we save for

273

and plan for, and which make the passing of time more meaningful, and yet which – come the end – will be wrapped in newspaper and driven to the charity shop?

She lies with her head against the radio and listens to a woman's voice, which is sometimes lost but emerges again, speaking Russian maybe, and then blends with two hands playing a piano. Chopin? Bill Evans? She never catches enough of it to know. When she wakes in the morning, only a faint crackle comes from the loudspeaker and she imagines to herself that the voice she heard has a life of its own which she can catch but never keep. She tries to find the same station, moving the dial so slowly she barely moves it at all, but there is no trace of the Russian woman and her friend the piano player. Like the shops on Unity Street, like the people who ran them, like their customers and all those people who loved vinyl, who loved talking about this and that, nothing in particular, they are ghosts—

Well, that's no excuse.

There are fifteen salons listed on the receptionist's computer. She scrolls through them one by one. In 1988, Ilse thought the only people with tattoos were bikers, prison inmates, men who liked heavy metal – and Maud. Now, it turns out, everyone wants them.

'Are you sure she's still here?' asks the receptionist. 'A lot of shops have gone, you know.'

No, Ilse is not sure. But if anyone was going to survive from that little bunch of shopkeepers, she has a hunch it would be Maud.

She drives all over the city, with the printed list of tattoo salons on the passenger seat. She meets young men and women, with colourful arms like sleeves. She speaks to several with shaved heads and beautiful symbols of love and peace tattooed where other people would just do something ordinary and grow hair. One old man shows how, when he flexes his pectoral muscles, two bluebirds on his chest flap their wings. She ends up buying coffee for a woman inked all over with hearts and words like *Pax* and *Happy*, who is, without a shadow of a doubt, the saddest person she has ever met. But no one has heard of a tattooist in her fifties called Maud.

'There *was* a woman,' pipes up a young blue man. 'She ran a salon in the nineties. Down a dead-end street. I don't know what I did to upset her but she told me once to fuck off. She runs a flower shop, near Castlegate. It's real posh—'

Ilse is already running for her car.

'*You?*'

Maud appears to be speechless. She stands with a bunch of chrysan-themums in one hand, and a dangerous knife in the other.

Her shop is cold, the interior more like a warehouse; a contemporary mix of glass, exposed brickwork, grey and steel. It's the last kind of shop Ilse would expect to find in this city. There are notices on slate boards – *Flowers of the day* – and bouquets arranged in stark, unusual ways which somehow make the blooms more spectacular, as if you have not seen things like roses and lilies before. A bouquet of olive branches and rust-brown dahlias; pink peonies with blooms like tissue paper held in a cone of willow twigs. From the walls hang wreaths made with scarlet chillies, twists of paper, apple rings. One sprouts fine wisps of blue wire like a Catherine wheel. '*You?*' she repeats. 'What do *you* want?'

For reasons she cannot begin to explain, what Ilse would most like is to hug Maud.

Instead she explains all over again. About her career as a violin teacher, about moving into her mother's apartment to nurse her, and then selling her own when her mother died. About hearing Vivaldi in Lidl and deciding to come back. About looking for Frank—

All the while, three shopgirls with smart aprons watch Maud and Ilse with a look of utter confusion.

'Don't just stand there,' snaps Maud. 'Go and do something useful.'

They scarper out the back.

Maud has changed. Her Mohican mane is now a geometric brown bob, greying above the ears and around the temples. She no longer dresses as a bad fairy. Instead she wears a charcoal-grey linen tabard over jeans, and brown lace-up boots. Patches of skin are still blue, though it is pink around her neck and hands.

'I had some of them removed,' says Maud, noticing Ilse's confusion. 'It was getting to the point where everyone had a tattoo.'

She seems to have focused her attention on her nails instead. They are long, filed to a point, and painted with swirls and stripes. Maud flashes her fingers a lot, like someone with a new engagement ring. She clearly likes those nails.

No engagement ring, though.

Maud explains everything she knows about Frank, and that is very little. 'Basically, he lost everything and refused help.' She hasn't heard about him since the mid-nineties. Maud finally sold her salon in 2000. Went away to college to learn floristry and then invested her money in this shop. She runs an online business. Deliveries. Big weddings. Corporate stuff.

'I saw Frank's shop. What happened?'

Maud softens a little, or at least she puts down her knife. She tells Ilse about the blaze that started the day the shrink-wrap machine caught fire. Ilse has not thought of the thing in years, but now that it is back in her mind, it is so real she feels she could reach out a hand and touch it. Smell it.

Maud sighs. 'Kit was badly burnt. Frank felt awful about that. I don't know what happened to Kit afterwards. I thought I saw his photo once in the paper but I guess I was wrong.'

And so Ilse learns what happened the day Frank walked away from her. She learns that he lost everything and tried to keep going for a while and then gave up. 'He'd got it all wrong about CDs. He hated the way everyone kept buying them. It seems so crazy now; no one wants CDs. But at the time it made him difficult. I heard he got involved with some dodgy people. The last time I saw him he was down in the park.'

'Did he say anything?'

'No.'

Ilse listens in a kind of dream. None of this holds reality. She realizes she has not taken a proper new breath in minutes.

'It's a long time ago now. He could be dead.'

After everything else, it's a punch to the stomach. Ilse gasps.

'No,' she murmurs. 'No. I can't believe that. No.'

Maud's voice jolts her back to the present. She asks if Ilse would like to see inside the shop? She's got a spare key.

By the time they're in Unity Street, it's getting dark again.

The music shop stinks of mould and cold and piss. Maud moves the white cone of light from her mobile phone, showing Ilse the damage. The turntable that crossed the back wall is a charred plank on the floor. The booths have gone. The counter too. The floor shifts beneath her feet; a dense wad of broken vinyl, dust, plaster, ash and glass. The walls are black. Someone has been using it as a shelter; in the corner there are bottles, cans, takeaway food boxes, an old sleeping bag. There is even an upturned shopping trolley, stuffed with a blanket and a baseball bat.

'You see?' says Maud. 'There's really nothing here. You see?'

Ilse feels so cold, she begins to shake. She clenches her fists to keep from crying. She tells herself it will pass, this feeling, it is only another moment, she need not stay with it, and briefly she succeeds, she thinks I am not hurt, I have money, I have food. But then the sorrow grips her again and it is like being occupied from the inside out. She has no idea how she will ever get over it.

In yet another café, Maud fetches mugs of tea. She seems uneasy. A blend of formal and kind. She snatches a packet of cigarettes from her pocket, swears and puts it away again. 'I bloody hate the new laws about smoking.' She searches for Nicorettes. 'Do you still—?'

'No. I never really did. I just smoked when I was with Frank.'

Maud shows Ilse a photograph on her phone of the thatched cottage where she lives. It takes her forty minutes to drive in. She strokes the image on her screen, like something she loves.

'Is there anyone else?'

'How do you mean?'

'The Williams brothers? Father Anthony? Mrs Roussos?'

The Williams brothers died a few months after moving out of Unity Street. Within a fortnight of each other. It was probably as well. Fort Development went bust and the people who had invested in them lost everything. Frank had been right; the whole thing was a scam. As for

Mrs Roussos? Maud does something uncharacteristic; she laughs. The old lady kept going for years. Died in '99. 'You wouldn't believe how many people turned up for her funeral. The last I heard, Father Anthony was in a home but if he's still alive he'd be in his eighties. I'm the only one left.' She checks the time on her phone. She needs to get back to her shop.

At the door of the café Maud briefly holds Ilse. It's an odd sensation. Not comforting as such; more like meeting a piece of armour. 'Safe journey home. Sometimes it's best if you move on. This city always was a dead end.'

As Ilse walks away, she has to take deep breaths in order not to cry. A man in a doorway asks her for money and – thinking of Frank – she empties her purse.

'God bless you,' he shouts. 'God bless you.'

His voice follows her the length of the street, like a piece of rope, pulling her back.

It occurs to her she has been searching for Frank in all the wrong places.

She visits pubs down by the docks, she approaches people selling the *Big Issue*. She stops people at bus stops, she asks at a refuge centre and an all-night kitchen. By 8 p.m., she has been to the cash point and emptied her purse all over again. She has listened to a woman telling her about the day her husband simply disappeared. She has been laughed at, shouted at, followed, ignored, passed by, bumped into. On more than two occasions she has felt pure white terror. Smoke lifts from the chimneys of the food factory. Her feet hurt like stings.

No one knows anything about Frank, or even a man who wanted to help other people find music.

'Sounds like a guy in a film,' someone laughs.

It is as though he never existed.

42

Last Night a DJ Saved My Life

ILSE LIES FULLY clothed on her bed at the hotel. She has no idea what time it is. She just lies watching the black square of window, lit up by thousands of tiny lights. Thoughts come to her and they are not so much words as things. Shapes. The air is so still, it seems as if every-thing has been taken away and there is only this unsettling feeling of something mislaid that shouldn't be. This absence.

It is already her third night in England. All day, she has lost Frank, only to find him and lose him all over again. There is no guarantee that just because you are ready to go back and claim something, it will be there. She tries to tune the radio into the woman's voice that she heard the night before, and her friend at the piano, but even they have aban-doned her. Instead she ends up with the local radio station. She listens to a phone-in chat show ('*Late Night Surger-y!*' the jingle sings every fifteen minutes) where ordinary people ring and talk about their problems and a DJ suggests ways to deal with them. Something about the programme is familiar and she listens with the volume turned very low so that she has to keep really still in order to hear. It is as if she already knows these stories – a man who can't sleep at night, a woman who can't make up her mind whether to leave her husband. The DJ makes zippy 'Mm mm' noises as he listens and then he gives unlikely advice to his callers like 'Try sleeping on the other side of the bed,' and 'Listen, lady, that man of yours sounds like bad nooooze.' He has a phoney American accent and a lot of enthusiasm. He plays records that affirm his message. Ilse thinks she will find him irritating but actually she finds herself more and more enchanted. There is something irrepressibly good-natured about him. He keeps repeating the phone number of the radio station and reminding his listeners to call the Late Night Surgery about whatever they like. Then out of the blue there's a terrible clunk – a direct assault to her ear – and he says, 'Oh shit,' only not in his American accent but in another one that she knows instantly.

She grabs the phone.

'How did you realize it was *me*?'

They sit opposite one another in the hotel bar. Ilse and Kit are the only customers. It's one in the morning and he has come straight from the radio station. He's still wearing his bicycle clips. His thick black hair is flecked with grey but his face is round and smooth and very pink. Unlike Maud, Kit has slimmed with age. He is dressed head to foot in Lycra and zips, and his cycling helmet sits on his lap like a plastic pet.

'I didn't know at first. Then you dropped something.'

Kit laughs into his fruit cider. The waiter has served it in a long glass with a cherry on a cocktail stick. It's a small piece of kindness but it touches Ilse; the only drawback being that every time Kit takes a sip, she worries he will lose his left eye.

She says, 'I found Maud.'

'I avoid Maud.'

At the bar, the waiter is alternately watching Kit and flipping through his newspaper, as if he thinks he might recognize Kit's voice and is a bit shy.

Kit tells her about himself. He has been doing his *Late Night Surgery* on the radio for years. He gets letters every week and he has a big following on social media. When he yawns, she can still see the teenager in him. She apologizes. 'I shouldn't have asked you to come. But as soon as I heard your voice— It's been a terrible day. Are you hungry?'

Of course he is hungry. This is Kit. He orders a BLT sandwich from the all-night menu. When the waiter brings it, it is served with a garnish of crisps and two pickled onions. The waiter asks if Kit is really KIT. From the radio? Kit says he is. 'Oh shit, no way,' says the waiter. 'I'd know your voice anywhere.' He asks Kit to sign a napkin, a beermat and his shirtsleeve. 'My mum loves you,' he says. And from the way he keeps blushing, it seems possible the waiter likes Kit too.

Over the course of another cider (and two more cherries), Ilse learns more. Kit was badly burnt in the fire. He still has the scars on his legs and upper arms. Frank sat with him in hospital every day. Afterwards he introduced Kit to a friend who was a DJ, and that was how things began for Kit at the radio station. But within about a year, Frank was going downhill. He spent a lot of time alone. Kit wonders if Frank pushed people away on purpose – or maybe he stopped caring.

For a while he stayed friendly with his old bank manager but he refused financial help. Then the bank manager took early retirement so that he and his wife could take the kids travelling. Frank's old customers would try giving him money or help if they ever bumped into him on the streets, but he could be unpredictable. He might agree to meet, and then not turn up. Or he might say he'd found the record you needed, but then decide to give it to someone else.

'After that it just seemed he'd had enough of music altogether.'

Of all the things she has heard in the last few days, this is the one that throws her most, as if a new cavity has opened inside her filled with nothing but sorrow.

'Frank gave up on music? But music *was* Frank.'

'I saw him around '98. I was leaving a nightclub. It was a shock. He looked terrible. I was with friends and he kept falling all over the place. I remember he said his head hurt a lot, it was clear he'd been drinking. I tried to help him, but he went away. I think he wanted to give up, you see, and he just couldn't do it.'

Ilse listens with her handkerchief to her face. But when she asks quietly, 'He *is* alive, isn't he?' it's Kit whose eyes bud with tears.

'Oh God, I hope so. I can't imagine the world without Frank. It would be a really terrible place.'

Kit does not go home. He sold his parents' house when they died and he bought a warehouse flat. He follows Ilse up to the executive suite (he brings another sandwich) and lies flat out on the bed beside hers. They talk for the rest of the night, remembering Frank and the music shop, and all the people he once helped. He tells her more about his radio show, and Ilse speaks about her career as a violin teacher. Twenty-one years can be condensed to very few words. Is that a good thing or a bad one? It's just the way it is.

'Frank was so in love with you,' he says. 'We all were. Even Father Anthony.'

Her heart begins to beat fast with the sudden shock of hope, and the relief too of hearing it spoken at last, Frank's feeling for her. She tries to breathe deep. She says, 'Maud wasn't in love with me.'

'Maud was in love with Frank.'

'Is she still?'

'I doubt it.'

'Nevertheless I felt it even today. As if she was trying to get rid of me.'

It occurs to her there is something, even after all these years, about all three of them, something separated. Unfinished. Unfinished symphonies, she thinks. Even Kit – with all his energy – has a loneliness stored in his smile. But what will it take to complete them? A miracle? At the very least, a small piece of human magic. Far away Ilse can hear sirens and drunken shouting. Where are you, Frank? She strokes her throat with her hand, trying to make the fingers of her left hand become his, willing him to be with her. To be safe. She thinks of herself, in this executive room, and herself in her mother's apartment, and herself as a young woman, walking beside Frank, and it is as though all those versions of her life exist concurrently. It is hard to work out which is the most real.

When Kit begins to snore, she eases the plate from his hands and pulls the covers over him.

It turns out there are even more care homes in the city than tattoo salons. The following morning, Ilse and Kit stand either side of the receptionist as she scrolls through the listings on her computer. They have happy names like Sunnyview and Meadowbanks through Ilse doubts they have a single sunny view or meadowbank between them.

The receptionist has turned a blind eye to the fact that both Kit and

Ilse emerged from the lift at eight in the morning. Though she *has* asked if he is really the *Late Night Surgery* DJ from the radio? She loves his programme, she says.

'I rang in once.' She blushes all round her blue uniform scarf.

'Oh?'

'I didn't know if I should leave my job and go to India.'

'What did I say?'

'You said the world's your oyster.' She clicks her mouse on PRINT. Six pages of care homes shunt from her printer. She fastens them with a stapler and hands them over. She gives him an embarrassed smile. 'One day I will go,' she says.

In the hotel restaurant, Ilse sifts through one page after another, marking up the homes she considers most likely. Really this is guess-work. She hasn't a clue. She points again at all the care homes on her list. She's supposed to be heading back to Germany tomorrow. It could take her weeks to drive round all these places.

Kit knocks back a glass of detoxifying green juice and laughs. 'Have you never heard of Facebook? The mobile phone?'

An hour later, he has sampled everything the breakfast buffet has to offer, and also located Father Anthony in a home called House of Hope.

'Frank?' the girl says. 'Oh. I know that name. Mr Anthony goes on about him all the time.'

The House of Hope is a vast single-storeyed building furnished with handrails and security buzzers, and does not look very hopeful at all. The girl leads the way along a corridor. She wears jogging trousers and a T-shirt over which she has a blue plastic apron, so thin it could have been made from a bin liner.

The girl's crepe-sole shoes go *shlop shlop* in the silence; the corridor is lined, wall to wall, in old brown carpet that feels sucky underfoot. There are windows on one side, doors on the other. Sunlight measures itself out in regular oblongs and there is a very strong chemical smell that has clearly been used to overpower other very strong smells that are more of the human variety.

Ilse glances briefly from one of the windows and finds a view of the car park, containing only her hire car.

'Frank this, Frank that,' says the girl. 'Sometimes we shut the door and leave him to it.'

'What if he falls? Or he's lonely?'

The girl shrugs. 'He can ring his buzzer.' She pushes open a door.

'Shouldn't we knock?'

But the girl is already inside the room and yelling, 'Here you go, Mr Anthony. You've got yourself some visitors.'

The room is small. There is nothing here except the necessities. Not even a photograph, and the buzzer is in fact held to the wall with a strip of Sellotape.

Father Anthony waits in an armchair by the window. Beyond the bars there is a view of a brick wall that can't be more than ten feet away. What is left of his hair stands up in peaks, his eyes are rheumy with age, his glasses held together with Elastoplast.

'Don't get up, don't get up!' yells Kit.

But the old priest does. He flies up and embraces them as if he has been praying for this day for years.

'I'm not sure we are allowed to abduct residents, Kit,' says Ilse, pulling left on to the dual carriageway.

'We're not abducting him. We're taking him for a day out. I told the girl we were family.'

'Did she mind?'

'No. She asked for my autograph.'

Father Anthony sits on the back seat. He has wound down the window and the cold air rushes through his hair. He holds his face up, smiling.

Ilse Brauchmann has lost track of how many cafés she has visited in the last few days. She orders another black coffee, Father Anthony orders a glass of milk; Kit asks if he could have the full English afternoon tea, even though strictly speaking it is only halfway through the morning.

The waitress blushes and says of course, and is he by any chance the man—

'I am,' he says brightly. 'Would you like a signed photo?'

Father Anthony holds Ilse's hand and tells her all he knows about Frank. Yes, it's true he lost everything. Yes, it's also true he turned his back on music. And yes, he is probably still alive.

'Where is he?' She's on her feet and grabbing her car keys before the old ex-priest has finished his sentence.

'I don't know.' Father Anthony rubs his face in his hands. 'I don't know where he is any more. He used to come and visit sometimes. Walked all the way there, and all the way back. People liked him. He had time for everyone. Then one day he said there was something he had to do, and he wouldn't be able to see me for some time.'

'When was this?'

'I don't remember. I get things confused.' His eyes well up. Ilse takes his hand. He might be frail but there is life in him.

'What did he have to do?'

'I don't know. He just said he needed a regular job.'

'Why would that be a problem?'

'I don't know.' Father Anthony's face puckers all over with emotion. 'Oh my goodness, I am so happy to see you.'

They drive back through the city. They go to the park, they visit the police station, they walk the length of Castlegate but they don't even know what they are looking for. Every time she feels she has Frank in her sights, he seems to disappear down another alleyway. They end up parking on Unity Street, and standing outside the boarded-up parade. It's mid-afternoon and a soft pink light fills the air so that the row of abandoned shops glows with a warmth of its own. Even the blackened bricks of the music shop have beauty.

'It was a good time,' murmurs Kit. 'We didn't even know how good it was.'

'Oh but we did,' says Father Anthony. 'We knew it was special. We loved helping people and Frank loved that more than anyone. But I think he lost his way. It happens sometimes.'

Ilse asks if he would like supper with her at the hotel. He nods and says he would like that very much.

As she drives them back to the old docklands area, Kit talking nineteen to the dozen, Father Anthony's face beaming in her rear-view mirror, she allows her mind to drift. She pictures the music shop as it once was, the boxes of vinyl, the booths with the little mother-of-pearl birds, the old Persian runner. She hears Maud's voice, all over again. *Sometimes it's best if you move on—*

She almost hits the pavement.

'Whoa!' says Kit.

If Maud has not seen Frank for fifteen years, why does she still have the key to his shop?

The answer is waiting in the hotel foyer.

'Oh shit. It's *her*.'

Kit actually leaps behind Ilse and grips on to her shoulders. Father Anthony raises his hands to his mouth, in wonderment. At her computer, the receptionist stares.

Maud stands in front of the decorative wall of moving water, hands on hips, legs astride, like some kind of official police barrier.

'I know what happened to Frank,' she says. 'I lied.'

Over dinner in the hotel restaurant, Ilse learns the final piece in the puzzle. Maud has to repeat herself many times because the acoustics do not lend themselves to whispering, and Father Anthony is now very hard of hearing and Kit is constantly interrupting with questions.

'Frank is *where*?' 'What?' 'How?'

She didn't tell Ilse the whole story two days ago because she thought it would be best for everyone to leave him alone. 'Besides,' she reaches for cigarettes and slams them back in her handbag, pulling out Nicorettes, 'you were the last person I expected to see. I've been angry with you for a long time.'

She needs them to understand. Frank isn't *Frank* any more. He's empty. 'In fact,' she says repeatedly, 'he's a twat.'

Ilse feels a light, hollow sensation in the pit of her stomach. Everything seems fluttery and liable to fall apart at any minute. 'So where is he? What does he do that's such a secret?'

Frank works in the food factory. He makes the cheese and onion flavouring for the cheese and onion crisps.

'That's it?' repeats Kit. 'That's what he does?'

Father Anthony shakes his head sadly. 'Oh my,' he murmurs.

He managed to keep a key for the shop and Maud looks after it. Sometimes – when things are bad – he sleeps there, or lends it to a friend. She has no idea where he spends the rest of his time.

'But why does he work in the food factory?' repeats Kit. 'He hated that place. He gave me a job so I wouldn't have to work there. He said there was more music in his little toe than there was in the food factory.'

Maud empties a bottle of red wine into her glass. 'It's like he doesn't want to be found any more. Like he wants to hurt himself.' She adds that it's getting to the point she expects to find his body one day, just curled up on the street. Every Saturday lunchtime, he eats a burger in the shopping mall. Apart from his job at the food factory, it's the only time he goes out in public.

'Why does he go there?' asks Ilse.

'The mall is a *dive*,' says Kit.

'It's what he does. Don't ask me why. I think there's some weekly voucher system with the factory.'

'Can we see him?' Ilse's question comes the same time as the pudding menu. 'What can we do?'

For once Kit doesn't even think about food. He waits, they all wait, for Maud's answer.

'You need to wake the fucker up. God knows how. But you need to do it big time.'

*

Ilse sits in her hotel room, writing everything down in order to understand. What has taken two hours to tell can be reduced to one half-page of foolscap paper.

All night she asks herself the same question. *How?* How do you find a man who has hidden himself away? Who has put himself to sleep? How do you wake up such a man? Why can't she just go to him? She knows the answer. Frank would run, and she can't afford to lose him any more times. Besides, there are occasions in life when the simple and the ordinary will not suffice.

Think, she tells herself. *Think.*

What would Frank have done, if this had been another customer? Someone who really needed help and didn't know how to find it?

She writes the question over and over, and underlines it.

Father Anthony is asleep on the extra bed. Maud has crashed out on the sofa. Kit is doing his *Late Night Surgereeee* on the radio. Ilse has promised to tune in and she does, she listens quietly with her ear to the speaker, as Kit tells people how to fix their lives, and gives them songs to help them feel better. At the very end, he says he has a special message for dear friends. He plays 'Keep On Keepin' On' by Curtis Mayfield.

'How?' she says aloud. 'How do we do it? How do we help you, Frank?'

By the time Kit returns in his Lycra and bicycle clips, she has the answer.

The cure is in the disease. She of all people should know that.

Frank needs to hear the one record he could never bear.

The following morning, Ilse Brauchmann is back at reception. She asks the woman with the blue scarf if she could possibly check into the

292

executive suite for an extra week? She tries not to think about her bank account.

'Will your friends be staying?'

'Yes,' she says. 'I believe they will.'

It's the first time she's laughed in days.

43

Hallelujah!

THERE ARE A number of ways of listening to the *Messiah*. You can go to a live performance. If you have a local music shop, you can buy it there. You can take it out from the library – so long as your library still exists, and also has a music department. You can buy it online and have it delivered without even having to leave your home. Easiest of all, you can download it. Search it; ping it; there you go. *Hallelujah*.

But how do you bring the 'Hallelujah Chorus' to a man who refuses to listen to music? Ilse, Father Anthony, Kit and Maud sit in the window of the Singing Teapot café. It is Kit who has led them here.

As soon as the waitress spots Ilse, she barks she's not open yet. Then she drops her Hoover. 'Oh my God, it's *you!*' Before Ilse can reply the waitress – no longer a young woman, but certainly a larger one – bear-hugs her. When she smiles, her whole face joins in the fun. 'Let me fix something for you.'

She disappears through her saloon doors.

Once again the group discuss the options. They have done nothing else all morning. How can they get Frank to hear the 'Hallelujah Chorus'? Maud suggests physical violence. An ambush, or something.

Father Anthony folds a paper bird and asks what about singing it? 'Me?' says Ilse. 'But where will I do that?' And anyway, the whole point about the *Messiah* is that it is a choir. Lots of voices must sing for it to have its full impact.

Kit counts heads. 'One, two, three, four—'

'I'm not fucking singing,' says Maud.

It is strangely reassuring.

No, they will have to surprise Frank. If they want him to listen to the 'Hallelujah Chorus', they have to catch him unawares, and the sound has to be so big he can't ignore it. Ilse suggests singing outside the food factory. Kit points out they will get mugged if they sing Handel outside the food factory. What if they sing on Unity Street? Nobody will hear them if they sing on the street, and anyway there is no guarantee that Frank will sleep in his shop. The only way to play it to him is to trap him somewhere very public where he can't run away, and where sound is contained.

'Ah ah ah!' says Kit, as if he has trodden on something ouchy. 'The shopping mall! On Saturday!'

Good idea. They need to play it to him while he eats his burger.

But how?

Could they play a CD on a ghetto blaster at the next table? suggests Kit.

'A CD?' barks Maud. 'Why not bash him on the head while you're at it?'

She is right. They have to play the record. So what about a wind-up gramophone?

Yes, they are getting warmer now.

'But we need to find a way of making the sound *big*,' says Ilse. 'So it really gets him in his heart. I don't know. Do we get several gramophones?'

Everyone makes a polite face. But not a convinced one.

'Ooo oo oo.'

'What's wrong with Kit?'

'I guess he's having another idea,' says Maud.

Kit explains several times but he is excited and the sentences are coming thick and fast, sometimes back-to-front. 'A happening! Lots of . . . ! People . . . ! A flash! A *mob*!'

'A what? A what?' says Ilse.

The waitress interrupts with her tray. She lays the table with tea, milk, slices of lemon, sugar and a selection of little homemade pastries. Pink iced coconut. Coffee macaroons. Red velvet cakes.

She draws up a chair and she can't help herself. She just has to take hold of Ilse's hand and stroke it.

'So what are we planning here?'

Kit draws a deep breath. He sits very still, as if he is balancing something precious on top of his head, and tries to explain all over again. A happening is an event. It's a thing that happens. And a flash mob is when a group of people get together in a public space, usually somewhere like a shopping mall, and they perform a piece of music or a dance or anything like that as if it's just happening by chance. 'It's brilliant!' he keeps saying. 'It's amazing!' The participants make it look like a spur of the moment decision, as if they all happen to want to do the same thing at the same time, in the same venue.

'But what is the point?' asks Maud.

The point, Kit explains, is that a flash mob event has *no* point. Its point is the sheer beauty of doing something joyful that is also unnecessary, unexpected and free of charge.

296

Ilse says, 'But it would take months to arrange a performance of the "Hallelujah Chorus". We'd have to advertise for singers. Find a rehearsal space. And what about the musicians? There's no way we can do that by Saturday.'

Kit wafts his hand. He has just eaten an entire slice of iced coconut in one mouthful.

('It does tend to stick to the teeth,' concedes the waitress. 'I don't think I've got the recipe right yet.')

He explains. Flash mobs are arranged mainly via social media. At a pinch, he reckons they could do it by Saturday. They won't have time to rehearse and that's a bit of a problem, but everyone knows the 'Hallelujah Chorus'. The main thing about a group of people singing is that Frank will have to listen. They'll have him surrounded.

'You're telling me that you will arrange an entire performance of the "Hallelujah Chorus" by putting a message into the ether?'

'Yes,' says Kit. That's roughly what he's saying.

'People will come to sing?'

'Yes.'

'Because they love Frank?'

'Or because they love vinyl.'

'In the shopping mall?'

Kit says, 'Twenty-one years ago, Frank tried to save vinyl and lost everything. This time we'll save him. We'll plan a *flash mob*.'

They have four days.

This is how it will work. Kit will phone the council to request permission to use the shopping mall. Then they will do a recce of the venue. Ilse will find a second-hand record player and a copy of the *Messiah*;

she'll only find that kind of thing in a charity shop but fortunately the city's stuffed with them. After that they will recruit singers. Kit will make leaflets, which they will print and hand out. Father Anthony will telephone every independent shopkeeper in the city and every amateur singing group. Kit and Maud will use social media. Sadly Kit can't mention the event on his radio show because the person who really mustn't hear anything about this is Frank.

'Such a shame,' says Kit.

The Singing Teapot waitress insists the refreshments are free of charge. She's not really the waitress any more. She bought the owner out fifteen years ago.

The glass doors of the shopping mall slide open. All the shops here have 'Bargain' in the name, or at least the promise of one. Poundland. Super Saver. The Eatery is a floor down, on the basement level. There are no windows. The only natural light comes from a glass-domed roof, which is mainly nicotine-yellow now. The group take the escalator and stare at the vast space as it comes into view. There are at least twenty different food outlets – Happy Wok, USA Chicken, Millie's Cookies, TexMex, Aunty's Pretzels, The Great British Potato, and those are just the closest – with white plastic tables and chairs arranged in the middle. Giant waste bins stand at regular intervals, made in the shapes of blue fish and squirrels, with wide-open mouths where you are supposed to throw your rubbish. There are also vast pots filled with vast plastic leaves. Presumably all these things are designed to make people feel nice while they eat, though in reality if you came across a giant squirrel or a blue fish with its mouth wide open, or even a plant with leaves that size, you would be wise to drop your fizzy drink and run for it.

The place couldn't make humanity look more shabby if it tried. Barely anyone is here. Just a woman mopping the floor, a man asleep, and a young mother feeding burger to her baby.

'Well, at least we can't miss Frank on Saturday,' says Kit.

He shows where the flash mob singers can station themselves. If there are about twenty of them, there will be room to stand in front of the potted plants. They can give a quick rendition of the 'Hallelujah Chorus' – and then disperse.

Ilse shivers. Something about this place makes her long for a green apple. She can't wait to be back outside.

Kit's years of craftwork have paid off. She drives him to a retail outlet on the edge of the city where they buy bulk packs of A4 paper, colouring pens, marker pens, string, ribbon, tape, glue, safety pins, badge pins, glitter pots, fabric shapes and trims, decorative tape, peel-off shapes, foils, films and flakes.

'This is so exciting,' says Kit. He does little Kit-like skips. Overhearing his voice, a man stops him and says he just needs to thank Kit. He rang in to his show once, when he felt really low.

'Oh? What did I say?' It touches Ilse that Kit seems to have no real idea of his influence.

'You told me to take a nice walk.'

'Did it work?'

'That was how I met my wife.'

Kit spends the rest of the afternoon designing leaflets in the hotel suite. They encourage anyone who knew Frank's music shop to attend the shopping mall on Saturday at 1 p.m. and sing the 'Hallelujah Chorus'. Ilse drives with Father Anthony to the printers. They have dinner in the hotel restaurant before Kit nips off to do his radio show. He returns that night with a spare set of clothes for both himself and Father Anthony. Maud comes late after work with a small suitcase.

The next morning, Ilse fetches boxes of button badges, which Kit has designed to hand out on the day. There are three different logos and they all come with exclamation marks. *I love vinyl!*, *Hallelujah!* and *Sing for Frank!* There is also a jumbly mix of all three, *I love Frank, Hallelujah!*

Time passes through her like glass. Every waking moment is spent planning the event. She barely has time to email her students and explain. She manages a few texts but they are simple messages, reassuring friends she is OK. She spends an entire day searching charity shops for a record player until she finds a second-hand Dansette Major, with a red leather trim and brass wire grille. The man at the till takes pleasure in showing her how to use it, and checking the stylus works. She riffles through hundreds of crates of second-hand vinyl and buys a 1959 recording of the *Messiah*, conducted by Malcolm Sargent on Decca. She also finds copies of the 'Moonlight' Sonata, Duke Ellington's *Satin Doll*, James Brown and Nick Drake. She buys the lot for 50p. Noticing her interest, another customer asks if she has heard of Record Store Day? 'Vinyl's making a comeback,' he tells her.

Kit and Ilse hand out their leaflets on Castlegate. Father Anthony sits on a bench and does the same. They explain to anyone who will listen, telling people about Frank and his music shop and how he just wanted to help. Over and over, they ask complete strangers to come to the shopping mall and, on a given signal, sing the 'Hallelujah Chorus'. A few agree they will try to come if they remember.

Meanwhile Maud has also mounted her campaign on social media. She has set up a group page on Facebook. *Friends of Frank.*

What about a rehearsal on the day? asks Ilse. Kit explains again that there will be no opportunity for a rehearsal. The only thing they can do is offer simple instructions via social media about the music and what to wear. Kit is adamant that everyone must look as normal as possible. Father Anthony suggests everyone brings a sign, like a placard or something, so that Frank sees how many people are here for him.

At the end of each day, they lie exhausted in their executive suite, staring at the lights in the city, and playing the 'Hallelujah Chorus' over and over on the Dansette Major. The sound is rich and deep, as if the music is reaching up to them from far away. Smoke lifts in pale columns above the food factory.

It's midnight; twelve hours to go. No one can sleep. There are multiples of things that might go wrong. They have no idea how many singers plan to turn up. So far, many people have liked Maud's Facebook page and Kit's leaflets have all been taken, but no one has made any promises. Father Anthony has been in touch with the music master at the cathedral to ask if he can spare a few choristers. He has also had a promise of support from a few of his friends at the home. But, of course, there is no guarantee that Frank himself will show up. The thought of seeing him slings her heart sideways. Part of Ilse just wants to run away. It would be so much easier.

They sit in her hotel suite at midnight, Kit, Maud, Father Anthony and Ilse, surrounded by Kit's artwork – he has been making placards ever since he got back from the radio station. Meanwhile Father Anthony has folded so many paper birds they are technically a flock and Maud has bitten off each and every one of her nice new nails.

'You instructed people to assemble by the potted plants, Kit?' says Ilse.

'Yes.' They have been through this over and over.

'Just before 1 p.m.?'

'Yes, Ilse.'

'Looking ordinary?'

'Yes.'

'With placards?'

'Yes.'

But why would people turn up to sing for a man they don't know? Why would they even do that for vinyl?

They lie in the dark and sometimes one of them says, 'Are you still—?' and another says, 'Yes,' and another says, 'Me too.'

When morning lifts into the sky, they get up solemnly and wash and dress. No one can eat. Not even Kit. They listen to the 'Hallelujah Chorus' but they can't sing. The receptionist wishes them luck and they check once again that they have the record, the Dansette, the placards.

'Have faith,' whispers Father Anthony as Ilse helps him with his coat. He's holding a plastic bag. It occurs to her that he actually seems robust and healthy.

She sighs. 'It's all so *unknown*.'

'That's because it's a flash-mob event,' Kit reminds her. 'It's a surprise.'

And here comes another surprise. As they approach the shopping mall on Saturday – so nervous they feel stunned – the glass doors slide open and Kit drops the Dansette Major.

44

Flash!

'WHY ME?' Ilse hisses in the entrance to the shopping mall. The glass doors slide shut.

'Because you're the musician,' Maud hisses back. The glass doors slide open.

'But I don't *play* any more. I just teach.'

'What kind of teacher is that?'

The doors slide shut. Open.

'Do you think we could possibly move away from the doors?' asks Father Anthony.

Forty minutes to go before the flash-mob event and they have no music. Actually they *do* have music. They have 'Toxic' by Britney Spears. It is playing through every sound system in the shopping mall. But in terms of Handel and the 'Hallelujah Chorus', they have no musical accompaniment unless Ilse agrees to play. She suggests she could run out to try and buy another Dansette, but she knows even as she says it, this is not an option. There is no time.

Kit paces with his phone. He is texting with one hand and scratching his head with the other.

'How can I possibly play?' insists Ilse. 'I have no violin. And no music.'

Father Anthony lifts his plastic bag. Kit has taken the liberty of borrowing sheet music, as well as a violin – he was just too frightened to mention it. It was in case the Dansette didn't work. The violin has a battered brown canvas case and the bow is missing some horsehair.

'But I can't really play any more.' Ilse's voice comes out as a raspy whimper.

'Now's your big chance, then,' says Maud.

Father Anthony is still holding the violin. He hugs it to his chest as if it is a small pet he has rescued. 'Do we need to tell someone we're here?'

At this point, Kit goes very quiet.

'Is something wrong?' asks Ilse, more than a little tense. 'Apart from the broken Dansette Major?'

Kit fiddles with his zip. He, uh, he hasn't liked to mention this before, but he never quite got round to phoning the council.

Maud swings round to face him. 'You mean this event is *illegal*?'

Um. Sort of. Yes. Did they seriously believe the council would give permission over the phone for a thing like this? It would take weeks just to fill out the paperwork.

'We can't do it, then,' says Ilse.

'We have to do it,' says Maud.

Kit agrees. It's not as though you get security guards in a place like this. In the circumstances, he suggests the best thing to do is to disperse and pretend they don't know each other.

'Suits me,' says Maud, already stamping down the escalator.

Kit says he will go incognito. He doesn't want Frank, or indeed any of his fans, to spot him yet.

As the moving staircase carries her down to the basement level, Ilse's hands begin to shake. It's small at first, but by the time she steps on to the floor her entire body is trembling.

Saturday lunchtime. The place is packed with people eating junk food. Why didn't they think of this? Couples, solitary shoppers, middle-aged women on outings, a group of men in football scarves, gangs of teenagers – practically entire classrooms of them – and even families, two or three generations. The noise is a roar, and so is the smell. So many people with takeaway dishes, and fizzy drinks in cups the size of lampshades. Others queue at the different food outlets. She wishes Father Anthony was beside her, but he is busy inspecting the crowd, searching for a sign of some choristers or anyone he recognizes from the home. She looks up at the domed yellowy roof light, hoping for comfort.

Sitting directly beneath it, she finds him.

Frank.

The breath goes clean out of her. She almost falls.

He sits erect and alone on a white plastic chair at a matching plastic table, eating a burger from a paper wrapper. He is wearing his factory overalls, even on a Saturday. His skin has a cheese and onion look, like a film of yellowy sand, and so does his long white hair, which he has tied back from his face with a rubber band. It's the tenderness with which he takes a chip and dips it in a sachet of ketchup that really gets her. He chews very carefully, making sure the taste is right. He adds a tiny sprinkling of salt.

305

She doesn't want to cry but she can't help it, she can hardly see him any more through tears.

He is the same, older, the dearest man in the world. He lifts his burger to his mouth, takes a small bite, puts it down, chews carefully, and then picks it up again. When a child stops and stares at his long hair, he nods.

But why is there another person with a beard waving at her, as if he is bringing a plane in to land?

It is Kit. God help him. He is in disguise.

He is letting her know he too has spotted Frank. He points to his watch. Twenty minutes to go.

There is no one else in the crowd she recognizes. Not even the Singing Teapot waitress has made it. A toddler spins herself to dizziness beside Sweet-you-like until a woman scoops her up and carries her, yelling and wriggling, to a pushchair. A young man in a jogging suit approaches a woman and she shakes her head, as if to say, *No, you've been late too many times.*

At another table, three overweight businessmen with briefcases eat pizzas, paper napkins tucked into their shirt collars to protect their businessmen suits. A pair of old ladies share a slice of cake. A woman drinks a plastic cup of coffee opposite her young son, and the look on her face is so empty, you'd think they'd been here years. When he starts bashing her mobile on the table, she just stares. Two cleaners drag their mops between tables.

At another table, a young man is fast asleep with his head in his arms. In the far corner, a woman with a baseball cap peels the crust from a sandwich and pecks at it with the tiniest bites, as if she is afraid it will turn round any moment and bite her back. Another woman is entirely shrouded in a yellow cagoule. People everywhere. And not one of them a singer. Ilse throws back her head in despair.

That's when she spots them. Two security men. Up on the first floor.

She takes the escalators to check. They are standing in front of Ann Summers and they don't look especially lively. In the shop window behind them, a mannequin wears a peep-hole bra, suspenders and a pair of pants that is more ribbon than pant. She's also holding a pair of handcuffs though presumably she is not trying to help the security guards.

Ilse returns to the Eatery. She stands with hands gripped in a ball. She can't stop shaking. Never mind playing a violin. In her present condition, she wouldn't even be able to unzip the case.

When she next spots Kit, he is flashing his fingers at her. Ten minutes to go.

Where is the joy, Frank? she asks herself. We had Bach. We had Mozart, you and I. Schubert, Chopin, Tchaikovsky. Even when she was teaching, there would be a child, once in a while, who got it, who really understood. But *this*? Is this where the world has been heading? To canned music and burgers and no daylight and plastic bins in a shopping mall? Every man for himself? Is this where it all ends?

Father Anthony appears at her side. 'OK?'

'No. I am terrified. There's no one here.'

'There are lots of people here,' says Kit, appearing at her other side, sans beard.

'But none of them have come to sing the "Hallelujah Chorus".'

'We asked them to look ordinary.'

307

'Not this ordinary. They're all eating burgers. And what about the placards?'

'Hm,' says Kit. 'You're right. There are no placards.'

'Have you seen the security guards?' She lifts her eyes in the direction of the first floor. The two security guards remain with their arms folded in front of the not-very-dressed lady mannequin.

'Shit,' says Kit.

Maud joins them. She carries a tray with bottled water. 'I thought you might need a drink before you start.'

Ilse's mouth is sandpaper. Her body is frail and nothing but air. She can't tell if she is very hot or very cold. 'How can this work? There's no one to sing with us. There's security upstairs. And Frank won't even hear.'

Kit says, 'How about "Happy Birthday"? We could do that. Or we could just join in with "Toxic"?'

Ilse stares at Kit. 'Are you serious?'

'We are trying to *save* Frank,' says Maud. She stops talking for a second and then remembers who she is. 'Pillock.'

Father Anthony glances up at the two security guards. 'I'm not sure this is a good idea, you know,' he says quietly.

On the other side of the Eatery, Frank continues to eat his burger.

'Three minutes to go,' whispers Kit.

'No. I can't do it. I can't. And it won't even be in tune.' Ilse puts down the violin. But before she can move away, she is caught by one small and very firm hand on her shoulder. It actually hurts.

Maud grips Ilse tightly by the collar and draws her face right up close to hers. They are nose to nose. Maud snarls through clenched-together teeth. 'Listen. We have waited twenty-one years. You need him. He

308

needs you. *We* need you to sort this out. So pick up your fiddle—'

'Actually it's a violin,' says Kit.

'I don't give a flying fuck what it is. Play the thing.'

Maud marches to one of the few remaining free tables, piled high with abandoned food wrappings, napkins and paper cups. She clears a space while Kit fetches a roll of blue paper towel and something squirty, in order to rub at the sticky patches. He presents Ilse with a chair. Tugging his Lycra jacket over his head so that his hair stands up in a wild halo of static, he then folds it into a careful square and makes a cushion of it. Father Anthony approaches with the violin case. He places it on the newly cleaned table and solemnly undoes the zipper. Ilse's heart jumps like a piston.

'This is not going to work,' she says. 'Look at my hands.' They are trembling with a life of their own.

'You're our only chance,' says Father Anthony. He takes her fingers, presses them inside his, warming them up. She steals one last look at the security guards. Kit holds out the old violin.

At this point – and to her eternal surprise – her body takes over. It knows what to do, without requiring the aid of the rest of her. Her back straightens, her neck lifts, her feet widen. Her arms welcome the violin, her left hand opens around the scroll, resting the broad end on her left collarbone. Her head lowers until it reaches the chin rest and angles itself a little to the left so that the chin rest now tucks beneath her jaw and ends at her chin. There is a direct line from her nose to the struts at the neck of the violin.

Britney Spears sings 'Toxic'. Ilse's right arm shakes so hard she can barely bring up the raggedy bow.

She remembers, *The cure is in the disease.*

She positions her left hand at the neck, supporting it between her thumb and forefinger, with her other fingers curled around the struts. Her thumb locks and she almost drops the thing. Kit gasps.

She lifts the bow in her right hand, resting her right forefinger on top of the bow's pad and her pinky finger on the screw. Her hands are stiff and the effort sends a shooting pain up from her wrists. Father Anthony reaches out and steadies her arm.

She manages the most basic introduction to the 'Hallelujah Chorus'. A child could do better. It is not strictly in tune and her notes are a scratch, a squeak. At her side, Kit hums the tune to keep her steady, and so does Father Anthony. But it is Maud who drops her mouth wide and sings loudest.

Nobody looks up. People continue to eat and drink. The little girl strapped in her pushchair is still crying. The three businessmen eat their pizzas, the old ladies continue with that slice of chocolate cake. Frank doesn't even notice.

Then – 'Hallelujah!' The girl with the baseball cap leaps to her feet.

She is holding her sandwich but her voice is clear. She tips her chin upwards so that she seems to be singing not to anyone in particular, but more towards the sky, or at least the yellowy glass roof.

One or two people turn to look. Most continue to eat. The couple right next to her stare, as if they have no idea what's come over her. They shuffle their chairs away, trying to create a distance. Ilse's hand can barely keep hold of the bow.

'Hallelujah!' The young man who was asleep springs to life and leaps on his chair. 'Hallelujah,' he sings loud.

The businessmen put down their pizzas and unlock their briefcases. A few waitresses laugh.

'*Hallelujah!*' A young couple waiting at USA Chicken throw their arms wide.

And now three attendants make a dash from the lavatories, wearing overalls. '*Hallelujah!*' they sing, as if to spread the marvellous news.

Ilse's left fingers move on the struts. They're too slow. She steals a glance in the direction of the security guards. They don't seem to have heard anything up there.

But everyone else has begun to notice. They don't know who is going to sing next. They glance around, waiting, uneasy, as if this thing might be contagious. The two old ladies sharing cake, the girl waiting for the man in the jogging suit, a waitress at Happy Wok; one by one they rise to their feet and sing. A minute in, and at least twenty people have joined in.

'*For the Lord God Omnipotent reigneth. Hallelujah! Hallelujah!*

'*Hallelujah!*

'*Hallelujah!*'

Will the security guards notice?

Will Frank?

'*For the Lord God Omnipotent reigneth.*'

The three businessmen snap open their briefcases and produce a recorder, a triangle and a shaker. Springing to their feet, they begin to play. This is not – by any stretch of the imagination – the purest version of the *Messiah*, it has a few alterations and mistakes and a lot of extra—

'*Hallelujah. Hallelujah!*'

Nevertheless people smile, entranced. Some pull phones and cameras from their bags and start to film. The woman whose son was banging her mobile now lifts him on to his chair for a better view. People exchange brief looks with strangers, checking this is for real. Even those who don't know the words are singing something like 'Hallelujah!' Thirty people now.

No, forty.

No, forty-five.

The person in the yellow cagoule shucks it off and reveals herself as the Singing Teapot owner. She climbs right on top of her table, throws her arms wide enough to embrace a mountain, and yells: 'Hallelujah!'

Fifty people.

The lift opens and two choristers dash out. 'Hallelujah!'

Sixty voices, all of them sent upwards. 'Hallelujah!'

Some people sing as if they have at last found the thing they were supposed to do – joyful, exuberant, dental work for all to see – while for others it is a tentative, private experience, more of a murmur than a song. The music is big enough to contain anything anyone could ever feel. The emergency exit doors swing open and a care-worker appears from the home, pushing an old man in a wheelchair.

And 'He shall reign for ever and ever!' The refrain resounds from Happy Wok, from Sweet-you-like, from among the blue-squirrel bins and the giant plastic leaves.

'King of Kings. For ever! For ever! Hallelujah. Hallelujah.'

One hundred people sing in a shopping mall. Outside, the air will stink of cheese and onion, people are being mugged, others are starving, the sky is grey, but for one brief and irrational gap in time, there is this beautiful human madness. The world is not terrible after all.

Then – just as the piece should begin to climb towards its crescendo – the security guards glance down and notice.

'Shit. Now we're for it,' shouts Kit.

312

But it's too late. Too many people are involved. There is no stopping this thing.

The security guards go straight from static to full running. They don't even do the walky bit that generally goes in the middle. They march down the escalators, leaping the bottom step, and, yes—

'*Hallelujah!*'

In his joy Kit runs forward to throw out button badges and people scramble to pick them up. *I love vinyl! Hallelujah!* The sleepy man dashes out to join Kit and they embrace, jumping as they laugh.

The chorus builds. Everyone is on their feet. Everyone is singing. In truth this 'Hallelujah Chorus' has taken a jazzy improvised turn of its own. It owes very little to Handel, and it has far outstretched its conventional running time of four minutes. But then – just as people reach the climax – something else happens.

They raise their hands.

'*Hallelujah. Hallelujah.*'

Kit has not planned any of this. The idea seems to be there in the shopping mall; it's just a question of going with it, and not messing it up by thinking too hard. Everyone – young, old, musical, non-musical – all these people stand with their arms raised, like three hundred trees. And what are they holding?

Record sleeves.

Albums, 45s, 12-inch singles, picture discs, coloured discs, bootlegs, collector's items, original pressings. Some people are even holding up their vinyl. They push it high for Frank to see.

'*Hallelujah. Hallelujah.*'

And now placards too.

You gave me Bach.

Hello from Stockport.

You gave me Aretha.

We love you, Frank, from Cardiff!

Remember us, Frank? The crazy couple from Düsseldorf!

And here it is. That last chorus. The one that made Peg bawl.

'*Hallelujah! Hallelujah!*'

Three hundred people PAUSE. You could hear a pin drop.

Then: 'HALL-LE-LOOOOOO-JAHHHH.'

In the silence that follows, one man sits. Eyes down. He doesn't eat, he doesn't drink. He doesn't even move.

'What happened?' asks a child, very loud. 'Didn't he hear?'

Of course he heard. But he remains as before, the old bastard, refusing to wake.

It's too much. Kit flops into the arms of the young man he danced with. Maud gropes for Father Anthony's hand and he in turn removes his coat and slips it over her shoulders.

Ilse weaves through the crowd. People stand, still holding up their records, and they part like water, allowing her to pass. She pushes through until she is right in front of Frank's white plastic table. If she reached out, she could touch his hair. He remains looking down.

'Frank.' Her voice wobbles. 'I have come back for you. All these people have shown up. They have sung. I have played. They brought their vinyl. Look at us. *Look!* But we can't do the whole thing on our own. The last bit is up to you.' She can feel the heat in her cheeks. Two blazing circles. 'You think you can just *sit there*? You bloody, bloody man. Wake up!'

Her pulse beats so hard she feels it in her neck and ribs. She can see nothing but the crown of his bowed head. The only movement is a slight tremble from his fingers.

It's too much. She turns. Pushes her way back through the fringe of the crowd towards Maud, Kit and Father Anthony. She feels their eyes on her like lead weights, pressing all the energy from inside her. Tears blur her path. She will get a flight home. She will sell her mother's apartment. Move on. She should never have come back—

She's a few feet into the crowd when something tugs at her skirt. A hand. She pushes it off – *No, go away* – but it comes back.

'Lady!' a voice calls. 'Miss!' It is the boy who banged his mother's mobile phone. 'Come back. Look.'

She turns. People dip their heads this way and that, trying to get a better view. There he is. Frank. Burger. Fizzy drink. Something is definitely happening. His shoulders lift and fall. His hands span the edge of the table and grip hard.

He slowly eases himself to his full height. His mouth drops. Amid the crowd, amid a hundred plastic cups and iced doughnuts and Great British Potatoes and Happy Wok meals, across a sea of *I love vinyl!* and *Thank you, Frank!* he finds Ilse Brauchmann and their eyes lock.

Silence falls over the entire shopping mall.

He gazes at her.

She gazes at him.

His mouth does something funny that says, *Is that really you?*

Her mouth curves to say, *I guess it is.*

Tears come, but he does not shake them away. His breath goes in, it goes out, and through it all, his tears. For a moment she is terrified it is too much for him, that he will fall, but no, he keeps his beautiful eyes locked on hers. Then with one movement, he lifts the plastic table and

315

clears it to one side. So now there is nothing between them but several feet's worth of infinite love.

He gives a little shake of his head. Not a *No*. It is a gesture of wonder. Followed by a look that is more of a question. *Are you going to stay?*

She laughs.

He lifts his arms. Clears the distance between them in one small step.

He draws her close.

HIDDEN TRACK

THERE IS A music shop.

From the outside it still looks like any shop, in any backstreet, in any city. The name is painted in big letters above the door and there is a colourful display in the window, along with an illuminated sign. WE LOVE VINYL! WELCOME!

Inside, the shop is packed with stock. To the left, to the right, and running along the centre, polished wooden units are crammed with records and there are separate racks for shining towers of CDs. Each one of them has been labelled with individual notes, describing the album and suggesting listening tips; things to notice, music that is similar, and why you might like to try it. Scented candles line the counter, along with a vase of flowers.

Behind it sits a tall man, wearing a bottle-green sweatshirt with the shop logo. His hair is a shamble of white. His wife sits beside him, a small woman, wearing a sweatshirt just like his with the same logo, *Frank's Records*. She has silvery hair – some pinned up, some dangling – and extraordinarily large eyes. A giant and his lady.

On the wall behind them hangs a framed photograph of a very old

319

man with a lopsided laugh. It must have been taken a few years ago because the man and woman at the counter are in the photograph too, and they look younger. In the photo, she is wearing a diddy hat with a veil. He has a big leaf in his lapel. Their wedding? Whatever the occasion, everyone in the photo is very happy, with the possible exception of a scowling short woman with geometric hair. *RIP, dear Father Anthony!!!* someone has written beneath it in bouncy metallic pen. *Jazzin' it up there with Miles!!*

You ease a record from its cover. It's years since you've held one but you do this without thinking. Slide your fingers inside the sleeve, careful not to touch the vinyl. Draw it out. Hear the rustle of paper. Balance it in the span of your palm, the outer rim on your thumb, the label on the tip of your middle finger. As it brushes your wrist, feel the soft static kiss of it. Smooth as liquorice and twice as shiny. Light spills over it like water. Breathe in the new smell.

'Can we help?' asks the woman behind the counter. Her accent has a little edge to it.

So you say you are looking for music, you don't really know what. Actually you threw out all your vinyl years ago. You don't even have a CD player any more. Mostly you shop online and if you want music you stream it on your mobile phone. But it shocks you, now you say it, how quickly the world dispensed with things like records and shops. Even your local bank has closed.

'Well, lots of us did,' agrees the woman, as if people think – and say – this all the time. 'Lots of people threw away their records. In 1988 all we wanted were CDs.' Two red circles ping into her cheeks. The man at her side takes her hand, lifts it to his mouth and kisses it. It is a gesture of infinite tenderness. 'Now how can we help?' she asks.

320

'I'm not sure,' you say.

The man turns his gaze on you. His eyes crinkle at the corners.

'What do you think?' she asks him. 'What do you think our new customer should listen to?'

He continues to gaze. He continues to smile. It is as if he has seen you before, somewhere in another part of your life. But it is not the strength of his gaze that stuns you, or even its steadiness; it is the kindness. He knows what you have been through, the losses and disappointments, he feels them too. It's like being charged with a whizz of light.

You begin to blush. Pull at your coat. Mutter about something you heard on Spotify.

But: 'Aretha!' he booms.

'Aretha?' repeats his wife.

'Oh yes.' They seem to think that's an inspired idea. Oh yes, they agree. You are going to love Aretha.

She says, 'Why don't you stay and listen? Our new Saturday boy will take care of you.'

She points to the back of the shop. And that's when you notice a whole gang of customers, sitting in easy chairs with headphones. People alone, couples, teenagers. Families even. How could they all know about this place when you didn't? They drink coffee. Some look up. A few nod as if to say hello. One or two are asleep. A teenage boy covered in badges darts forward. Cappuccino, he asks? Biscuit? In his eagerness to take your coat, he narrowly misses flooring a scented candle.

You glance back at the outside world. A lot of the streets are dangerous these days. A lot are run-down. People rush past the shop window in the dirt-grey city light.

321

'You know, you can stay here as long as you like,' says the woman at the counter. 'Isn't that right, Frank?'

He nods with solemn authority and smiles.

'You can come any time,' she says. 'We're always here.'

PERSONAL NOTE

IN ORDER TO write about music and healing, I did a lot of research, and even though little of it appears in the book now, I wouldn't have been able to write very much without it. So as well as reading many books, articles, blogs, online references and record sleeves, I relied on the wisdom, passion and kindness of many people – music-shop owners, record collectors, healers, music lovers, and most of all my husband, Paul Venables. I relied on him all the time.

In particular I would like to thank Graham Jones; Simon Vincent at Trading Post Records, Stroud; Robert Nichols; Gabrielle Drake; Michael Odell; the assistant with the polo-neck sweater in the jazz section of Soundscapes, Toronto; Larus Johanneson and everyone at 12 Tonar, Reykjavik; Tim Winter and the staff of Harold Moores Records; Johnnie Walker; Cathy Thompson; Jumbo Records, Leeds; Sophie Wilson; Peter Macdonald; Lucy Brett; Vinyl Vault; the bewildered and extremely young assistant who explained to me about master bags at Phonica Records, London; Susanna Wadeson and Lizzy Goudsmit; Alison

Barrow; Clare Conville; Susan Kamil; Kiara Kent; Susanne Halbleib; Steve Gibbs; Chris Rowe; Myra Joyce; Amy Proto; and Emily Joyce.

Any mistakes in this book are entirely Frank's or Peg's.

Rachel Joyce is the author of the *Sunday Times* and international best-sellers *The Unlikely Pilgrimage of Harold Fry*, *Perfect*, *The Love Song of Miss Queenie Hennessy* and a collection of interlinked short stories, *A Snow Garden & Other Stories*. Her work has been translated into thirty-six languages.

The Unlikely Pilgrimage of Harold Fry was shortlisted for the Commonwealth Book Prize and longlisted for the Man Booker Prize. Rachel was awarded the Specsavers National Book Awards 'New Writer of the Year' in December 2012 and shortlisted for the 'UK Author of the Year' 2014.

Rachel has also written over twenty original afternoon plays and adaptations of the classics for BBC Radio 4, including all the Brontë novels. She moved to writing after a long career as an actor, performing leading roles for the RSC, the National Theatre and Cheek by Jowl.

She lives with her family in Gloucestershire.